Daughter of Ishmael

PROMISED LAND, BROKEN HEART

Daughter of Ishmael

PROMISED LAND, BROKEN HEART

DIANE STRINGAM TOLLEY

BONNEVILLE BOOKS

An Imprint of Cedar Fort, Inc.
Springville, Utah

This is a work of fiction. The characters, names, incidents, places, and dialogue are products of the author's imagination and are not to be construed as real. The opinions and views expressed herein belong solely to the author and do not necessarily represent the opinions or views of Cedar Fort, Inc. Permission for the use of sources, graphics, and photos is also solely the responsibility of the author.

ISBN 13: 978-1-4621-1966-0

Published by Bonneville Books, an imprint of Cedar Fort, Inc.
2373 W. 700 S., Springville, UT 84663
Distributed by Cedar Fort, Inc., www.cedarfort.com

LIBRARY OF CONGRESS CATALOGING-IN-PUBLICATION DATA ON FILE

Cover design by Priscilla Chaves

Edited and typeset by Jennifer Johnson

Printed in the United States of America

10 9 8 7 6 5 4 3 2 1

Printed on acid-free paper

To Caitlin.

Daughter. Editor. Friend.

And quotation mark sheriff.

ALSO BY DIANE STRINGAM TOLLEY

Carving Angels

Kris Kringle's Magic

PROLOGUE

Hannah sank onto a log a short distance from the fire. Velvet darkness shrouded the rest of the camp—shadows made deeper by the light of the towering flames in the exact center of the compound.

Even from where she was, she could feel the heat. She wondered how the figures leaping and dancing between her and the flames could stand it. Their bodies were glistening with moisture. She could see streaks of it in the dark, forbidden blood they had used to paint themselves.

Hannah sighed, then realized there was moisture on her own face. She reached up to brush at the offending, telltale tears. It would not do for any of the camp to see her grief. Especially for such animals.

Another tear trickled down her cheek and she wiped at it impatiently. They were just poor, dumb animals!

But deep down, she knew it was not the pitiable, slaughtered creatures she grieved for. It was something else. Some intangible sense of "right." Some line crossed that could never be uncrossed.

Another figure joined the writhing, gesticulating group near the fire, a tall, boyishly underdeveloped figure newly bedaubed with gleaming blood and sporting a freshly shaved head.

The breath went out of Hannah as if from a blow. Her eyes blurred and her ears began to buzz. For a moment, she felt faint. She struggled to force air back into her lungs and blinked her eyes to bring her vision back into focus.

Then she was blinded once more. This time, by tears.

Samuel was joining, for the very first time, his father, uncles, and cousins in their horrifying and hideous victory dance.

Her son. Named for the great Israelite prophet.

"Ah. You must be as proud as we are to see your son finally find his place with the hunters."

Hannah straightened but did not need to look up to know that Uzziel was standing, tall and imperious, beside her. "Proud?" She prayed that her elder sister did not detect the quaver in her voice.

Uzziel laughed. "Of course. He's wanted this for so long! And Laman has been as eager as Samuel's own father to have it happen. And today, in our moment of utmost triumph, when at last we have truly shaken off the foolish traditions of our fathers, he has made his first kill!"

Hannah shivered. "They slaughtered some swine," she said dully.

Uzziel nodded and lifted her head proudly to watch the dancers. "What better way to show those who would enslave us that we will not be enslaved! That those who cling to the old, ancient, and outdated traditions are nothing but fools!" She smiled. "The upstart knew, finally, that it is not as easy as he thought to take what does not belong to him. And so he fled the natural justice that was reaching out for him."

"You think this of Nephi?"

"Of course. Chosen of the Lord. Pah!" Uzziel waved one hand dismissively. "As the fourth-born son, he has no claim to the rule of these people. He has been made to understand that." She smiled. A rather nasty smile. "And when our hunters find him—and those with him who fled like frightened goats—justice will be meted out."

"But—" Hannah closed her lips on the words. No one here would listen. Or agree.

She watched as—with the flames forming a towering background and the madly gyrating, blood-soaked dancers adding the last chilling touch—Laman brought out the hollowed-out head of a boar and, laughing, placed it over Samuel's.

Her son danced around for a few moments, wearing his horrifying headdress, then pulled it off and handed it to someone else. Laman embraced him warmly, both of them covered in gore. Hannah's husband stood to one side smiling at them proudly.

Her family.

How far they had all come.

What distance had been covered, both in space and spirituality since her idyllic girlhood days on her father's property on the outskirts of Jerusalem.

CHAPTER 1

"Hurry, girls! Your father will be waiting!"

Seven-year-old Hannah pushed her head cloth back on her black hair, carefully picked up the jar of water in its large bowl, and followed her two elder sisters to the stairway. Tall, dark-haired, brown-eyed Moriah importantly bore their father's morning drink of herbs and honey, and Uzziel—she of the shining auburn hair and dark eyes—the tray with the jars of cleansing balm and ointments. Behind Hannah, the six-year-old, brown-eyed, flaxen-haired twins, Amanna and Anava, shared between them a stack of clean, folded cloths.

"Now do not spill, Hannah!" her mother cautioned.

Hannah turned to give her mother a nod and a hopeful smile, and then tripped on the rug at the bottom of the stairs and watched in dismay as the bowl in her hands tipped, the jar slipped to one side, and the precious water sloshed onto her sandaled feet, across the rug, and onto the thirsty stone floor.

The little train of girls stopped at her gasp.

Moriah, patient and kind, smiled, and the two little girls giggled. Uzziel rolled her eyes, straightened the head cloth over her shining hair, and glared down at Hannah. "Can you not do anything without spoiling it?"

Hannah felt close to tears. She looked at her mother, apologies already issuing forth, but her mother merely smiled. "Bring the jar back, dear. The Lord has blessed us amply with water."

Her mother refilled her bottle, and this time she was able to make the trip across the courtyard and up the staircase without incident, though Uzziel kept up a constant mutter of dire predictions for her, her bowl, her water, and all who had the misfortune of following her.

When they reached the top of the stairs, Moriah stopped, turned to her sister, and protested quietly, "Enough, Uzziel. Why must you be so discontented?"

Uzziel whispered back, "And why must I be forced to endure—" She got no further.

"Is that my daughters I hear? Come, come, my beautiful sprigs of sunshine! Come to me, my angels, my golden spray of God's flowers!"

The two littlest girls giggled happily, squeezed their small bodies past their elder sisters in the doorway, and hurried across the room. In an instant, they were enfolded in their father's warm embrace.

Hannah smiled as she watched them doing what she had so often done herself.

Her tall, black-eyed father, his dark hair and beard liberally streaked with grey, bent his head and whispered something to his two youngest daughters. Something that made them giggle loudly.

"See? They have no idea or care for proper decorum." Uzziel had obviously not been cheered—or muted—by her father's presence.

"They are little girls, Uzziel," Moriah explained patiently. "They may be excused if exuberance overcomes them at times."

"At times? All of the time!"

Moriah ignored her sister and moved further into the room. "Good morning, my father," she said, gracefully bowing her knees in a slight curtsy and smiling at her parent. "I pray I find you well this morning."

Ishmael smiled at his eldest daughter. "I am blessed with good health and much to be grateful for, my chosen one." He reached out a hand. "Ah! You look more like your lovely mother with every sun! Come and bless me further with your cheery face!"

Moriah moved closer and held out her mug. "Here is your morning drink, my father. Iscah tried a little something different in it today."

Hannah's father disentangled himself from his small daughters and, taking the cup, peered into it suspiciously. "What did she try today? Another of those ghastly mushroom pastes she is so fond of?"

Moriah laughed softly. "You are instructed to taste first and question after."

He snorted, "The disrespect to your father is astonishing."

Moriah's face coloured profusely as she threw herself down onto her knees on the floor. "Oh, Father, I meant no disrespect!"

Her father laughed. "Rise, my daughter, rise. I meant nothing by it!"

Moriah got to her feet and moved to one side as Uzziel came forward bearing her tray of unguents. "Father, if you are ready to cleanse yourself."

He looked at her. "You have the face that all heaven smiles down on, my Uzziel," he said, raising a hand and touching her softly rounded chin. "And yet you wear the frown of discontent upon it. It reminds me of a beautiful flower with a smelly fisherman's net thrown over it." He smiled and drew her closer. "Remove the net and let me see the father's flower."

Uzziel took a deep breath and managed a smile for her father.

"Ah, there is my girl!" Their father put an arm about her slender shoulders and hugged her tight. Then he turned to Hannah. "Ah, my little, faithful Hannah. You have brought my water?"

"Well, she had to spill it all first," Uzziel said.

Moriah looked at her. "Hush!"

"Ah, I see we have already had some incident," their father said. "Come, my treasured one, and tell me about it."

Hannah moved closer and, in an almost perfect re-creation of her accident in the courtyard, tripped over the rug at her father's bedside. Her bowl tilted once more and the jar resting inside slid toward the floor.

Her sisters held their breath as disaster threatened, but their father reached out and nabbed the bottle.

Smiling broadly, he turned to Hannah. "I said tell me, little one. No need to show me!"

"What is it with you and rugs?" Uzziel demanded.

"We know that they are mere adornments, do we not, Hannah?" Her father put his arm around her and held her tight. "Useless and unnecessary and very often something to trip over."

Hannah summoned up a smile.

Her father handed back the jar and held out his hands. "If you would be so kind, my angels."

It took only a few moments to pour his water and help him with his morning ablutions. Then they packed up their offerings and left him to his dressing.

"Ah, my daughters," their mother said. "Your father is well this morning?"

"Yes, Mother," Moriah said. "Well and happy. He will join us shortly."

Zedekiah was sitting on a cushion near the fire, Berachah next to him. Both boys, black-haired and dark-eyed like Hannah, were sneaking dates from a large bowl between them.

"Boys!" their mother said. "You must wait for the food to be blessed!"

"I am sure it was blessed last night when this same bowl sat in the center of our evening meal," Zedekiah whispered just loud enough for Hannah to hear.

She stared at him in surprise as Berachah started to laugh.

Her mother put her hands on her hips and glared at them. "What was that?"

"Nothing, Mother," Zedekiah said, smiling sweetly. "Merely discussing the size, taste, and texture of this season's harvest."

Their mother reached down and grabbed one of the dates, then held it to the morning sun. The light shone through it, making it glow a light green in her hand.

"Yes, we truly have been blessed." She dropped the date back into the bowl and looked at him suspiciously. "But I do not think that is what you were discussing."

Zedekiah put a hand to his breast and blinked his eyes innocently. "Why, Mother, how can you suspect me?"

She smiled, "How can I not?"

Just then, their father appeared at the top of the stairs. He waved his arms toward them. "What a sight there is before me! I see every arrow in my quiver gathered and awaiting me."

"And blessed by your presence, husband," Hannah's mother said. "Come. Let us break the fast."

The men gathered on cushions around the leather cloth laid over the swept stones of the courtyard. After their father had pronounced a blessing, they fell on the food with the appetite of men who spent their lives in outdoor labor.

The five girls—with their mother and the servants Iscah and Vashti guiding—served them.

Sometime later, their father sat back, patted his stomach, and smiled at his wife. "A wonderful meal, my dear wife."

Hannah's mother smiled back. "Thank you."

She nodded to her daughters, and they repeated the ritual of pouring the water so their father could wash his hands. Then they turned to their brothers and performed the same service.

"Well, this is an important day," Hannah's father said.

Her mother and the rest of the family gathered closer.

"It is to be today, husband?" her mother asked.

"I will attend the temple today, and afterward, meet with the servant of Amoz."

Zedekiah straightened in his seat. "Amoz?"

His father smiled. "Yes, my son. Today is the day we begin the bargain for your marriage!"

Zedekiah started to breathe deeply and his face went pink.

Hannah frowned. "But he is not yet nineteen. How can this be?"

Her mother put her arm around her daughter and said, "Ah, these things take time, my daughter. First there is the negotiation and engagement. Then the betrothal. Then the marriage."

"As you well know," Uzziel put in.

A marriage! Hannah thought. *The first in our family!* She smiled at her eldest brother, then sighed as her willing mind began to weave scenarios that featured her as some future bride to some handsome prospective bridegroom.

"Hannah! Wake up!" Uzziel marched past, carrying a platter. "There is work to be done!"

A short time later, the menfolk went outside. Hannah stood at the entrance of the house and watched them separate, her brothers moving out into the orchards and her father going off along the road into the great city of Jerusalem.

She stood there until they were out of sight, then drifted dreamily back inside.

Her mother and two elder sisters had started their spinning. The twins were taking turns carding the soft wool and getting in the way.

Just as Hannah reached them, her mother set down her spindle. "Anava! Amanna! Go with Hannah to help her tend the goats."

Sighing, Hannah, with her younger sisters tagging along, turned back and went out to the animal pens.

The three girls spent the rest of the morning milking the goats, tending to animals' needs, cleaning the pens, and talking.

"I cannot wait until it is my turn to get married!" Hannah told them. "Think of the handsome man who will ask for me and bargain for me and—"

"I'm going to marry Father," Amanna announced.

Hannah made a face at the little girl. "Girls do not marry their fathers!"

"Well, Berachah, then."

"Or their brothers."

Amanna's bottom lip went out and she plumped her round bottom down in a pile of clean straw. "You just do not want me to marry at all!"

Hannah laughed. "I do, little lamb. Do not worry. You will have a handsome bridegroom too. Just as I will."

"I just want someone kind," Anava put in. "Like Father. To read to me and tuck in the blanket just so."

Hannah smiled at the twin sisters. They were really only a year and a few months younger than she, but sometimes they seemed very young indeed.

Early in the afternoon, when the sun was high and the heat was rising in waves over the landscape, Hannah escaped into the bedchamber she shared with her sisters and threw herself down on her pallet.

Then someone outside began shouting.

Sighing, Hannah rose and looked out the window.

Her father had returned and someone was with him. Someone who seemed familiar. Hannah watched them as they grew closer. Finally, she recognized the man. Father Lehi, her father's cousin.

She also realized that the shouting she could hear was her sister, Uzziel, calling her to come and help prepare for a guest.

The men were relaxing after their meal. Hannah went to each one, offering to fill his mug.

"There has not been anything more than words thrown so far," Father Lehi was saying in his quiet voice. "But tempers are high and simmering. And no one wants to hear that what they are doing is wrong in the sight of the Lord."

"It has always been thus," Hannah's father said. "Even I have trouble with someone correcting me."

"But not when it comes to the important things," Father Lehi went on gently. "Not when it comes to your standing before the Lord."

"Well, that is true," her father said. "Our standing before the Lord has, and should always be, of utmost importance."

"You would think so," Father Lehi sighed. "But it is not always so."

"Well, sometimes I think that the Lord has a little too much say in our lives," Zedekiah spoke up. "After all, He is not the one living here and having to make a living and get along with people."

Father Lehi looked at him and said, "But He should have all say in our lives, my son. Is not He the one who has given us everything? Is not He the one who provided this earth for Father Adam and Mother Eve and the rest of us to live and grow and progress? And what does He ask in return for all of these gifts? Merely that we learn to govern ourselves by walking in obedience throughout our lives." He shook his head. "It seems so little to ask."

"But the people of Jerusalem are righteous!" Zedekiah said. "I have seen them at Temple and attending to their duties throughout the city! Seen them giving to the poor and the widows. I've seen them!"

"Ah yes. You've seen them," Father Lehi said sadly. "And that seems to be the exact reason that they do those things. To be seen."

"I do not understand," Zedekiah said. "What does it matter why something is done as long as it gets done?"

Father Lehi smiled, "Why indeed."

Hannah's father cleared his throat. "I would speak to you of another matter, if I may."

Father Lehi took a sip of his drink and nodded, "Of course, my brother."

"This is something I have been giving a lot of thought to—" Her father paused.

"Go on."

"Well, you have your two daughters and your four sons."

Father Lehi nodded, "Yes, my brother. Sariah and I have been well blessed. My quiver is filled."

"Well, I have a full quiver too. Of two sons and five beautiful girls. What do you think of our really making our families one?"

Hannah's heart seemed to freeze in her chest. Her sisters, for the first time since they had finished serving, stopped their whispering to listen.

All eyes were on Father Lehi.

He looked surprised, then thoughtful, then pleased. "You have a beautiful family, as I have often told you," he said finally. "And I can think of no other family more suited to combine with mine." He offered his hand to Hannah's father. "Let us speak of this more. My daughters, Rachel and Talitha, are just reaching the marriage age. Your Zedekiah and Berachah would make them fine husbands. And Laman is just now thirteen. Time to start thinking seriously of the girl who will become his help meet. And his brothers'. I am quite sure your daughters would make fine wives for my sons."

CHAPTER 2

"Well, all I can say is I hope mine is handsome! And tall!" Uzziel was sitting cross-legged on her mat, admiring her face in her small mirror, her tunic pulled above her knees and exposing long limbs.

Hannah shook her head and went back to her sewing.

Moriah came through the doorway and said, "Uzziel, pull your tunic down. Modest in dress and action whether inside or out."

Uzziel made a face, but did pull her dress down to cover her legs. "It's only us women here."

"Inside or out," Moriah repeated.

Anava and Amanna burst in, chattering excitedly.

Uzziel dropped her mirror into her lap and covered both ears with her slender hands. "Oh, please, do we have to have this babble?" she asked.

The little girls were instantly silent, staring warily at their elder sister.

Moriah moved to them and put an arm around each small figure. "Of course we do," she said. "When a child speaks, it is with the voice of an angel."

"Well could we please find an angel that is a little less shrill?"

Moriah shook her head and looked down at her youngest sisters. "Are you excited, my little angels?" she asked them.

Both little girls burst into speech at once. "Oh, it is so exciting, Morrie! To think we will meet our husbands!"

"Do you even know what a husband is?" Uzziel demanded.

Amanna lifted her head and looked at her elder sister. "A boy like Father." She nodded at Hannah. "Hannah told us."

"That's right. A boy. Who might grow up to be a horrible man with a twisted face and body who will beat you with a big whip."

Anava's round eyes looked up at Moriah. "Is it true, Morrie? Would Father give me to such a man?"

Moriah frowned sharply at Uzziel, and then smiled down at the little girl. "Of course not, my angel. Father will only give you to someone who will cherish and love you as he does. A man who will honor his priesthood and take his vows to the Lord very, very seriously."

"I hope mine is handsome!" Amanna said, plopping herself down on her pallet.

Uzziel laughed. "They have no idea what you are talking about, Morrie. They are six years old!"

Anava turned to Uzziel. "I know I want a man like Father," she said steadily, looking suddenly elder than her six years. "A man who will be kind like he is."

Uzziel lay back on her pallet. "Well, good luck, my small sister."

Moriah frowned again at Uzziel. "Uzziel, why must you always be so cross?"

Uzziel shrugged, "You call it being cross. I call it being truthful."

Suddenly, all five girls straightened as a shout drifted in through the open window and door.

"They're here!"

Hannah could not help staring at the four boys sitting with the other men around the meal. Even as she, her sisters, and Father Lehi's two daughters quietly helped the two women servants prepare food and bear dishes and platters back and forth to the male guests across the courtyard, she found time to look each boy over carefully.

The eldest, black-haired Laman, was large. At thirteen, he was already showing the unmistakable signs of his first facial hair growth. He was gruff, outspoken for his age, and just a bit scary.

Lemuel, the next in line, was tall with sun-streaked brown hair. Still smooth-faced, he seemed colorless—simply doing whatever his elder brother said or did.

Samuel was a happy boy, full of sunny smiles and good humor.

Nephi was the youngest son and, though he was the same age as Hannah, was already much taller than she. For some reason, he seemed to draw her eyes the most. Though dark like his eldest brother, any similarity ended there. Unlike his elder brother who continually talked in muttered undertones to the second brother, Nephi was serious and respectful, giving the men his full attention and ignoring the youthful antics of Sam and the insolence of his two eldest brothers.

Father Lehi's two daughters, Rachel, who at fifteen was just older than Moriah, and Talitha, just younger at fourteen, were both surprisingly outspoken, voicing opinions and ideas freely. They seemed to become quick friends with Uzziel, exchanging gossip and giggles as each glanced with interest toward Hannah's two brothers.

Hannah noticed that the two girls were not the only ones showing interest. Both of her brothers' eyes often wandered toward them as well. It made Hannah tingle with the possibilities.

The evening was warm. A light breeze smelling of grape vines and earth drifted across the courtyard, and Hannah noticed how it brushed Nephi's dark hair and lifted it briefly from his broad brow.

"Hannah, my favored one, why are you dawdling?" Moriah had come up behind her, bearing a tray of cheeses. "Take your tray in. The men need their bread."

Hannah blinked and shook her head. Then, careful to watch her feet, she approached the seated men and boys.

"Well, it is unfortunate that I do not have quite enough sons to satisfy both of our families." Lehi was saying. "A great pity one of your daughters will not be joining my household!" He sighed. "But she will be as great a blessing to another family as your other daughters will be to mine."

Hannah's heart seemed to freeze in her chest and she stopped short, completely losing track of what she had been doing. The tray she carried tipped, showering its entire contents onto Lemuel's head.

The boy scrambled to his feet, scattering fresh, warm bread everywhere.

Hannah stared at him, horrified, as she clutched her now-empty tray.

Lemuel's eyes narrowed as he looked at her, still brushing at imagined crumbs, but a great shout of laughter behind him made him turn his head.

Laman had gotten up as well, and he grabbed the large chunk of bread that was teetering dangerously atop his brother's head and, folding it, took a big bite. "Now that's what I would call personal service," he said, slapping his brother on the back and looking down at Hannah with approval in his dark eyes. "Perhaps we've found the wife for you!"

Hannah's eyes went wide. She gasped sharply and, spinning around, fled past her mother to the kitchen area. She glanced back and saw that Laman was continuing to look after her. "Maybe she does not think it is such a good idea," he said loudly. Then he laughed again.

"Laman, you are embarrassing her!" Father Lehi had pitched his voice low, but still it reached Hannah's ears.

She ducked her head and dropped her tray into Iscah's surprised hands. Then, pulling her head cloth further forward to cover her face, she fled to her chamber.

CHAPTER 3

"It was not so bad, dearest." Moriah's gentle hand rubbed Hannah's back as the younger girl sobbed on her pallet.

"Yes. I am quite sure the way to a man's heart is by quite literally showering him with bread," Uzziel added, sounding immensely satisfied with the entire day but especially with Hannah's blunder at dinner.

"Sister, do not you have somewhere else to be?" Moriah was losing patience, something Hannah had never before seen happen.

Hannah blotted her eyes on the coverlet she had gripped tightly in her hands and choked down another sob.

"You mean cleaning up Hannah's mess in the courtyard? Iscah and Vashti will have cleaned that up long ago."

Moriah straightened and looked at her next younger sister. "I mean somewhere else to go," she said, sounding firm and unwavering.

Uzziel sighed and got to her feet. "Yes. I suppose I do," she said. "Perhaps one of our suitors needs something. Maybe Hannah's. I'll just go and ask."

Moriah was silent for a moment after Uzziel left. Then she resumed rubbing Hannah's back.

"Why does she hate me so?" Hannah whispered.

Moriah sighed. "She does not hate you, dearest. She really does not hate anyone. She is just one of those people who—takes life hard."

Hannah looked at her. "I do not understand."

"Nor do I, dearest."

"So Lehi was thinking of Rachel for our Zedekiah, Talitha for Berachah, Moriah for his Laman, Uzziel for Lemuel, Hannah for Sam, and one of the twins for Nephi."

Hannah was seated in her special place, a tiny, warm corner behind the oven—too small for anyone but her. Or her two younger sisters, if she ever showed them how to wiggle inside, which she had vowed never to do.

The night was soft and dark around her, and she snuggled into it like an old friend and listened contentedly to her parents as her father drank his cup of herbs and honey before bedtime. She heard them say her name, but the topic was so remote it was as though they discussed someone else.

"That sounds wonderful," Hannah's mother said. "Our sons and almost all of our girls spoken for by one of the leading spiritual families of Jerusalem."

"Lehi also expressed a bit of concern about our standing in the community."

"What? Does he not think we are good enough for him?" Her mother's voice rose suddenly.

"No, my dear, no. He does not want to—expose our family to ridicule. Or worse. He has received threats to his person and his family if he does not stop teaching."

"That's foolish. He is a prophet of the Lord. How can he simply stop teaching?"

"You know he is a prophet, my dear. And I know. But those he is calling to repentance will never admit that. It is easier to silence the messenger than to change one's behavior."

Her mother sighed, and then was silent for a moment. "Hmmm. Now that you do mention it, it shines a whole new light on something that happened this morning in the village."

"What was this?"

"I was visiting Jeshua's widow—Oh, Ishmael, she is in such need!—and Martha stopped me as I was leaving. You remember that she has recently married again and that her new husband is—well, let us just say that he has a much higher standing in the community than her first husband."

"Yes?"

"Well, she put her hand on my arm and said, 'Judith, I have great concern for you.' Of course I stopped to listen to what she had to say."

There was a pause and Hannah could hear liquid being poured.

"Thank you, my dear. You see to my every want," her father said. Another pause. Then, "And what did Martha have to say to you?"

"It was quite garbled, but now, with this new information, it seems to make more sense. She told me to be cautious of the people I welcomed across my threshold. I could not understand to whom she referred, and we were interrupted before she could clarify. I just put it down as the ramblings of someone who continually has some other person's business on her mind."

"Well, you were right to put it there. Because that is what it is." Hannah's father sighed. "It all seems so simple to me. Spend your life pleasing man and what do you have? Nothing. But spend your life pleasing the Lord? You have eternal riches beyond measure."

Hannah's mother sighed, "There are those who think riches of the world are more important."

"Then what do you have hereafter? Because we know you cannot take any of them with you." Her father sounded tired.

"But if you simply deny that a prophet is a prophet, then you are free to do whatever you want and still promise yourself eternal rewards."

"All of which disappear the moment you cross the veil into the hereafter," her father sighed. "I am quite ready to find my bed, my dear."

"Have faith, Ishmael. All will turn out as the Lord wills."

"I know, my dear. Sometimes I just wish that every good thing would not be accompanied by trials and opportunities for growth."

Judith laughed softly. "When we have Lord-given trials, we receive Lord-given strength to withstand them and Lord-given rewards for our obedience."

"Our fathers were so wise to give you to me," Ishmael said, his voice was moving across the courtyard to the stairs.

"And to gift me with a man of true strength—the Lord's strength. My life has been many times blessed."

Hannah poked her head out of her special place and peered around the oven. She watched as her parents disappeared through the doorway to their chamber.

Then she sat back against the sun-and-wood-warmed wall and thought about what she had heard. Some of it her seven-year-old mind just could not quite grasp. But she did understand that some people would not like to see her family marry with Father Lehi's and that some people did not follow the prophet of the Lord.

She had understood that. She just could not understand them.

Hannah looked at her eldest brother and asked, "So it is settled?"

Zedekiah nodded. "Father and Father Lehi have spoken and agreed; it is settled. The deal has been struck. Rachel and I are to be officially betrothed. In one year, we will wed."

"So you will be a married man?"

He smiled slightly and said, "It sounds a bit strange."

"Oh, no, Zedekiah!" Hannah protested. "I think it sounds wonderful! And you will be a fine husband. Strong. Kind. Honorable."

"You sound like Mother."

"Good."

Zedekiah stubbed the toe of his right foot into the dust of the vineyard and said, "It is all happening so fast."

Hannah tipped her head to one side and looked at him. "I thought you were the right age for a betrothal."

"Well—yes. But when it is happening to you, it suddenly happens very fast."

Hannah giggled. "I would love to be married!" she said as she looked at her brother. "And guess who I would choose for my husband."

"You're seven. Who do you know? Your parents and about three other people."

Hannah giggled again and tucked her hands together behind her back. Leaning forward, she grinned at her brother. "Guess!"

"Well, you know you cannot marry one of the servants' sons."

"Oh, this is not a servant's son."

"And I, Berachah, and Father are all out."

"Ye-es."

"Okay, I bet it is Sam."

Hannah frowned. "Sam?"

"Yes. Is he not the one Father has chosen for you?"

"Well—yes—but he is not the one I would choose."

"Well, who, then? I am out of options."

Hannah's brown eyes twinkled and danced with glee. "It is Nephi," she whispered. "Do not tell!"

Zedekiah frowned. "Nephi? Is not he the baby of the family? The one who looks so serious and studious all the time?"

"Yes!" Hannah hugged herself and spun around in a circle. "I think he is so handsome."

"Handsome? Do you even know what that word means?"

She stopped. "I think so. I heard Uzziel say it about Laman and we use it all the time." She clapped a hand over her mouth and stared at her brother in horror. "Have I been saying something I should not?"

He laughed. "Not really. It is just not a word I thought I would hear from my little sister. At least not yet." He reached for one of the tightly-braided plaits that had escaped her head scarf and gave it a pull.

"I am not that little," Hannah said indignantly, pulling her hair out of his hand and smoothing it back under its covering. "I've been milking the goats for over a year."

Zedekiah laughed again. "Maybe it is one of the servant boys you should marry."

Hannah thrust out her chin and glared at her eldest brother. Then she spun around and stomped off through the vineyard, her brown, bare feet raising little puffs of dust with every step.

Behind her, she could hear Zedekiah laughing.

Bright lamplight illuminated the scene. Rachel and her parents were seated across the snowy cloth from Zedekiah and his parents. Everyone wore wide smiles.

Hannah could not take her eyes off Rachel. Her brother's future wife looked much different than when Hannah had seen her before. Her dark hair was cunningly twisted into many plaits, twined with gleaming jewels, and left to hang down her back. Her tunic was a work of art—richly embroidered and finished. She wore chains of gold about her throat and rings on her slender fingers, and her wrists clinked and sparkled with precious jewels and gold coins whenever she moved her arms. Even her ankles bore signs of the same ropes of gold and jewels.

Her brother was marrying the daughter of a very wealthy family indeed, and Hannah thought Rachel was the prettiest girl she had ever seen.

The four parents and the couple chatted for several moments in low tones. Then Zedekiah stood up and approached Rachel. Kneeling beside her, he lifted her hand, pressed it gently against his chest, and released it. Reaching into his pouch, he pulled out a long, golden chain, which had at its end a large, gleaming stone.

Rachel gasped and stared at the stone, which was much larger and brighter than any she possessed.

"Rachel, my beautiful, see by this token thou art set apart for me, according to the law of Moses and of Israel."

Rachel leaned forward, and Zedekiah lifted the chain and placed it over her head and around the her neck. The bright white jewel nestled among her other necklaces as though it had always been there.

Rachel smiled at Zedekiah and bowed her head.

"The token is given and accepted," Father Lehi announced. "The betrothal is done!"

Everyone cheered, then began to talk and laugh excitedly. One of the musicians who had been set up in one corner of the courtyard began to play a lively tune, and soon people were dancing enthusiastically.

From that time, the evening was a blur of filling mugs and passing trays of foods and sweetmeats.

Father Lehi and Hannah's father were happily seated in a corner of the courtyard with several of their friends, discussing politics and other issues of the day.

The hour grew late and the people still seemed unwilling to leave. Some of them had consumed so much wine that they were acting foolish. Hannah watched, horrified, as one young man, a friend of both Zedekiah and Berachah, decided to test himself to see if he could walk on the top of the courtyard wall across its entire distance. Partway around, he lost his balance and disappeared into the hedge on the far side with a crackle of branches and a loud "Oof!"

The fact that Hannah later saw him engaged in some sort of drinking and gambling game assured her that the young man was no worse for his encounter with the bushes.

As dawn filled the sky with deep, rosy tones, the last of their guests found either the road home or a cozy corner to sleep in.

Hannah watched her brother and her parents accompany Father Lehi's wagons up the road to the top of the hill. There, Zedekiah took his newly betrothed's hand and said something to her and her parents, then both groups separated and Hannah's parents turned to come back home.

Zedekiah remained there at the top of the hill, obviously watching Rachel and her family as they continued down the other side.

Finally, he, too, turned back toward the house. He looked—happy.

CHAPTER 4

"I am glad they are coming. It has been far too long since we saw them."

"It has only been a month, Uzziel," Moriah said, sounding disinterested. "Just since Zedekiah and Rachel's wedding."

Uzziel smiled and stared dreamily out the window. "The wedding," she whispered.

Moriah stopped what she was doing and stared at her sister. "Your head is certainly in the clouds this morning," Moriah said.

Uzziel glared at her eldest sister. "You have to admit that our brother's wedding was beautiful!"

"I have never said otherwise."

"And that our new sister looked amazing with her dress and finery."

"I've never seen so much gold and jewelry on one person," Moriah said, smiling. "I was surprised the girl could even stand, let alone walk."

"Father Lehi gave her what he could. Besides, if she and Zedekiah should ever part—"

"Uzziel how can you even think of such a thing?"

"I just know my brother," Uzziel said, looking down at her fingernails. "I would not want to live with him."

"May I point out that you have always lived with him?"

"As his wife! As his wife!"

Moriah put her hands on her hips. "You are in an odd mood today, my sister."

Hannah laughed. "It's because Father Lehi's family is coming. Whenever they come, Uzziel forgets what she is doing and stares into the heavens a lot."

"I do not." Uzziel said as she stood up, stung.

"You do. I've watched you."

"Well stop watching me!"

Hannah merely smiled.

Moriah gave a light laugh. "So, back to what we were discussing—"

"I've forgotten, Moriah," Hannah said. "What were we discussing?"

Moriah looked sideways at Uzziel. "How long it has been since Father Lehi's family was here for a visit."

"Oh, yes. And Moriah said that it had only been a month."

Uzziel frowned. "Once a month is still not enough."

"But if you add up that it has been once a month for over two years? That should be enough." Moriah smiled, and then sobered and went back over to her mat. "And I am quite sure Laman has not forgotten you in a few weeks." She folded the coverlet from her bed and stacked it neatly aside with her pillow. Then she pulled at the linen sheet that covered her mat, balled it up, and tossed it into a basket.

Uzziel sat down on her own pallet and watched their oldest sister with her chin in one pink palm. "You have got to be the cleanest person I have ever met," she said.

Hannah moved between them. "I like it." She, too, stripped the bedding from her sleeping mat. "I like being clean."

"Well, I hope Sam likes that, good little wife!"

Moriah turned and fixed Uzziel with a glare. "Stop it, Uzziel. You know we are to keep ourselves and our surroundings clean and tidy. Gifts from the Lord are not to be ignored or abused."

Uzziel sighed and stood up. "You are right, of course, Moriah. Too bad it is not going to get you a husband." She stretched and then smoothed the soft fabric of her new tunic about her waist and hips. "It has been more than a year since Laman even spoke to you."

"But I thought they were betrothed—" Hannah was confused.

"No," Uzziel shook her head, "And a non-betrothal can easily be broken, so . . . " She let the last word dangle.

Moriah sighed.

Uzziel laughed and disappeared through their chamber door.

Hannah looked at her oldest sister. "Are you sad, Moriah?"

"No, dear," Moriah shrugged. "I am not even sure I like Laman. He is so outspoken and—" she paused. Finally, she frowned. "I guess disrespectful is the word I am looking for."

Hannah put her arms around her sister's waist and hugged her tight. "Well I hope you find someone who is a little less disrespectful."

Moriah smiled. "And I hope the same for you—with your Sam." She wandered over to the window and looked out across their father's land with its acres of tidy grape vines and date and olive orchards.

Hannah joined her.

The afternoon was hot, but not unaccountably so, considering it was one of the months of summer that usually smothered them in its heat. A goat bleated from somewhere close by, but nothing in the landscape seemed to stir.

"I like the quiet in the afternoon," Hannah said, bracing her elbows on the sill and planting her chin in her hands.

Moriah smiled. "I do, too, my little favored one. It is like the moment of calm reflection between the tasks of the morning and those later in the day."

Hannah looked up at her elder sister. "Moriah, if you do not marry Laman, who will you marry?"

Moriah traced the wood in the windowsill with a fingernail. "I do not know, Hannah. But the Lord knows me and He will provide." She took a deep breath and straightened. "Now we have some clothes to wash. Are you coming with me?"

Hannah giggled and went to fetch her bundle.

It took only a few minutes for the two girls to make their way to the well that serviced much of their family's acres.

Drawing water, Moriah poured it into a nearby trough and the two of them went to work, scrubbing and pounding the lengths of cloth expertly. Hannah admired Moriah's strength and found herself wondering if she would be as strong and sure when she was fifteen.

A shout went up from the compound just over the rise and both girls lifted their heads alertly. "Our guests have come," Moriah said. "We must finish. It is unseemly that we not be present for refreshments."

They hurried and were just wringing the water from their final garments when movement off to the right caught Hannah's eye. She turned and looked.

Seeing her, Moriah turned as well. "What is it, sister?"

"Someone—" Hannah finally spotted a figure as it came out from behind one of the oldest trees in the grove. "Look! There!"

"It's Uzziel," Moriah said. She watched for a moment. "What on earth is she doing?"

Uzziel was taking care to stay out of sight of the house. She dashed across from tree to tree until she was at the farthest point of the orchard.

Then the girls saw a man coming from the opposite side. The pair met behind one of the trees and a package exchanged hands. They spoke briefly and clasped hands for a moment, and then Uzziel was running off toward the house clutching her prize to her chest.

The man waited for a few minutes more, then followed her along the same path toward the house.

Hannah looked at Moriah. "What was that?"

Moriah shook her head and replied, "I do not know. But that was Laman out there giving something to Uzziel. Something that neither of them wanted any of us to see."

"Well, we need to get back to the house anyway," Hannah said. "Come!" She grabbed her sister's hand and started to pull her.

"Wait! I need my basket." Moriah stooped and picked up her load of sodden clothes. Then the two of them quickly crossed the dusty earth toward their home.

Setting their baskets in the cool milk room, they quickly washed their hands, tidied themselves, and hurried around to the porch to greet their guests.

Uzziel was there when they arrived, slightly out of breath and looking just a bit disheveled, especially when standing next to Zedekiah's bride, Rachel, who as usual was perfectly and exquisitely groomed.

Hannah smiled at them both and received a bright smile from Rachel in return, but Uzziel turned away, appearing to concentrate on their recently arrived guests by offering drinks and water for washing.

The men gathered on the far side of the courtyard, already deep in discussion.

Hannah hurried over with yet another tray of drinks.

"It is getting worse," Father Lehi was saying. "Yesterday, I stood in front of the temple to discuss the Lord's instructions to our brothers and sisters in Jerusalem and—"

Laman interrupted, "Someone threw a stone at him!"

Hannah's father sucked in a breath. "My brother, were you injured?"

"Show him the bump, Father," Laman said as he got to his feet and started pacing. "Every time Father goes into the city, he seems to gather a crowd of people willing to call him names and heap every indignity upon him."

"Your concern for your father says much of you, Laman," Hannah's father said approvingly.

"Yes, well—" Laman's frown deepened.

"Laman and I were discussing this very thing last night," Lemuel spoke up. "It's getting harder and harder for us to spend any time with our friends. Why, just last week, one of our closest associates informed us that it was too dangerous—dangerous—for him to continue to be seen with us."

"Ah." Hannah's father looked thoughtful.

"Dangerous!" Laman repeated. "And dangerous for an old man who cannot seem to keep his thoughts to himself."

Father Lehi was watching his eldest son gravely. "Your concern is touching, son. But you know that the words I speak do not come from me, but from the Lord."

Laman shrugged. "Well then the Lord should deliver them Himself and not put our family in harm's way."

"The Lord is delivering them himself," Father Lehi said quietly. "I will be with thy mouth, and teach thee what thou shalt say."

"Let's agree to disagree on this one, Father."

"No, son," Father Lehi said as he got to his feet. "On this theme, we must be of one mind!"

Laman stared at his father for a moment, then ducked his head slightly. "As you wish, Father," he said and sat down.

Hannah realized that she was still standing beside them, holding her forgotten tray. Self-consciously, she set it down on the cloth between them and made her escape back over to the other women.

"What are they discussing so seriously over there, Hannah?" Moriah asked as her younger sister joined them. "Here. You can help me grind the grain."

Hannah grabbed the dipper and poured a cupful of kernels onto the stone Moriah was using. "Something about Father Lehi preaching the Lord's word and someone throwing a stone at him."

"A stone!" Hannah's mother gripped her shoulder. "Someone stoned Father Lehi?"

"Well—one stone. But it hit him and Laman is very upset about it."

"That speaks well of Laman," her mother said, looking pointedly at Moriah and smiling.

Moriah shook her head and turned away.

"It does." Uzziel said. "He is strong and protective. He'll make a fine husband."

Her mother frowned, continuing to watch both Uzziel and Moriah.

"Mother, it is embarrassing!" Uzziel sat down on the sun-warmed stones of the courtyard and picked up her spinning.

"Hush, dear. There is nothing wrong with it."

"But they hang around him like bees around the hive. Always buzzing—and giving him things."

Hannah's mother smiled and replied, "Well, one of the twins will be his wife. It is natural that they should want to hang about him. He is already showing the makings of a fine man, a man who will honor both his wife and his priesthood."

"Pfff—all of that is in the future," Uzziel waved dismissively. "As will be their marriage. It is now that I am talking about!"

"I think they're cute," Hannah put in. "And Nephi shows no sign of resentment. He is endlessly patient with them. And kind. Do you know that he was teaching them from a little roll of scripture he carries about with him?"

Uzziel snorted. "He carries scripture with him?" She looked at their mother. "Is there a rule about that?"

Her mother smiled. "Yes. That we should know the scriptures and apply them to our daily lives."

"That's not what I meant," Uzziel sighed. "How old is Nephi? Nine?"

"He is the same age as me," Hannah said. "So, yes. He is nine."

"What does a boy know at nine?"

"What does a girl know at thirteen?" Hannah challenged.

Uzziel straightened and glared at her. "I know a lot more than a little girl like you."

Hannah shrugged, "I never claimed to know anything." She smiled. "Besides, we were not talking about me. We were talking about Nephi."

"You always want to talk about Nephi," Uzziel said. "Have you forgotten that you are intended for Samuel?"

"No."

"Well, you should get your head out of the clouds and your nose in its own business."

"As you do?" Moriah had been quiet through the whole discussion, but she spoke up now. "Were you not the one who was worrying about the little girls bothering Nephi, who will take one of them to wife? Whose business is that but theirs?"

Uzziel dropped her spindle and got to her feet. "I was only trying to save our family from embarrassment."

"Like you did when you met my intended out beyond the orchard and received a gift from him?"

Hannah's mother's head came up, her brown eyes fixed on Uzziel.

Uzziel's face flushed crimson and she floundered for something to say. "You were not supposed to—! How did you—! Where were you?"

"Hannah and I were washing clothes. We saw you meet someone at the edge of the orchard." Moriah gave a little laugh. "It is strange because we would not have noticed you if you would have just been walking. It was the running from tree to tree and the looking toward the house that attracted our attention."

Uzziel's lips set into a hard line and she thrust out her chin when she said, "Well, we met there. Laman said he had something for me." She glanced at her mother. "We have done it before. These past two years, we have become—friends."

Her mother dropped her spinning and reached for her second daughter's hand. "Uzziel, my strength, is that what it is? Because you know that Laman is intended for Moriah."

"We have become friends, Mother," Uzziel said firmly.

"But—meeting alone," Hannah's mother said. "Being friends with a righteous young man is a good thing, but not alone. Never alone." She peered up at her daughter. "Has he been promising you—anything?"

"What could he possibly promise, Mother? He is fifteen, like Moriah. What say does he have in anything?" Uzziel let out a sob, put one hand over her mouth, and fled.

Everyone sat in silence for a moment, then Hannah's mother picked up her spindle. "Carry on, my daughters," she said quietly.

Hannah and Moriah went back to their spinning.

"Do you think the little girls bother Nephi?" Hannah's mother said some time later.

"No," Hannah said immediately. "He enjoys their company. As I was telling you, he brought out this little roll of scripture that he had in his pouch, and he was teaching them to read from it."

"Scripture," Hannah's mother said as she took a deep breath. "He is remarkable for one so young."

"He says he loves the scriptures," Hannah smiled. "I think his exact words were that his soul delights in the scriptures."

Her mother shook her head. "Remarkable," she said again. "I must learn more of the young Nephi."

Hannah nodded. She, too, would like to learn more of this Nephi.

CHAPTER 5

"Uzziel, could I please speak to you for a moment?"

Hannah lifted her head from the grain she had been grinding. When Father spoke in that tone, he had something he was worrying about.

Uzziel set down the bowl she had been filling with grain and dusted her hands. "I am not clean, Father," she said. "Could you wait until I have a chance to wash?"

"I am needed in the orchards, my strength. I must discuss something with you now."

Uzziel sighed and crossed the courtyard to where her father was reclining on his cushion on the cobblestones following breaking the fast.

Hannah's brothers had already gone out and Hannah's mother and sisters were busy elsewhere, so there was only Hannah, Uzziel, and their father there in the bright morning sunlight.

Uzziel stopped and sank down on her knees beside her father. "Yes, Father?"

He looked into her eyes for a moment. Then, "What did you receive as a gift from Laman?"

Hannah saw Uzziel's eyes widen and heard her take a deep breath. "I—it—it was nothing, Father."

"Uzziel. You know that it is unwise to accept gifts from a young man who is not your intended."

Uzziel hung her head.

"You do know this."

"Yes, Father." Her response was a mere whisper of sound.

"What did Laman give you?"

"It was nothing—"

"He gave you nothing?"

"Well, it was—it was just a small—"

"Uzziel, please bring it to me."

Uzziel looked as though she would faint. Her face got very red. Then white. She got to her feet and slowly started toward the chamber she shared with her sisters.

"Uzziel, I am a patient man, but there are places I am needed and I prefer not to wait while you take the day."

Uzziel's steps quickened and she disappeared inside, returning moments later holding a cloth-wrapped bundle. She moved back to her father's side and stopped, still clutching the object.

"Let me see it, my dear."

Slowly, Uzziel knelt once more and lowered her bundle to the mat spread out before her father. Then she sat back.

Ishmael gently unwrapped the cloth, finally exposing what it had covered. He took a quick breath and looked at Uzziel.

Hannah could not see the object, nor her father's expression, but she could see Uzziel. Her sister's face was the dead white of newly carded sheep's wool. Even her lips were colorless.

"Uzziel, you brought this into my house?"

A tear made a path down one of Uzziel's cheeks. She nodded.

"You know the commandments."

Again, she nodded. Another tear.

"My daughter, I do not know quite what to say." Hannah's father lifted the object and now Hannah could see it.

It was the figure of a woman with her hands raised and her skirts flaring as if she had been caught in the middle of a dance.

It was beautiful. And, at the same time, repulsive.

Hannah knew the laws against creating anything having the form of a human. Only the Lord Himself could create the human form.

And if Hannah knew, then Uzziel certainly did.

"Laman gave this to you?"

"He made it for me!"

Again, Ishmael drew in a quick, shocked breath. "Made it for you?"

Her words came out in a rush. "He has been at it for weeks. He was tending the olive trees in the oldest part of their orchard, and there was this old tree that had died. The wood was beautiful and he said it reminded him of me and—"

"Enough."

Uzziel clamped her lips shut and bowed her head.

"I will think on this, daughter. You have deliberately encouraged this young man, who you know is intended for your sister. You have met him without a proper chaperone, ruining both your reputation and his. And he has flouted both the law and the sanctity of his father's house and mine." He looked at her. "There will be—punishments," he sighed. "I will think on this." He waved a hand, dismissing her.

Uzziel reached for the figure, but her father stopped her and shook his head. "You will not touch it again, daughter. It must be destroyed."

Now the tears were flowing freely down Uzziel's face. "But it is mine, Father! It was a gift for me."

"How can you not understand?" Ishmael's voice had risen. "It is a sin to have it here! You have sinned! You have brought the spirit of evil into our h-home!" His voice broke on the last word.

Uzziel rose to her feet and ran out of the courtyard.

A moment later, Hannah could see her flying figure as she crossed the yard and disappeared into the olive grove.

Ishmael leaned forward and placed his face into his large, calloused hands. Hannah watched wide-eyed as those strong, beloved shoulders shook with obvious emotion.

Her father's anger she could barely withstand. Her father's grief was beyond her.

Sensing that what he needed most now was her absence, Hannah, too, fled.

Hannah's father stood before all of them. Even the servants had been summoned and waited, silent and respectful, with the rest.

Ishmael was standing quietly, his hands folded together, his head bowed.

For several seconds, the only sound were the cicadas shrilling somewhere in the garden.

Then Hannah's father lifted his head.

Hannah was shocked at how old and tired he looked. Much older than his forty years.

He sighed heavily. Then, "Our daughter has sinned," he said at last.

Hannah instantly focused on Uzziel. Her elder sister's face was again the white of sheep's wool and the picture of guilt.

The group looked around, but finally, everyone fixed on Uzziel.

The girl fell to her knees. "Papa, please—"

Her father shook his head and Hannah saw a tear trickle down the weather-beaten face. "No, my daughter. We must admit our mistakes and make our amends. Then rely on the Lord's forgiveness to take away our stain."

Uzziel buried her face in her hands and sobbed softly.

Ishmael turned back to the waiting crowd. "Uzziel has been meeting a man unchaperoned and alone. She assures me that they have only exchanged gifts and talked, but her reputation has been shattered." He took a deep breath. "I have met with the young man's family, and we have crafted a solution." He looked at Uzziel. "Daughter, please stand."

Hannah's mother moved to her second eldest daughter, offered her a hand, and helped her to her feet.

Uzziel was openly crying now, her tears falling unheeded to make spots of moisture on her tunic and the recently-swept courtyard.

Ishmael cleared his throat. "Father Lehi and I have discussed this and have agreed that the best solution and the one that will save both parties will be to wed the two, Uzziel and Laman."

Uzziel's head came up and she caught her breath in a gasp.

Moriah gasped at the same time, and Hannah turned to look at her eldest sister, whose eyes were suddenly swimming with tears.

Her father shook his head and closed his eyes for a moment. Opening them, he went on, "This may sound like a reward to you my daughter, as you profess to have feelings for this young man and he for you, but know this, that many lives have been touched—and hurt—by your actions."

Uzziel was wiping hastily at her tears and nodding eagerly at her father.

He sighed again. "Not the least of which is your sister," he said, glancing at Moriah's woebegone face, "who had been chosen for this young man."

Uzziel glanced at Moriah, then turned back to her father.

Some of the people started to speak, but Hannah's father put up one hand and silence was instantly restored.

"It has been an unusual situation and the normal traditions could not be observed, but Father Lehi and I have agreed that the betrothal ceremony will take place soon." Again, he held up one hand as people tried to speak. "What I have not mentioned is Uzziel's payment for her actions."

The smile that had started to peep through Uzziel's tears disappeared.

"From now until Uzziel is the wife of Laman, she will be accompanied for every moment of every day and night by either her mother or one of her sisters."

"Father!"

He ignored the outcry and, looking steadily at Uzziel, went on, "She will neither receive nor make any calls off our property, but will stay within sight of her mother and continue with her chores and duties. Except for the betrothal ceremony, she will neither see nor hear Laman until the time that they are man and wife." He looked at his once-more sobbing daughter. "Is that clear to you, Uzziel?"

It took a moment, but Uzziel was finally able to nod.

Her mother led her from the courtyard.

"The commandments are given to us to keep us safe," Hannah's father said quietly. "They may seem like rules designed to complicate our lives. But understand this: they have been given for the sole purpose of keeping us clean before the Lord. And staying clean, while not easy, is always best." He looked down for a moment, then lifting his head, said, "Once we have broken those laws, we must do our utmost to make reparations. And serious sins require lengthy reparations." He looked around the group, focusing especially on his sons and daughters. "Remember that. And remember, too, that sin can happen to any of us at any time. It courts all and cherishes none. We must always—always—be on guard."

He nodded, then turned and moved toward the stairway to his chamber.

"Father?" Moriah had followed him.

Ishmael turned. "Yes, my daughter?"

A tear slowly made its way down one smooth cheek. "With my intended gone elsewhere, what happens to me now?"

"Oh, chosen one!" Her father enveloped her in a warm hug. Then he leaned back and took her by the shoulders. "Do not worry, my dear. The Lord will provide someone special for you in time."

"But Father, already I am of an age to marry."

"Then we shall urge Him to hurry." He hugged her again, then started up the stairs.

Moriah dabbed at her eyes with a corner of her tunic.

Hannah hurried to her and put her arm around her eldest sister. "Do not worry, Morrie. You are too special for the Lord to ignore!"

Moriah let out a gasp of laughter. "Let us hope so, my treasure. Let us hope so!" She brushed at the last of her tears. "You will not hear me speak of it again. And I certainly do not want to hear you speak of it either."

Hannah nodded.

"Now. To our chores, my sister. Work. Work will heal us faster than anything."

CHAPTER 6

The midwife has been sent for. It is time. I must go back up and join Uzziel, who is sitting with Rachel."

Hannah stared at her mother and then, as her words sank in, she squealed aloud and grabbed Anava in a hug. The two girls giggled and swung about in a circle.

"Your first grandchild, Mother!" Moriah said.

Hannah's mother smiled, her dark eyes twinkling. "Children are an heritage of the Lord," she sighed happily. "Hopefully this will be the beginning of a great heritage!"

"Well, with Zedekiah and Rachel already bearing children and now Berachah and Talitha betrothed and their wedding quickly approaching—"

"You think our heritage is upon us?"

Moriah put her arm through her mother's. "I know it is, Mother."

All of them heard the sound of the knock on the heavy planks of the front door.

"Ah. The midwife has arrived," Hannah's mother said. "I will take her up."

The rest of the day passed in delicate tasks in the birthing room, the usual care of the household, the constant and exciting watching, and the reassuring of Zedekiah that things were progressing "normally."

Finally, just as the sun was dipping toward the western horizon, Hannah's mother, trailed closely by Hannah and the twins, came out of Zedekiah's room bearing a swaddled bundle. She walked over to Zedekiah, who got to his feet, his eyes wide and his face flushed.

"My son," his mother said with a smile. "You have a son."

Zedekiah looked as though he would faint. His mother held out the tiny bundle, but he made no move to take it.

"Son. The Lord's heritage has come to your house."

Zedekiah reached out his arms.

His mother placed the tiny, wrapped bundle in them.

For several moments, the new father stared into the little face—the tightly closed eyes and fine eyebrows and hair. Smudges of the salt that had been rubbed onto the baby skin to purify and cleanse showed white on the little cheeks.

"Is he—is he—he is—"

Hannah's mother smiled again. "He is fine and strong, my son. He will be a credit to your house into the next generation."

Zedekiah moved gingerly toward the door, as if concerned any sudden jarring would injure his tiny son. As he stepped finally into the evening light, he held the boy up and announced to anyone within hearing, "I have a son!"

The servants hurried over, as did Ishmael himself. For a moment, the great man simply stood and looked down at the small face. Then he placed one of his large, calloused hands on the small head. "A great heritage, son," he said softly. "A great heritage indeed."

There was a burst of laughter from the courtyard. Hannah, carrying a stack of cloths, hurried outside. "What is it?"

"Little Thaddeus is trying to walk!" Amanna said. "He weaves around on the cobbles—"

Just then, the small boy appeared, black hair standing straight up on his little head and dark eyes twinkling merrily. With his mother holding one small hand, he was walking successfully. As they watched, he stopped and let go. Gleefully, he waved both fists in the air and crowed loudly. Then he sat down abruptly.

Instantly, his face puckered and turned red.

"Oh, dearest! Here. Sister Anava will help." Anava reached down and grabbed one little hand. In a moment, heartbreak was forgotten and the little boy was, once again, toddling about, babbling happily.

Hannah watched him for a moment. "How fast they grow," she said.

"Like little flowers in a heavenly garden."

Hannah turned. Her mother was carrying a large bag of wool, ready for carding and spinning. Uzziel, following closely, held the wooden box containing the carders and spindles.

Thaddeus saw them come in and his small face broke into a wide smile. "Mamamamammmm," he said. He dropped to his hands and knees and crawled toward his grandmother.

Hannah's mother laughed. "He recognizes the wool! Let's hope he does not get into as much of a mess as he did last week."

Rachel hurried after her son. "I'll take him out, Mother Judith."

"No need, dear," her mother-by-marriage said. "He will have to get used to the process at some point."

"Maybe the time will be better when he's learned not to eat the wool, Mother," Hannah said.

Her mother stopped and looked at her. "But how will he learn if he is not allowed around what he needs to learn?"

Hannah frowned, but then nodded. "You are right, Mother."

Her mother smiled. "Of course I am right. I am your mother."

Hannah laughed. "I will put these clean things away and join you." She turned toward the house.

"No, dear. Your goats need you more right now."

Hannah looked at the sun and realized that sunset was imminent. She had not noticed how near they were to the end of the day. She set her pile down. "Amanna, Anava, come and help me, please."

The girls looked at their mother.

"Go."

Anava released Thaddeus's hand, which immediately caused him, once more, to sit down. "Sorry, my little wise one," she said, kissing the tips of her slender fingers and pressing them to his soft hair. "You must learn to walk on your own!"

Rachel picked up her son. "Actually, I think it is time for a feed." She disappeared into the house.

Hannah retrieved her bowls and skins from the milk room, and she and the twins hurried out to the goat pens. Once there, they slipped into their milking tunics. The goats pressed around them and one by one they milked the gentle creatures out.

The sun had set by the time Hannah was pouring the last of the precious milk through a clean cloth and into the largest milk skin. She and her sisters slung the heavy bags over their shoulders and started toward the house.

Then Hannah saw a figure come over the hill from the city. Curious, she chose a route through the olive orchard. This way, whoever was walking along the road would have to pass right by her and her sisters.

They reached the turn in the road at the same time as the stranger, who turned out to be no stranger.

"Father Lehi!" Hannah exclaimed.

The man took no notice of her, but continued to make his way along the road toward the house. It was then that Hannah noticed that his steps were unsteady. He was walking with his body angled far forward and looked as though he did not quite know what he was doing.

She lowered the heavy milk skin to the earth and ran forward. "Father Lehi!"

The man lurched to a stop.

Hannah gasped. Blood from several wounds on his face and head was soaking into the collar of his tunic and into his prayer cloth. He had obviously been in an accident of some sort.

"Father Lehi, what happened?" She reached out her small arm and tried to offer him some support, but the large man swayed back and forth a couple of times, and then collapsed to the hard-packed dirt of the road, nearly taking her with him. "Quick!" Hannah said to her sisters. "Run to the house and fetch someone!"

The girls started to walk up the road, their pace slow because of the heavy skins they still carried.

"No! No! Drop the skins there beside mine and run!"

The girls did as they were told. Their small, bare feet made little sound in the dirt as they ran as fast as their legs could manage.

Hannah tried to help Father Lehi into a more comfortable position on the bare road. Then she pulled off her head cloth and dabbed at some of the wounds on the man's face and head. Many of them still oozed, but some were already dried.

He moaned and his eyes fluttered open and he stared at her for a moment as though trying to figure out who she was.

"Father Lehi, it is me, Hannah. You are at the house of Ishmael."

For an instant, he seemed to understand what she had said and one of his large hands gripped her arm tightly. Then his eyes closed once more and he gave a long sigh.

"Father Lehi!" Hannah called out in alarm. In a panic, she pressed one palm against the older man's chest. It rose and fell. She let out a quick breath of relief. He was still breathing.

She looked down at the long, capable fingers still gripping her arm. They too showed signs of abuse—deep scratches and cuts both on the backs and the palms.

"Hannah!"

She turned. Her father had arrived. Her brothers and several of the servants were running up the road behind him.

"Amanna and Anava said—" her father got no further. "Lehi, my brother!" He sank to his knees beside Father Lehi and touched a gentle hand to the man's wounds. He looked at Hannah. "Run to the house, daughter. Make sure there is plenty of hot water and salt and herbs for dressing. Oil. Wine. Hurry! Tell your mother!"

Hannah scrambled to her feet and sped toward the house.

She burst into the courtyard as if demons were following her. "Mother!" she gasped. "Father Lehi—!"

But her mother was already preparing. She had moved the nearly ready evening meal from the cooking pit and, together with the help of Hannah's sisters as well as Iscah and Vashti, had set a large pot of water in the coals. Flasks of oil and wine, dishes of salt, and stacks of bandages had been arranged.

A few minutes later, the men came through the door, carefully carrying Father Lehi's limp, bloodied body.

Rachel appeared and threw her arms about the still figure, smearing herself and her tunic with his blood and spreading her tears on his still face. "Father!" she wailed. "Father! Speak to me!"

Hannah's father put a hand on the girl's shoulder. "He has been badly injured, my daughter. Let us help him."

Rachel released her father and sank to her knees on the warm stones of the courtyard as they laid Lehi down on the meal mat and proceeded to remove his outer tunic.

Then Hannah's father looked at her mother.

The women dipped wooden bowls into the already hot water and poured in a measure of wine. They took bits of clean cloth and, soaking them in the water, used them to gently sponge away the blood from Father Lehi's wounds.

Hannah's mother handed Rachel a wet cloth and instructed her to wipe her face and arms. Rachel scrubbed absently at the blood staining her skin and clothing.

Hannah helped where she could, her bottom lip clasped tightly between her teeth.

After some minutes of careful ministering, they concluded that most of Father Lehi's wounds were upon his face, head, and upper body.

Carefully, they washed and treated the numerous wounds, then they bound them up with clean cloths soaked in oil and wine.

Finally, Hannah's mother sat back on her heels. "I do not think there are any broken bones. But he has received several severe injuries to his head, and I am uncertain if we should summon a healer."

"We will anoint him," Hannah's father said. "The Lord will direct us."

He and his sons placed their hands gently on Lehi's head and pronounced a priesthood blessing. Then Hannah's father looked up. "The Lord will heal him. His work is not yet finished."

"Oh, I am so grateful!" Hannah's mother and Rachel said at the same time.

The men carefully lifted Father Lehi and, with Rachel trailing along behind, transported him to one of the guest sleeping mats. Hannah's mother spread a blanket over the unconscious figure and found a pillow for his head.

As the women tidied the area, Hannah asked the questions that had been spinning around in her head since she first saw Father Lehi on the road. "But what happened, Mother? Did he fall?"

Her mother paused and, straightening, looked out across the courtyard toward the vineyard. She sighed. "We do not know, dearest. I think we can safely guess that he did not get his injuries in a fall. But the rest—I do not know. We will have to wait until he wakes."

"But if he did not get them in a fall, then what—?" Hannah was confused.

"I think it is more a matter of who," her mother said cryptically.

Hannah stared at her mother. "You think someone h-hurt Father Lehi?"

Her mother sighed, "It has happened before."

"But why would someone hurt him? He is so kind and generous."

Her mother shook her head sadly. "People do not like to be told that the Lord is not pleased with what they are doing."

Hannah awoke to bright sunlight filling the room. Her sisters were gone. Quiet voices rose from the courtyard. She gasped and hurriedly dressed and groomed herself. Twisting her hair into a new braid, she joined her mother and sisters as they moved back and forth between the cooking area and the dining mat.

Hannah was a bit surprised but very relieved to see Father Lehi sitting with the rest of the men and being assiduously tended by Rachel with some questionable help from little Thaddeus. The wounds on Father Lehi's face had stopped bleeding, but the many bruises were much more obvious in the morning light.

Someone seated beside Father Lehi turned and looked at her, and Hannah received an even greater surprise as she recognized Laman. Lemuel was also there.

Hannah turned to see how Uzziel was handling this, then realized that her next elder sister was nowhere to be seen. "Ah. The punishment," she said softly to herself. She looked toward the house and saw Uzziel's face in one of the ground-floor windows, peering out.

"Good of you to join us, daughter," her mother said, handing her a jar of milk. "Here. Serve the men."

Hannah hurried over and began to pour fresh, creamy milk into the men's cups.

"So you do not know who did this to you?" Hannah's father was neglecting his meal to speak with Father Lehi.

Father Lehi slowly shook his head. "There was the shouting crowd. Apparently, they do not care to hear of the coming of Christ or of the Lord's disappointment in their actions and choices." He frowned and rubbed a hand across a particularly large bump on one side of his bandaged head. "One large, well-dressed man approached me, shouting something, but I could not understand him. I leaned closer to hear what he was saying and he clubbed me with a rock. After that, I remember very little."

Hannah's mother sucked in a breath and put a hand on Hannah's arm.

"Were they intent on killing you?"

"I think they know very well how to kill a man," Father Lehi said sadly. "If they were intent on it, it would have been accomplished."

"But they were intent on doing some damage, that we know!" Laman, too, was ignoring the food on his trencher. He leaned toward Father Lehi. "Father, you have to quit this silliness. People are going to do what they are going to do. And nothing you say or do is going to change them."

Father Lehi turned to look at his son. "But son, it is not me that is saying it."

"Well, it sounds and looks a lot like you!"

Father Lehi smiled slightly, then winced and touched a sore spot near his mouth. "It is the Lord's message. It is He who wants them to repent and change their ways." His voice dropped in volume. "He who is threatening to destroy them."

Laman snorted. "Father. Think of how great the city of Jerusalem is, how large. What army could ever conquer such a vast stronghold?"

"They have been warned, my son, by the Lord. Are you saying that the Lord Himself does not know what He is saying?"

Laman was silent for a moment. "What I am saying, Father, is let someone else do the warning. Let a younger, stronger man be the bearer of these evil tidings."

Father Lehi smiled again. "But it is I whom the Lord has called. Even this old man."

"Who has nearly reached the great age of forty years." Hannah's father smiled and nodded at his cousin.

Father Lehi tried to smile. And winced.

Hannah's mother handed Hannah a jar of salve. "Give this to Father Lehi," she said softly.

Hannah did as she was told and Father Lehi smiled his thanks, then gingerly rubbed a bit of salve on the sore near his mouth.

Father Lehi handed the jar back to Hannah and looked at Laman. "Son, the Lord Himself is warning the people of Jerusalem that if they do not repent, they will be destroyed. Do you not think He can do this?"

"But look how great, how vast—"

"Son, think how vast the entire world is. And yet the Lord had the power to destroy it—the entire world—in a flood."

Laman said nothing.

"If the Lord says it shall be destroyed, I think we should listen."

Just then, there was a knock at the front gate. Hannah's father turned to look. "Ah. The morning reports from my herdsmen. Would you brethren excuse me for a few minutes?" He got to his feet.

"We must be on our way as well, brother," Father Lehi said as Laman and Lemuel helped him up.

Hannah's father stopped and looked at him. "But surely you should not travel—"

"My sons have brought the wagon. I can ride the short distance quite comfortably in it."

Ishmael nodded and embraced Father Lehi. "Then you are in good hands. I will wish you a good trip and better health."

Father Lehi smiled—and winced—once more. "I thank you for your hospitality, brother," he said. He also looked at Hannah's mother. "And to your good wife as well." He pressed his hands together and bowed slightly. "You are true, true friends to a man who was in great need."

"And I will be forever grateful that my land is near Jerusalem and that you were able to make it this far."

"As shall I." Father Lehi turned to his sons. "Let us go."

Laman and Lemuel each put an arm behind their father and steadied his steps as he walked across the courtyard and disappeared into the porch with Rachel, Hannah's father, and her brothers following closely behind.

A moment later, Hannah could see Father Lehi and his sons as they helped him into a large wagon. Soon, their team of oxen was pulling them out of sight over the hill.

"Well, that is that," Hannah's mother said. "Let us find our own meal and then get the chores started." She looked at Hannah. "I am sure your goats will be wondering what has happened to you."

Hannah reached for a large piece of bread and set it on a clean platter together with some cheese and fruit. "I could not sleep last night," she told her mother. "Things just kept turning and turning in my head."

Her mother and the twins sat down beside the mat and began to fill their own trenchers. Moriah joined them soon afterward, bearing a large jug of milk.

Uzziel rushed out of the house. "Have they—" She stopped and looked around. "Oh."

"They are gone, my daughter. Here. Come and eat with us."

Uzziel sighed and went to sit beside her mother.

Hannah's mother patted her second daughter's hand. "I know it seems a long time, my strength. But soon your sentence will be finished and you will be reunited with your young man."

Moriah looked down and concentrated on her meal.

"It is so hard to wait," Uzziel said. Then she hummed softly to herself as she took a fresh trencher and chose food to break her fast.

"So what did Father Lehi remember this morning?" Hannah asked as she wrapped some of the soft, warm bread around a lump of tasty goat's cheese and took a bite.

"Well, he was in the square just a short distance from the temple, speaking to the people."

"Yes?" Hannah prompted.

"Simply doing what the Lord has asked him to do—warn them."

"I should think they would appreciate it," Hannah said stoutly.

"Hannah, no one likes to be told what to do." Uzziel dropped a large olive into her mouth. "And they never want to be told that they are doing something wrong."

"Do you know what I find peculiar about this?" Hannah's mother asked.

Her girls looked at her.

"Well, every prophecy that the Lord has given us—every prophecy—has been fulfilled. And still we tell ourselves that, this time, the Lord made a mistake."

Hannah nodded. "That is what I have been saying. Why do we not simply obey?"

Uzziel snorted softly, "Hannah, you are such a child!"

"And a little child shall lead them," Hannah's mother said softly.

CHAPTER 7

Moriah's eyes were sparkling, and she was fairly skipping with something momentous. "Hannah, I have exciting news!"

Hannah set her spindle down and turned to her eldest sister expectantly.

Moriah sat down beside her and clasped her hands together in her lap. "You know that the servant of Banaiah was here to see Father this morning?"

Hannah shook her head. "I was out with my goats this morning, sister. One of them put her foot into something and required the care of the healer."

"Well—he was. Here this morning—" Moriah paused and giggled softly.

Hannah nodded impatiently. "And?"

"And Father Banaiah has asked to approach Father. For me. For his son, Benammi!"

Hannah gasped and put one hand over her mouth. "Really?!"

Moriah nodded and giggled again.

Hannah laughed and threw her arms about her sister. "Moriah, that is momentous news indeed!"

Moriah leaned back and brushed at happy tears. "They are a good family—" she began.

"—and Benammi is a handsome man!" Hannah said.

Moriah shrugged. "Well, that is still to be seen. But he wants me!" She hugged her arms about herself. "He wants me. He will have me for his wife!"

Hannah laughed happily and embraced her sister again. "And now you do not have to worry about Laman—"

Moriah nodded. "We never have to mention his name again—"

"—except as the husband of your sister—"

"—and all will be peace and serenity." She sighed and leaned back against the wall. "Oh, Hannah, this is finally coming true for me."

Hannah laughed. "I am so happy for you, my sister."

"As am I," someone said.

Both of them looked up. Uzziel was standing a few paces away. "I never meant to hurt you, my sister," she said, moving closer. "The heart does what the heart wants. Can I now be forgiven for the sins I have committed?"

Moriah got to her feet. "From a full heart, I forgive you, sister." She put her arms around Uzziel. "It is forgotten. I will never speak of it again. Except to congratulate you on your wedding day."

"And I shall do the same for you."

Hannah joined them, putting her arms around both of her elder sisters. "Then there is nothing left but to rejoice!" she said happily.

As her two sisters continued talking, Hannah turned away, frowning. Why did her words suddenly fill her whole soul with unease?

Hannah had never seen her eldest sister so excited. Usually, Moriah was the one sister in the family who showed the most sense and decorum.

"And just look, favored one! Look!" For the tenth time that day, Moriah was holding out her hand on which she wore a gold ring with a large, sparkling blue stone.

Hannah smiled. Moriah had waited such a long time for this moment. Perhaps she could be justified in her exuberance.

"And was not it the most beautiful ceremony ever?" Moriah's eyes were shut and Hannah knew her sister was not seeing the animal pen they were cleaning, but the quiet, joyous assembly of the evening before.

Moriah had been dressed in a soft, white, linen tunic, beautifully and cleverly embroidered with many colors. She had jingled and tinkled with every movement of her slender figure as the necklaces, bracelets, and the golden headband of jewels and coins she wore clashed together.

Hannah, together with the rest of her sisters and sisters-by-marriage, had witnessed the scene from one side of the lamplit room in Benammi's parent's home. Her parents, the groom's parents, and the soon-to-be-betrothed couple had seated themselves on a large rug made of sheepskin in the center of the room. There they had carried on a low-voiced conversation for a few minutes. Then Benammi, who had turned out to be pinch-myself-I-cannot-quite-believe-he-is-real handsome, had risen to his feet, stepped gracefully across to where his intended was seated, and presented her with the ring.

Hannah had not been able to see the token clearly at that time, but she was definitely making up for it now. She sighed as, once more, it was thrust under her nose. "Is it not the most beautiful thing you've ever seen?"

Hannah laughed. "The most beautiful. On the most beautiful girl in the world!"

Moriah giggled and leaned on her pitchfork, forgetting what she was doing for a moment.

"Almost finished, my daughters?" Hannah's father poked his head in the doorway. "Your goats are getting hot out there in the sun."

"Nearly done, Father!" Hannah said.

Moriah giggled happily and thrust her fork into the matted straw. "Nearly done," she echoed.

Their father laughed and disappeared.

A few minutes later, dirty straw removed and clean straw spread, the girls hung up their forks and opened the gate that kept their gentle herd of goats from the now-tidy shelter.

Throughout the operations, Moriah kept up a stream of happy chatter.

Hannah smiled. To see her sister this happy was worth anything.

"Just a few more hours and the garment will be finished, my chosen one," Hannah's mother said as she laid the nearly completed linen tunic across Moriah's pallet and spread the skirt. It was beautiful. And it had taken nearly a year to complete. Hannah's mother had been able to create a soft purple-blue color by mixing the berries of two different plants. The resulting cloth was at once unique and eye-catching.

Moriah picked it up reverently. "To think that, in a little more than a day, I will be the wife of Benammi. Me." She sighed happily. "Did I tell you that he told me I was the most beautiful woman he had ever seen?"

Hannah and her mother laughed. "Well, it is true," Hannah said. She reached out and touched her sister's new tunic. "And just wait until he sees you in this."

Moriah giggled and twirled about the room, holding the tunic in front of her. "Oh, Mother, I did not think it was possible for one person to be so happy!"

Her mother smiled. "And you do not know how happy it makes me to see my eldest daughter so happy." She stopped and looked toward the window.

Someone was shouting down below.

"Now what could that be?" she poked her needle into the tunic and, hurrying to the window, peeped out. "How odd. It is the servant of Banaiah. Oh, and your father has arrived and is speaking with him." She watched for a moment, and then frowned and looked at her daughters. "Wait here, my dears. I will go and see—" She was out the door, which she closed firmly behind her. But the closing door did not shut out the great shriek that rose from below. The death wail.

For Hannah, Benammi's funeral registered only as a series of impressions: People wailing and shrieking. Floods of tears. Men carrying the tightly wrapped body to the sepulchre and disappearing inside. People strewing flowers.

At one point, she noticed that Benammi's mother was seated near Moriah. The two women were saying nothing, staring at nothing. Though people paused to speak to them, they showed no signs of having heard and did not react in any way.

Hannah kept her eyes on Moriah. Her sister was wearing the tunic her mother had sewn for her wedding, which would have taken place on the morrow, but Hannah doubted that Moriah even realized it. She had been so toweringly happy, and now, with her dreams once again wiped away, she was in the very depths of despair. Hannah wondered if Moriah would ever be able to climb out.

She turned to look at Benammi's mother. What must this sweet mother be feeling? She had lost her only son to a chance encounter with thieves—and on the eve of his wedding.

The two women who loved him best and who least wanted to let him go.

For the first time since they had heard the news of the tragedy, Hannah felt the sting of tears. Then, suddenly, it was as if someone had opened floodgates. Great drops of water rolled down her soft cheeks and dripped from her chin. For the first time, her tears mingled with those of the other mourners.

It was, at once, a sympathetic gesture and a cleansing.

CHAPTER 8

"But, Mother, it has been three years! The betrothal was already two years ago!" Uzziel's words were a wail.

"Hush, my strength," Hannah's mother said. "There is a reason."

"What reason could there possibly be?" Uzziel stomped across the room and flopped down cross-legged, on her pallet. She suddenly sucked in a breath. "Do you think, because of my—reputation—?" Her face had turned quite pale.

"No, Uzziel. Your father has not mentioned any difficulties of that sort to me. I think that the family of Lehi has simply been busy and trying to live their daily lives."

"They have not even come for a visit in over six months!"

"Yes, my strength. But you have to admit that they have been having their problems."

"What problems?" Uzziel flopped backward on her mat and stared up at the ceiling.

Hannah spoke up, "Well, there are all the troubles with the people."

"Hmmph," Uzziel mumbled.

"You cannot have missed the almost daily updates from the servants and your father." Hannah's mother said. "The people are becoming more and more agitated by the things that Father Lehi has been saying."

"Then he needs to stop saying them," Uzziel said sulkily.

Her mother shook her head. "How can he stop doing what the Lord has commanded him to do?"

"Mother, how do we even know that the Lord is the one directing him?" Uzziel lifted her slender shoulders in a shrug. "For all we know, he is simply coming up with these things himself!"

Judith sucked in a breath. "Uzziel, you know that the things he says are of the Lord."

"No, Mother, you know that. I know only that my wedding has been postponed time and again and no reason has been given. And I am now seventeen years old!"

"Uzziel, your self-absorption amazes me!" Moriah spoke up, her voice growing more and more shrill. "You are complaining because your marriage to the man originally intended for me has been postponed. Look at me. My intended taken by my sister, my betrothed the victim of a band of robbers, no one speaking for me. I am nearly nineteen, past the time of marrying, and I have not complained. Before Father helps you, he needs to find a husband for me. The world does not revolve solely around you!"

"My world does." Uzziel waved a hand dismissively and sat up. "I am sorry that your betrothed was taken, but I have been imprisoned here for nearly three years, never going anywhere, never seeing anyone. Three years!" She slipped to her knees before her mother. "Mother, I am being held by a mistake made when I was only approaching marriageable age. Please, can you do anything? Speak to Father?" She sank back on her heels and bowed her head. "I am so weary of this!"

Her mother grasped her eldest daughter's hand and put a gentle hand on Uzziel's head. "I will speak to him, my daughter," she said. "I will speak to him."

"We can do what?" Hannah dropped her spindle and got to her feet.

"We are to go into the city to do some marketing for my wedding!" Uzziel's face was suffused with joy. "Mother spoke to Father, and Father spoke to Father Lehi. The wedding is to happen in three months' time. And today, we are to go with Father into the city."

Hannah felt her heart speed up. A trip into the city! Though they only lived a half-day's journey from the great walls of Jerusalem, she could count on one hand the times she had actually made the journey. "When are we going?"

"Mother says as soon as we get our chores finished." Uzziel disappeared through the porch doorway. "You are to call our sisters from the garden."

Hannah wasted no time, but slipped through the porch and out into the morning sunshine flooding their large garden plot.

Moriah, the twins, and Rachel, with baby Naomi peeking from the cloth wrapped about her and her mother, were carrying dippers of water from the large barrel to the various plants. Thaddeus was doing his two-year-old best to help, and had succeeded in soaking his tunic and most of the ground between him and the nearest plant.

Beautiful Talitha, Berachah's wife, great with their first child, was sitting on a large stone waving a fan before her flushed face. She smiled at Hannah as the girl approached. "Ho, little sister. Come here to relieve us?"

Hannah smiled back. "No, sister. I have come to take what help you have."

Talitha laughed. "Sure. Leave all the work to the most encumbered."

Hannah stopped and looked at her. "Sister, I can stay—"

Talitha got to her feet and put her hands out. "Oh, no! I did not mean that at all. You go with your family."

Hannah grasped the outstretched hands. "If you are sure—"

"Of course! Of course! My sister, Rachel, and I can continue the work. Come, let us call them." She lifted her head. "Sisters!"

Before an hour had passed, Hannah, her mother, her sisters, and the two servants, Iscah and Vashti, were in the wagon and being pulled along by their oxen at a steady, ground-covering gait.

Ishmael and two of the manservants, Ebed and Hurai, kept pace.

Throughout the morning, the women alternately hid from the beating sun under the cloth that formed the top of their wagon, or they walked alongside their father and servants on the hard-packed road.

They met many people coming from the great city. Most had been there on one business errand or another and were anxious to share stories of purchases and encounters. Though Hannah's father was pleasant and civil to all who approached, he was careful to continue moving and not to encourage lengthy conversation.

The road grew more and more crowded the nearer they crept to Jerusalem. Enterprising shopkeepers had set up booths beside the busy road. Beggars of various levels of need stood or sat and importuned those passing by. Steadily, the noise level increased.

As the sun reached its zenith, they approached the walls of the great city.

Hannah's father directed the team onto a flat piece of land to one side of the road and stopped them. Then he turned to his family. "Let us take some nourishment here, and then go on into the city," he said. He drove his staff into the ground, then left the two manservants to loop the lead ox's nose ring chain about it and care for the animals while he came around to the back of the wagon to help his womenfolk.

Hannah and her family helped the servants unpack bread, fruit, and cheese, and in a short time, all were happily eating and discussing which of their exciting possibilities they would do first.

A short time later, appetites satisfied and baskets repacked and stowed, they were back on the thoroughfare and passing through the enormous David's Gate into the city and following David's Road.

The crush of humanity was incredible. It seemed to Hannah that every person who lived in Israel was trying to get either into or out of Jerusalem at that moment. The noise everyone made as they went about was, to country ears, painful. The smell, a blended combination of washed and unwashed human and animal, food fresh and spoiled, dung, and the ever-present dust that drifted over everything, was even more painful.

Her father directed the placid oxen toward a crossroads, then turned them down a new street. Here, the din of humanity seemed somewhat lessened. Hannah peered out. There were still many people moving back and forth, but the crush had definitely diminished. Her father stopped the team at the side of the street. "Come, my flowers. The day is wasting and we must do our errands so we can return home."

Hannah, her mother, and her sisters scrambled out of the wagon and stretched their cramped muscles while their father once again drove a stake into the ground and tied the lead ox to it. Then he nodded to Hurai, who pulled a small barrel and a large wooden bowl from the back of the wagon and proceeded to water the two great beasts.

Hannah and her sisters smoothed their tunics and secured their headscarves. Taking hands, they followed Ishmael, Judith, and Ebed back out into the crush of the great David's Road with Iscah and Vashti bringing up the rear.

At first, all Hannah could see were the people. People walking. People riding. People in carts and wagons. Even people with other people on their backs. At every crossroad Hannah's family approached, there were inevitable snarls as different streams of traffic attempted to occupy the same space.

A short distance from where they had left their wagon and team, they passed a small square—more of a widening in the road. There, dozens of men were gathered—some dressed as richly as Hannah had ever seen— and all bursting with something to say. Several of the discussions looked as though they were becoming quite heated, the reddened faces and thundering voices of the participants attesting to opinions strongly felt.

Hannah watched the men curiously as her family skirted the little square until the crowd and the walls of buildings hid them from her sight.

For several minutes, the family continued, the girls holding tightly to each other so as to not lose anyone.

Unexpectedly, the street widened out once more and Hannah was staring at booths and stalls set up in a massive square.

The people were just as numerous here, but now the pace had slowed considerably, with most content to drift past the booths and step out of the gently-flowing stream of humanity to speak to shopkeepers and peruse goods.

Hannah's mother and sisters moved to join this much quieter group.

Hannah's father stopped and let them pass. "I will make my way to the temple," he told them. "I will return for you when the sun touches the spire of the church." He nodded toward a tall building forming one side of the square.

"Yes, husband," Hannah's mother said, smoothing the sleeve of his tunic.

"Ebed will accompany you." Hannah's father nodded to the second manservant, who, with Iscah and Vashti, moved to surround the family.

Her father then touched his daughters on the shoulder affectionately, briefly gripped his wife's hand, and disappeared alone back into the crush of humanity that was David's Street.

Within minutes, the market had completely absorbed Hannah and her sisters. For the next two hours, they watched as their mother haggled over spices and beautiful lengths of fabric with exotic-looking shopkeepers from exotic-sounding places. They giggled nervously as shopkeepers tried to draw them into conversation by holding up some choice piece of merchandise, and they shyly shook their heads and hid behind their mother when fruit vendors offered a taste of the "finest dates" or the "sweetest figs in all of the known world."

At one point, a scuffle in the crowd resolved into a man being dragged away by a local official, who was recognizable by his insignia and his long, curved sword.

There were whispers of "thief!" through the crowd, and a pathway opened for the official and his prisoner to disappear through.

Hannah watched them go, her eyes on the pitiable prisoner. The man was dressed in rags and looked as though he had not eaten in a very long time.

Hannah looked at her mother.

Judith's eyes were on the same man.

"Why would he do something that is so wrong, Mother?" Hannah asked.

"Hunger drives people to desperate deeds."

Hannah frowned. "But are we not expected to look after such people?"

Her mother smiled and looked over at her. "Yes, my favored one, and blessings on you for your generous heart." Her smile disappeared. "But, as you can see, it is an expectation that is poorly followed."

"Can we not go after them? Help him?"

Again her mother smiled at her. "Ah, my generous, loving girl. No. He has now broken the law and must be punished according to that law."

"But if he was hungry and none of us helped him, are we not as guilty as he?"

Her mother turned to her, surprised. "My child, only you would have ever made that conclusion." She put her hand on Hannah's shoulder. "And you are very right." She sighed. "By our own inactivity, we force the poor into desperate acts and then punish them for those acts." She shook her head. "A sad and sorry state indeed."

Hannah looked back toward the place where the man and the official had disappeared. The crowd had closed in and no trace of their passing remained. It was as though the men, and the experience, had been neatly erased.

Her sisters soon drew her back to their browsing, but part of her remained with the desperate, starving man.

Their time in the market proved a strange and exhilarating experience and, except for witnessing the poor thief, Hannah enjoyed every single moment. Her heart fell into her sandals when, looking up, she noted that the sun was just touching the spire of the great church.

A few minutes later, her father touched her on the shoulder and she knew that her time in Jerusalem was drawing to a close.

Sadly, she watched as her mother gathered up the family's purchases and distributed them between her daughters and the three servants.

Then, once more grasping each other tightly, they were underway.

The traffic on the street seemed to have lessened somewhat, although the noise level remained high. Hannah found that they could quite easily navigate the busy street, even while carrying their bundles and bags.

Her sisters were chattering excitedly, most especially Uzziel. A bolt of beautiful red cloth had been purchased to make Uzziel's wedding gown, and the bride-to-be was ecstatic and insisted on carrying it herself.

The family made steady progress through the crowd, and a short time later they were once again passing the small square Hannah had noted earlier.

Now, though, something was different.

One man was standing near the wall of the building that marked one edge of the square. Everyone about him seemed intent on what he was saying, but from the expressions of those nearest to Hannah, not everyone was agreeing with it.

Two of the men turned abruptly and stepped into the road beside Hannah at the precise moment that all movement on the street ceased.

"All he ever does is talk!" said the one of the men.

The disgruntled man's companion snorted loudly. "Who does he think he is? Standing there pretending to be so righteous and telling us that we need to change. I have been an attender at Temple my whole adult life. Everyone I know keeps the commandments. Just who is he calling to repentance?"

The first man nodded. "And to say that our city will be destroyed if we persist in our ways. This great city? The greatest city in all the known world?"

"He suffers from delusions. Or perhaps he is possessed of a devil."

"Ah!" the first man said. "That must be the reason for his actions. He is possessed of a devil."

The second man smiled. "Imagine. Him telling a high priest of the temple that he needs to repent!"

"Well, now that we know what is actually controlling him, we can end our concern. Except for the poor bedeviled man's family."

"Yes. We should—take up a collection!"

Both men laughed.

"Please, kind sirs. Could you spare some coins for my poor children? I am incapable of work and they are starving."

Hannah looked down.

A legless beggar in a tiny, crude cart was pulling himself along the crowded street. The man was filthy and ragged and extremely thin. Through the shreds of his tunic, she could see the bones of his spine and stark ribs.

He held a chipped earthenware cup in one hand and propelled himself up the street with the other.

The two men looked down at him. One of them gave the man's cart a heavy push with one foot and they both laughed.

The crude conveyance immediately shed a wheel and the legless man tipped precariously toward the stones of the street.

He gasped and reached out with both hands to stop himself from falling. As he did so, he dropped his cup, which shattered into a dozen pieces, scattering the couple of mites it contained.

The precious money was instantly kicked away as traffic on the street once more got underway.

The man, now braced on two hands, stared down at the shattered remains of his only livelihood, then looked frantically around for the lost coins.

Hannah, acting without thought, thrust her burden under one arm and, using feet and her free hand, scrambled through the countless feet and legs of the sea of passersby, looking for the precious money. She managed to find one of the tiny coins, but the other eluded her.

"Hannah!" She looked up. Her mother was trying to hold a place in the surging sea of humanity. "Where did you go, treasured one? We thought we'd lost you!"

Hannah held up the legless man's mite. "I was helping him," she said.

"Who?"

"Him," Hannah said as she pointed toward the man.

He had collapsed onto the dirty stones of the street and was being tripped over and stepped on by heedless travelers.

"Oh!" Her mother stepped into the street and made her way the short distance to where the man lay. "Find your father!" she shouted.

Hannah gripped the coin and her bundle and started through the crowd, calling at the top of her voice, "Father! Ishmael!"

Soon she spotted her entire family, grouped together and braced against the wall of a nearby building as people poured around them.

"Father! Come quick!"

Hannah fought to turn around. If making headway with the crowd had been difficult, moving against them was nearly impossible. "Please, Lord, give me strength!" she prayed over and over.

At that moment, someone picked her up in strong arms. Hannah looked down. Her father's concerned eyes were looking into hers.

"Father!" she said, rather breathlessly. "There is a man in need. Mother is helping him." She pointed.

Her father followed the pointing finger. "I cannot see—oh!" Through a small break in the traffic, he spotted his wife, crouched protectively beside the legless man.

He shouted out above the babble. "Everyone! Make way!"

Astonishingly, an opening appeared, just large enough for Ishmael and Hannah to make their way to Hannah's mother and the injured man.

Between the three of them, they managed to pull the man and his crippled cart off the street and into the square, out of the heaviest of the traffic. Then Hannah's mother knelt beside him on the rough stones.

"What can we do, Mother?"

Hannah looked up. Her sisters and the servants had managed to find them.

Hannah's mother handed the basket she carried to Iscah and said, "Iscah, Vashti, and Ebed, please take the purchases and my daughters to the wagon. Let the women remain with them. Ebed, you come back with a waterskin, tools, and some food."

"I want to stay," Hannah said. "I want to help!"

"And I," Moriah spoke up.

"Moriah, I need you to help watch the twins," her mother said. "But if Uzziel wants to stay—"

Uzziel looked down at the legless man and her lips curled slightly. "He's filthy!" she whispered loudly. Then, "Perhaps my talents will be better used in helping Moriah."

"Well, I will stay!" Hannah declared stoutly.

Her father looked at her, then he smiled and nodded.

The servants reached for the bundles held by Hannah and her mother. Hannah handed hers over gratefully and turned back to the stricken man.

Finally, the servants looked at Hannah's mother, who nodded. "Now go. Watch our daughters carefully and send back some supplies."

The three servants, with Moriah, Uzziel, and the twins shepherded cautiously before them, disappeared into the crowd.

Hannah's father squatted down beside the legless man.

"I dropped it," the man said. He pulled himself upright and stared down at his ruined cart. Tears dripped down his cheeks, making streaks in the filth and dirt. "I dropped it. I lost it all."

The man blotted his streaming eyes and nose on the ragged sleeve of his tunic.

Ishmael put a hand on the painfully thin shoulder. "We're here to help you, sir," he said gently. "Tell us what you need."

The man, overcome by emotion, simply looked at his cart and sobbed.

Hannah's father nodded and tipped the cart up on one side to examine the damage.

"I think you will need some tools," a voice spoke behind them.

Hannah and her family looked up.

Father Lehi was standing beside them, his hands folded together in front of him.

Hannah's father got to his feet, a welcoming smile on his face. "Brother!" he exclaimed.

He and Father Lehi embraced.

"But what brings you—ah!" Ishmael nodded. "You have been preaching."

Father Lehi nodded, "For all that anyone listens. Yes." He looked down. "But now I see someone who could benefit from my actions. What can I do?"

"Well, we have sent the servants for tools to try to fix his conveyance."

"And for food and water," Hannah put in.

Father Lehi put a hand on her small shoulder. "Then I can see his needs are being well taken care of."

Hannah nodded.

"Here you are, master." Ebed had wasted no time and was standing beside them, a trifle out of breath and holding a basket and waterskin.

"Well done, son," Hannah's father said.

"Thank you," her mother said. "Hand me the basket."

Ebed handed it to her, and she set it down beside the legless man and threw back the lid. Inside were the remains of their lunch. Ebed had made room as well for a hammer and other tools.

Hannah's mother handed bread and cheese to the man. "Here. Eat this. It looks as though it has been days since you were fed."

The man gratefully wrapped some of the soft bread around a piece of cheese and took a large bite. He coughed and choked and Hannah's mother handed him the waterskin. He tipped it and took several long swallows, then handed it back and devoted more time to devouring his small meal. Moments later, he was licking the crumbs from long, dirty fingers.

Hannah handed him another piece of bread and more of the soft goat's cheese. "Here," she said gently. "Have more."

The man took this second helping and stared down at it. Then he looked up at the faces around him. "My children," he said. "I need to take this food to them."

Hannah's father again touched the man's shoulder. "Let us see if we can fix your cart, then you can take this to them." Once more, he squatted down beside the little cart.

This time, the man joined him and, using the tools Ishmael supplied, they soon affected repairs to his little conveyance.

After taking another swallow from the waterskin, he maneuvered his body back into the little cart and, wrapping the rest of the food into his ragged tunic, turned to his rescuers. "I thank you for the time and trouble you have taken to aid me this day. May the Lord smile upon you all for your kindness and your charity."

He started to turn away.

"Do not leave until we have aided you properly," Hannah's father said.

The man looked back. "Oh, but you have helped me. You have pulled me from harm and helped repair my cart and, most importantly, given me food for my children. You have assisted more than any other in this great city."

"Well, here are some coins to further aid you," Hannah's father said, handing the man several pieces of silver. He reached down and picked up the tools the man had used so expertly in repairing his own cart. "I am certain that you are no stranger to these tools."

The man looked at the tools. "I am not. Before my accident, before the rolling wheels of a wagon took my legs, I spent much of my life with these exact tools in my hand."

"You were a carpenter?"

"Yes. And I took great pride in the work accomplished with the guidance of the Lord and my two hands."

"Then take these tools, my brother, and use them," Hannah's father said, handing them to the man. "You are clever and wise. You will once again build great things with them."

The man stared at the tools, then at Hannah's father. "Do you think so?"

"I know so," he said, smiling.

Father Lehi smiled too. "To be a carpenter is an honorable profession." He looked off into the distance. "A humble and a noble calling that will be practiced by the greatest that shall ever live."

The man frowned and nodded uncertainly.

"But what we have given you is not enough," Father Lehi added. He pulled off his own leather pouch and hung it about the man's thin shoulders. "Take this. It will see you through for many days."

The man's eyes filled with tears. "So much," he said. He smiled at everyone and turned away.

Hannah suddenly remembered the tiny coin she still clutched. "Wait!"

The man looked at her. "What is it, daughter?"

"I found this when your cup broke." She reached out and dropped the coin into his outstretched hand.

The man was crying freely by this time. "Oh, thank you, daughter! I cannot tell you what this means." He looked at them all. "May the Lord of Heaven smile upon you this day and always." He bowed to them and once more started to move toward the street.

Father Lehi stopped him once more. "My son—"

The man turned.

"—my son, leave this city. If you believe in the Lord of Heaven, know that my words come from Him and, because of sin and pride, His hand of destruction is over this place. Leave here and find refuge in Egypt. Use the coins you have received this day. Take your son and your daughter and leave."

The man blinked. "How do you know—?"

"Heed the word of a loving God who desires only your happiness. Leave this place and find refuge in Egypt."

The legless man nodded. "Yes, my lord."

Father Lehi nodded and heaved a great sigh. He reached out a hand and clutched Hannah's father's shoulder. Hannah was startled to see that he was trembling. They turned and started back up the street.

"Come, my family," Hannah's father said.

Hannah glanced back as she and her mother started walking, with Ebed close behind them.

The legless man was staring after them at Father Lehi. Once more, tears were coursing down his dirty cheeks.

A short time later, after saying farewell to Father Lehi, Hannah and her family were reunited with her sisters and on their way out of the great city.

The shadows were growing long when they emerged from the gate onto the highway. Hannah saw her father glance toward the western horizon, concern on his face.

"What is it, husband?" her mother asked.

"We are behind time," Ishmael said. "It will be dark before we arrive at home."

"Is this a worry?"

He glanced at Moriah seated in the back of the wagon and lowered his voice. "It never used to be, but too well we know of the incidents of robbery along the public roads."

Hannah's mother nodded. Taking a deep breath, she said, "We have been about the Lord's business. We will ask now for the Lord's protection."

And even as their father and the servants kept the wagon rolling steadily toward home, Hannah's mother bowed her head and poured out her heart to the Lord.

Watching her, Hannah felt instantly relieved. Warmed.

They arrived without incident a trio of hours later. The light of a full moon gilded the land and made the quiet countryside nearly as bright as it was at midday.

Servants who had obviously been watching for them hurried out with lamps to help them with the cart and team and to unload their purchases.

One of them reached for the bundle containing the beautiful wedding cloth. "No!" Uzziel cried, grabbing the parcel from the helpful but unwitting hands. "That is mine! I will carry it."

With the bundle held tightly in both arms, she started toward the house.

Partway there, one of the resident dogs, intent on some private game, dashed across the drive, right under Uzziel's feet. Unable to see him, she caught her toe under his ribcage and, completely overbalanced by her burden, effected a spectacular fall.

Her precious material ended up in the dust of the road. Uzziel then followed it, landing heavily and raising a small cloud of fine dirt around her and her beautiful length of cloth.

"Oh!" she said. She scrambled to her feet and frantically rescued her bundle, whose color was now unrecognizable. "Noooo!" she cried, looking up at Judith. "Mother!"

Hannah's mother moved quickly to Uzziel's side. She lifted a fold of the cloth. "Never mind, my strong one." She pointed. "Look. Only the outer layers were affected."

Uzziel looked where her mother indicated, then, great tears starting to make streaks on her dusty cheeks, she clutched her bundle tightly to her and started once more toward the house.

After her sister had disappeared into the house, Hannah turned to her father. "With the dust streaking Uzziel's face and clothing, it is amazing how much she looked like the beggar man we helped in Jerusalem."

Her father looked at her. "How often we despise in others those things we know exist within ourselves," he said quietly. He put a hand on Hannah's shoulder. "You are wise beyond your years, my daughter."

Hannah turned to him. "Father, just before I met the crippled man, I overheard a conversation between two men."

"Yes?"

"They were talking about someone preaching repentance and being possessed by a devil." She looked at her father. "Soon afterward, Father Lehi joined us and I heard him telling you he had been speaking. Could those two men have been talking about Father Lehi?"

Ishmael sighed. "Yes, daughter, I am sure they were."

"But Father Lehi is not possessed of a devil, is he?"

"Absolutely not. But let me ask you this. If you are doing something wrong, and you know you are doing something wrong, how would you react if someone pointed it out to you?"

Hannah frowned as she thought about it. "Well, if I knew it was wrong, I would not do it."

Her father smiled and placed a large hand on her head. "That is my beautiful child of grace. But not many people are as you." He looked out over the darkened countryside. "No. Man's usual response to correction is to find something to discredit the corrector. If one can prove that the messenger is wrong or evil or just plain mad, one does not have to admit wrongdoing or change one's actions. Throughout our history, from the time of Father Adam, prophets have been treated thus."

"But the things they prophesy come to pass."

"They do. Every. Single. One." He tapped the palm of his left hand with the tip of the finger of his right hand to emphasize each point.

"So the things which Father Lehi prophecies?"

"Will all happen. Count on it."

CHAPTER 9

Hannah, humming a happy tune, descended the stairs from the chamber she shared with her sisters. She stopped halfway down and stared at the people in the courtyard below.

They were standing motionless.

Her father and brothers, seated on the courtyard stones awaiting their morning meal, Hurai standing beside them. Her mother, sisters, sisters-by-marriage, and servants. All looked as though they had simply—stopped.

Only Thaddeus, clutching at his mother's tunic, and little Naomi, just beginning to creep around, were moving.

"What is it?" Hannah asked. She jumped down the remaining steps. "What has happened?"

Her father stood up. "All are gone?"

Hannah crept closer.

Hurai nodded. "They, their servants. Even their flocks and herds. The storehouses are empty. The harvest taken."

Hannah's father looked pale.

Hannah turned to her mother. "What is happening, Mother?"

Her mother spoke without expression. "Hurai has just returned from Lehi's lands. He was supposed to deliver a message to Father Lehi for your father. He found the place deserted." She moved toward Hannah's father.

"Noooo!" Talitha moaned. Carrying her new baby, she moved to where her sister was sitting and fell more than sat beside her. The two of them immediately wrapped an arm around the other and began to weep.

"Deserted?" Hannah followed her mother.

"Have they been taken?" Hannah's mother asked her father. "Has Lehi angered the wrong people?"

He shook his head, still seeming rather dazed. "I can hardly think so. Why the flocks and herds? Why the women and children?" He looked back at Ebed. "There were no signs of battle? Fighting? No—bodies? Of animals or—people?"

"None, master! It was as though they had simply taken everything and left. Pens were shut tight. Doors and windows latched. Neat. Orderly." He frowned. "There was one other thing. There are many possessions still in the house. Furniture. Household equipage."

"But no people or animals."

"No, master."

"And no crops or food."

"None that I could see."

Ishmael sat back and shook his head. "This is more than odd." He got to his feet.

"Husband, where are you going? What are you going to do?"

Hannah's father looked at her mother. "I am going to see what I can find out."

"You!" Her mother cleared her throat. "You will be cautious?"

He smiled. "My wife, as Lehi's kin, and on behalf of our two new daughters—" he looked toward Rachel and Talitha, weeping quietly together, "—it is my duty to try to discover what has happened. But yes, I will be cautious."

Hannah's mother nodded.

Ishmael looked at his sons. "I am afraid that breakfast will have to wait."

The three left through the doorway to the porch, with Hurai following closely behind. Rachel and Talitha got to their feet and, brushing hurriedly at their tears, caught up with Hannah's father at the doorway.

"Please, Father Ishmael, may we accompany you?" Rachel said, indicating herself and her sister. "It is our family!"

Hannah's father turned to them and put a hand on each of their heads. "My daughters, I think it would be wise for you to remain here and care for your children. We will discover what has happened." He smiled a bit sadly. "I know that the woman's role is far too often one of waiting, but I think at this time it is for the best."

Rachel nodded and stepped back, new tears starting to flow.

Talitha looked as though she would have argued, but Berachah moved to her and touched her hand. She looked at him and she, too, nodded unhappily.

The men filed out through the porch and into the yard.

Those remaining turned to Hannah's mother and began asking her questions. Uzziel was most vocal. Her face was pale, her eyes dark and enormous. Her headcloth had slipped back on her shoulders and her hair looked as though she had been pulling at it.

She appeared quite wild.

Their mother put up her hands. "My family, Uzziel, I know only what you know. This has come as a shock to me as it has to you. We can only wait until your father returns to discover more."

With that, she insisted that the day's chores be undertaken.

Hannah found that work helped occupy her mind and was very soon grateful for her mother's direction. She milked goats, ground grain, swept the courtyard, helped her younger sisters weave some baskets, and pulled weeds in the garden. By the end of the morning, she had almost stopped looking over toward the road.

Uzziel, however, did not seem to benefit from her labor. She could work half-heartedly at one chore or another for only a few seconds before drifting to the edge of the orchard and peering down the road.

Hannah saw her mother watching her next elder sister, but the woman said nothing.

Finally, just after midday, Hannah's father, brothers, and servants rode over the hill on their donkeys. The group turned off the road, cutting under the trees of the olive orchard toward the pens.

Dropping the weed she had just pulled, Hannah hiked her tunic to her knees and ran after them. But even as fast as she ran, she found that Uzziel was ahead of her, running frantically behind the little procession of donkeys.

Finally, as the group reached the donkey pens, Uzziel and Hannah joined them.

"Where are they? What did you find? Is everyone—?"

Hannah's father held up a hand and stemmed Uzziel's stream of questions. "One moment, my daughter," he said. "I will tell you what I know."

He dismounted and left the others to care for their animals. Then he beckoned to his daughters and started toward the house. "We found nothing," he said.

"Nothing?" Uzziel sounded as though she could not get enough air into her lungs.

"Nothing. Everyone, every animal, all the food, and many of their possessions are gone. Just gone. There are no signs of battle or raiding, no bodies, no signs of disturbance of any form. Even the neighbors heard nothing and know nothing." He shook his head. "It is most strange."

"But what about me?" Uzziel could hold it in no longer. "What happens to me?"

Ishmael stopped and put his hands on his daughter's shoulders. "My daughter, we will wait. We will see. But for now, it looks as though your betrothed has left. And by the looks of it, he will not be coming back."

Uzziel gasped and one hand clutched the front of her tunic convulsively. Then she tore herself from her father's grip and fled toward the house, her sobs floating back to them in the still air.

"So we know no more."

Hannah's father looked at her mother. "My wife, I have done what I can. I am relying on the Lord now to direct and protect my brother and his family, wherever He has chosen to send them."

"You think this is from the Lord, then."

"I am certain of it." Ishmael took a deep breath. "The Lord has been warning Lehi for years. The fact that he and his entire family have fled suggests to me that the days shall shortly come to pass that his prophecies will be fulfilled."

Hannah's mother sucked in a breath. "But that means that our family, too, is in danger!"

He nodded gravely, "I think we should seriously consider preparing to leave."

"But husband, where would we go?"

"The Lord will direct us."

Hannah's mother was silent for a moment. "Should I begin to instruct the servants?"

Ishmael was silent for a moment. "No. The Spirit constrains me," he said. "We will do nothing until I know from the Lord it is what we should do."

Hannah's mother nodded. "I, too, bow to the Lord's will."

Hannah closed the door of the girls' chamber behind her. "Uzziel has been crying for two days," she said to her mother.

"Yes," Judith said. "She grieves for all that she has lost."

"She refuses to eat and has torn up the tunic she was wearing."

Her mother nodded. "Her grief is indeed deep." She sighed. "I know of no way to help her. What comfort I can give, I have been giving. She will simply have to feel this way until she no longer feels this way."

"But what if that never happens?"

"My daughter, when grief presses upon us, it seems as though it will never go. Then one day, though it remains, some of its weight has lessened." She looked at the closed door. "No matter what the tragedy, life goes on. And we must go forward to meet it. Even if we go forward on our knees." She shrugged. "Perhaps the best way to go forward is on our knees."

Hannah and the twins picked up the last of the olives on the ground and packed them carefully into a basket.

"I do not understand why we have to be so careful when the olives have already fallen and must be bruised," Amanna said.

"Well, I suppose it is to avoid further bruising," Anava responded practically.

"Still, it seems silly. Why not just toss them into the basket and say it happened when they fell to the ground?"

Hannah looked at her and responded, "Because that would be lying!"

"But only a tiny bit."

"A little sin is okay?"

Amanna squirmed a bit and mumbled out, "No."

"Exactly." Hannah looked around the light-colored soil for any olives she may have missed. Seeing one on the other side of the tree, she walked over.

From the corner of her eye, she spotted movement on the road. Turning, she saw one of her family's servants on a donkey. At first, she dismissed his presence as normal farm business. Then, as he and his mount grew closer, she noted the hurried pace and intent expression.

Something had happened.

CHAPTER 10

"Well, I think we have found all there is to find," Hannah said to her sisters. "Please take this basket to the press. I have to—" she did not finish her statement. She was already running toward the house.

The servant had slid off the donkey and was just fastening its lead rope to a convenient ring when she arrived. He walked behind her into the porch and from there to the courtyard.

Hannah's mother looked up from the bread she was mixing and said, "Shalom, Hurai."

"Shalom, mistress. I have news for the master."

"I will send someone to find him, Hurai." She looked at Iscah, and the woman bowed and hurried out. "You have been to Jerusalem this morning?"

The man nodded. "It is like a great beehive this day—abuzz with news."

Hannah's mother frowned slightly. "News that would impact our household?"

"Nay, mistress. Or, at least I do not think so."

She nodded. "Sit, Hurai. Take some refreshment. You have traveled a long, weary way today."

"I thank you, mistress," Hurai said, accepting a cup of wine and sinking to one of the cushions in the eating area.

Hannah's mother turned to her. "Hannah, my treasure, could you—"

"Oh please, mother, may I stay? I so want to hear the news from Jerusalem!"

Her mother smiled. "My little jackdaw. Always after every shiny bit of news."

Hannah felt her face go warm, but she remained.

Hurai had finished his drink and stood up to hand the cup back to Hannah's mother when Hannah's father hurried in. The servant quickly turned to his master.

"What is your news, Hurai?"

"Master, the city is alive with the news of a murder!"

Hannah's father blinked. "A murder? But Hurai, there are murders there from time to time. Everyone knows that."

"But this murder is so—different. And they think they know who the murderer was!" Hurai turned slightly pink in his excitement. "Apparently, one of the church elders was found dead this morning. It took a while to identify him because his clothing was missing. As was his head."

Ishmael straightened. "His head was missing?"

"Well, it had—rolled away—"

"Hannah, you should not be hearing this!" Hannah's mother said sharply.

Her father looked around, noticing her for the first time. "No, daughter, you should not be hearing this."

Hannah sighed and walked very slowly toward the stairs to her chamber. She glanced back. Both of her parents were once more engrossed in what Hurai had to say.

Hannah slipped into the porch and flattened herself against the outer wall. From here, she could hear everything perfectly.

Hurai was proceeding with his story. "Apparently, the man, Laban, by name—"

Ishmael sucked in a breath.

"Do you know him, master?"

"Yes. He is a cousin to both Lehi and myself."

There was a pause. Then, "Do you want me to proceed?"

"Of course, Hurai. We have heard this much; we must hear the rest."

"Well, the man's body was found on one of the streets between his home and the inn. Apparently, he had been at the inn earlier that night, drinking with others of the town's younger leaders, making a lot of noise and bragging about how he had just made a lot of money on a deal with some foolish boys. The servants say that four brothers were there earlier in the day trying to buy something from Laban and so the speculation is that the two parties struck a bargain."

There was silence for a moment. "Four brothers?" Hannah hardly recognized her father's voice.

"That's what everyone is saying. He said he had made a deal with four foolish boys."

"Husband," Hannah's mother said. "I know what you are thinking and there is no reason to suspect he is speaking of Lehi's sons. There are thousands of boys in Jerusalem."

"You are right, my wife. You are right. It is just that he was cousin to both Lehi and myself. My thoughts just made the leap." He turned. "Go on, Hurai."

"The man was dressed only in his under tunic. His clothing, as well as his armor, was missing. The odd thing was that all of his jewelry was still on his body."

"Jewelry?"

"Yes. He had several heavy chains of gold as well as bracelets, rings and—well—a golden head circlet. Which they found—after—"

"After they found the head."

"Yes."

"So the murderer killed him, then took the man's clothing but nothing else?"

"Well, his sword is missing and I understand it was quite a valuable sword. Fine steel and heavily ornamented in gold and jewels."

"Perhaps the robber was interrupted before he could take the jewelry."

"Perhaps. But there is more."

"Say on."

"Laban's servant, Zoram, who had been serving as the night guard over Laban's treasury, is also missing. And now there is speculation that he may be the murderer."

"Was anything stolen from the treasury?"

"There have been men from Laban's household in there all night taking an inventory, and so far it looks as though nothing of worth was taken."

Hannah could hear her father shifting on his cushion. "That is an odd story."

"The whole city can speak of nothing else. This Laban—please excuse my speaking of one whom you call kin—had a reputation for many evil things. But he was a community leader, and no one should die on an empty street at violent hands."

"And yet, it happens to even the best people, Hurai."

"Yes, master. Well, I will go back to my duties now."

"Did you get the blades sharpened?"

"Oh, yes, master. They are still in my pack on my mount. I will fetch them to the overseer."

"Thank you, Hurai."

Hannah gasped as she realized that the servant would have to pass her to reach the outer door. She flew to the portal, threw it open, and fled.

"Why are we the ones doing this?" Uzziel brushed at her face, inadvertently leaving a long streak of brown soil on one cheek. "Do we not have servants for this sort of thing?"

Hannah pushed her head cloth back on her hair and looked up at her next elder sister. "Because we need the knowledge. A good wife is required to know all the operations of her husband's property."

Uzziel snorted. "And when am I likely to ever have a husband?" she sneered. "The only man—" the words stopped abruptly.

Hannah sighed. "Please, Uzziel, help me with this. I cannot hold the branch and cut at the same time."

There was no answer.

"Uzziel?" Again, Hannah pulled back her headscarf and looked up at her sister.

Uzziel stood frozen, her eyes focused on something over Hannah's shoulder, her face the white of new wool.

"Uzziel!" Hannah waved a hand before her sister's face. "Uzziel, what is it? What is the matter?"

"I think she has seen a spirit."

Hannah spun around to see who had spoken.

Laman was standing there, the reins of a camel in his hand.

CHAPTER 11

The camels were taking their time at the trough.

"Hurry!" Hannah urged. The large creature stopped drinking and looked at her with great, soft brown eyes. Hannah bit her lip. Who knew what was being discussed up at the house, and she was stuck here watering and feeding camels!

"Do not talk to them," Anava said softly. "They must like human voices because every time you say something, they want to stop what they are doing to listen."

As if in answer to her, one of the two camels she was leading lifted its head to look at her.

She giggled. "See?"

Finally, the thirsty creatures turned away from the trough and Hannah and Anava were able to lead them to one of the pens and fill their manger with fresh dried grasses.

Then they stowed the tack.

Satisfied, Hannah nodded and turned to Anava. "Race you to the house!"

In answer, her younger sister hiked her tunic up to her knees and took off at a run.

"Hey!"

A giggle floated back on the still air.

Hannah also lifted the hem of her dress and started after her sister. Laughing, the two of them reached the doorway to the house together. Then they smoothed their hair and clothing and moved slowly through the porch and into the courtyard.

Her sisters and her mother were sitting on cushions along the wall of the courtyard. Her two sisters-by-marriage were hovering about their four brothers as they sat with Hannah's father and brothers about the meal mat. The men had been served refreshments, but everyone was ignoring the bread, cheese, wine, and fruit before them in favor of talking.

All eyes were on Laman as he got to his feet. "Father Ishmael," he said, bowing slightly. "We apologize again for the disarray into which your household, so closely allied with ours, was swept. Again, it was not our will, but the Lord's. And I hope that, in the future, you will find it in your hearts to forgive us." He bit his lip. "And now I come to the reason I and my brothers are here today." He cleared his throat. "The God of Israel has decided that it is not wise that we brothers go into the wilderness without wives."

Hannah and Anava moved quickly and quietly to where the women sat and found a place for themselves.

Hannah saw Laman steal a look at Uzziel, who had seated herself squarely in his line of sight. "He instructed our father to send his sons to the household of Ishmael." He nodded at Uzziel and smiled. "Father's instructions from the Lord were that his sons should take Ishmael's daughters to wife and bring them through the wilderness to the land of promise."

Hannah felt her heart begin to beat faster. Through the wilderness to the land of promise? Where was that? And was not this the land of promise?

Her father held up a hand and Laman stopped speaking. "Laman, because you are your father's eldest son, I accept your words as though they came from him. But are you proposing to take my daughters, my precious flowers, into the wilderness?"

"The Lord of Abraham has commanded that our family, the family of Lehi, leave our possessions here in Jerusalem and travel into the wilderness. We know not where we go. We know not how we will survive, but the Lord has commanded it. And when the Lord of Heaven commands—" he stopped.

"Man can do nothing but obey." Hannah's father kept his eyes on his womenfolk. "But to take my daughters away from me into someplace unknown without a guarantee that they would be provided for, that they would even be able to survive?"

Laman started to speak, but again Ishmael lifted a hand and said, "You have expressed yourself clearly, my son. Now—" He got to his feet. "If you will excuse me, I will retire to my chamber and think on all you have said. And pray." He got to his feet, made a slight bow to those assembled, and disappeared up the stairway to his room.

Laman sat down and looked at his brothers.

Lemuel shrugged.

Sam and Nephi exchanged a look and Nephi stood up. "May I again issue an apology for our abrupt departure and for our sudden reappearance. If it is uncomfortable for us to remain with you, please say so. We can easily make our way to our old home and remain there until such time as Father Ishmael has an answer for us."

Hannah's mother stood up. "No, my sons, it is not uncomfortable for our family—" she emphasized the words "—to again be with us. We rejoice in your safe return. Although the tidings you bear are somewhat difficult to hear, you are always—always—welcome in our home." She waved a hand toward the untasted food on the mat before them. "Please eat. Drink. You must be greatly fatigued by your journeyings."

"I thank you, Mother Judith," Laman said. "We are indeed hungry. Your hospitality is most welcome."

With that, the four brothers fell hungrily on the food.

When Hannah awoke the next morning, the light in their chamber was still gray with the pre-dawn. But already the house was astir.

She could hear someone moving about below. She sniffed the air. Already the fire had been kindled in the great oven and fresh bread was breathing out its come-hither fragrance.

Then Hannah caught her breath and sat bolt upright on her pallet as the events of the previous afternoon and evening washed over her. Father Lehi's sons! They had come here! They still wanted her and her sisters for wives! Hannah tingled from head to foot, then shivered suddenly as she remembered that, if they indeed married Father Lehi's sons, they would not be traveling the few miles to Father Lehi's house and lands. Instead, the boys had proposed taking them into the wilderness. To an unknown place. An unknown fate.

Hannah felt her heart start to beat heavily.

She looked around.

Uzziel's pallet was empty, but the twins still slept peacefully.

Moriah, who had the mat nearest her, was also awake. Lying on her back with her hands behind her head, she was staring silently and gravely up at the ceiling.

Hannah lay back down, facing her sister. "Moriah," she whispered.

Moriah turned to look at her. "What is it, my treasure?"

"I did not have a chance to hear what happened to Father Lehi and his family last night. Everyone was either too busy or too self-absorbed to answer my questions."

Moriah smiled slightly. "I am sorry, Hannah. There was much to think about."

"So what happened?"

"Well, my understanding is that Lehi was having greater and greater difficulty as he tried to preach the words of repentance to the people of the city." Moriah stretched and yawned.

"But that's been happening for years!"

"Well, you remember how he was that night he stumbled in here trying to get home?"

Hannah shivered. "Yes."

"And how he had been so badly injured?"

"Yes. Father wondered if he had not been stoned."

"Well, he had been."

"But usually, when someone is stoned—" Hannah could not go on.

"They are killed. Yes, I know. But on this occasion, perhaps the people were just a bit cautious about killing a prophet of the Lord."

"But they do not believe that he is a prophet of the Lord!"

"Oh, they know exactly who he is. Make no mistake about it." Moriah rolled her head on her pillow. "Anyway, Father Lehi was warned to leave with his family and flee into the wilderness."

Hannah sucked in a breath. "They were warned to leave?"

"Yes. The Lord told them that their lives were in danger and that it was time to go."

"But why did they not say anything?"

"They were told to pack up and leave, not run through the neighborhood spreading gossip."

"But warning another family of believers—one who has direct ties—would have made sense."

"I think Father Lehi was only being obedient. Obviously it was more important to the Lord to get them to a safe place than it was to canvass for wives." She looked at the ceiling. "And now that they are safe he is sending them back to secure those other things that are important."

"Other things? We're things now?"

Moriah laughed. "Well, apparently, they were sent back to Jerusalem a few days ago to get a record from a kinsman in the city."

Hannah caught her breath. "So they were the four brothers who visited that man—the cousin of Father and Father Lehi—in Jerusalem. The ones Father heard called 'foolish.' "

"It sounds like it."

"Morrie, you do not suppose they had anything to do with that man's death?"

Moriah shook her head. "I cannot imagine it. That simply does not fit with what we know of Father Lehi." She took a deep breath.

"Besides, the servants of Laban chased them through the streets to one of the gates of the city, and Laban was very much alive when that happened."

"Good."

"Is it morning already?" someone said.

Hannah looked across Moriah to Anava's sleepy face. "It is, gentle one."

"Ah," the girl stretched, then looked across at Uzziel's empty mat. "Where's Uzziel?"

Hannah shrugged. "She was gone when I woke up a few minutes ago."

"She was just leaving when I woke up," Moriah added. "I could hear Mother in the courtyard, so I am fairly certain she is well chaperoned."

"It is a worry with Laman back in the house," Anava said.

"Though," Amanna spoke up, "now that he is back, it looks as though our agony really is about to end!"

"Ah. Amanna. You are finally awake?" her twin poked her with an elbow.

"Finally? With the three of you cawing like a flock of crows?"

Moriah laughed and sat up, thrusting her light quilt to the foot of her pallet. "Time to get up, my sisters. Father needs his wash water."

"I have spent the night in prayer and I am ready to tell you what the Lord would have us do."

Hannah's father looked tired and at the same time exhilarated. He swept the group in a glance. "While on my knees last night speaking with my Maker, I was carried away in the Spirit into a new land." He looked around. "It was a place different from this, a land of milk and honey, of grain and game, of flowing water. A land of plenty. A land that will support our sons and our daughters and their families. A land that will give all that we ask of it."

He looked around again and said, "And it is to be our home."

Hannah and the rest of the family stared at him, startled.

"Our home?" her mother asked.

Her father nodded. "Yes. Our Lord wants our daughters to travel through the wilderness to this new land. This blessed land. I will give my permission only if the rest of the family is permitted to join them."

"Husband!" Hannah's mother spoke in a single gasp.

"Father!" Zedekiah said a heartbeat later.

"Father Ishmael!" Laman said at the same time. He paused and looked at Hannah's mother and brother, then turned back to her father. "You—you would actually choose to remove your entire household to the wilderness?"

"Is it any more than your family has done?"

"But our father is a—visionary man. We go because our father had been directed. Why would you go?"

"Because your father has been directed," Ishmael said quietly.

"But you would uproot your home? Leave all this?" Laman waved a hand, indicating Ishmael's home and possessions.

Hannah's father smiled. "This," he, too, waved a hand, "is just worldly possession. Easily replaced or done without."

"Excuse me, sir, but possessions do make life more comfortable."

Ishmael smiled and asked, "Is life supposed to be comfortable?"

Laman opened and closed his mouth without speaking.

Hannah's father raised his hand. "Enough discussion. I will obey the Lord's wish and I will take my family into the wilderness, following after our prophet."

He sat back and let the discussion go on around him.

Hannah's thoughts crashed together inside her head. Was this really happening?

Her marrying one of the sons in Father Lehi's family had seemed a remote notion. Even when Nephi and his brothers had reappeared, their presence had sparked no real emotion, other than relief that

Uzziel would finally get what she wanted. But now, with her father's pronouncement, everything had suddenly become all too real. She was going to marry. She was going to leave her home for her husband's—wherever that may be. She was going to be a wife and—

For a moment, panic threatened. Then she looked at the calm, peaceful expression on her father's face. Her father's faith was great enough to follow his prophet into the unknown.

And suddenly, so was hers.

CHAPTER 12

The next few days passed in a blur of activity. An entire household had to be reduced to the few baskets and crates that could be carried by the family camels, donkeys, and mules. Flocks and herds needed to be gathered and culled; beasts sorted and sold; newly picked crops of grapes, olives, grains, and dates packed into baskets, ready for a long trip to wherever.

A thousand decisions had to be made. What to take, what to sell, what to leave.

And not just for her, her parents, and her sisters. Her brothers and their young families must also choose and sort and pack. And decisions become that much more complex when one is considering infants and tiny children.

Fortunately, most of their servants had decided to remain in Jerusalem so their needs did not have to be considered. Still, with Hannah's family and the three servants who had begged to come with them, there would be nearly twenty persons. A great number of people to transport and provide for.

It was early on the morning of the fourth day, after three days of sorting and selling and packing, that Hannah's father gathered everyone together. First, he led them in a solemn prayer of thanksgiving and a plea for protection and safety during the trip. "We are ready," he said simply, looking at Laman. "If you brothers will lead us, we will follow."

Laman nodded and mounted his camel. Lemuel did the same, and Hannah was surprised when the two of them made a show of slinging bows and drawing swords.

Without looking back, they started out of the yard and up the path to the main road. They were trailed by her father's two cypress mules who pulled the great wagon, directed by the manservant, Ebed. Hannah's mother, two sisters-by-marriage, and their small children sat inside amidst a heap of household goods.

Hannah's father, also mounted on a camel, came next, followed by the long string of camels, each heavily burdened with baskets and boxes containing household goods. These were shadowed closely by Hannah and her sisters on donkeys. Behind them were the family's large flock of sheep, shepherded by Hannah's two brothers. Then came their herd of cattle, carefully watched by Nephi and Sam, who brought up the end of the caravan on yet more camels.

Hannah could see that these two younger brothers had also armed themselves with bows and swords. Nephi's long weapon gleamed in the morning sun, the hilt unusually shiny for a sword.

The train was long and took some time to wind its way to the main road.

As Hannah urged her little donkey forward, she turned for one last look, saying good-bye to the home she had always known. Then she turned and looked forward toward the future.

She wondered what it would hold.

To Hannah's surprise, Laman and Lemuel only followed the main road for a few hundred paces. Then, just after they crossed the creek, they turned off toward the east, leaving the road behind and following a faint cart track across the countryside. Within a pair of hours, the settlements had grown sparse—people seemed to like to settle nearer the main roads. They passed flocks of sheep with solitary shepherds, but few buildings and no towns or cities.

Hannah looked around. She had never visited a place with so little human life. She felt—vulnerable. She nudged her donkey closer to Moriah. "Why are we going this way?" she asked.

Moriah had fastened a gauzy piece of cloth over her nose and mouth to try to combat the constant dust kicked up by the portion of the caravan that preceded them. Hannah could just make out the shape of her sister's mouth as she smiled.

"I think they do not want anyone to know where we've gone," Moriah said. "I think they are trying to avoid having people follow us."

Hannah frowned. "Are they that worried about people harming their father?"

Moriah shrugged. "Perhaps. There were many people who were not happy with Father Lehi's preaching. And they were angry enough with the Prophet Jeremiah that they have imprisoned him. Maybe Laman and his brothers are just trying to avoid a conflict."

"Hmm. Well, it is lonely out here."

Moriah's lips curved into a smile again. "How can you say that? You have your family—and your Sam."

Hannah glanced back to the tail of their caravan to the steady young man seated on a camel. She shook her head and sighed. "He's not yet 'my Sam.'"

"How can you say that? Father and Father Lehi—"

"Also said that you would be marrying Laman, and look how that turned out."

Moriah turned slightly pink. "I guess you have a point."

"I am sorry, Morrie. I should not have brought it up."

Moriah managed a small smile. "Do not worry your pretty head about it, my treasure," she sighed. "We, none of us, know what is in store." She glanced up and down the long train of people and animals and possessions. "For all I know, there will never be a man for me to marry. The brothers of Laman, like Laman himself, are all spoken for. There simply are not enough men to go around."

"Unless one of them chooses a second wife."

"Look how well that turned out for Father David and Father Solomon." Moriah gave a little chuckle. "No, I'd rather take my chances that someone will come along who does not have another wife or two in his entourage."

Hannah shrugged. "You'd still be married."

Moriah shrugged. "There are worse things than not being married."

The two rode companionably for the rest of morning, talking only occasionally.

As the sun reached its zenith, Moriah looked down at her donkey. "He senses something."

Hannah looked at Moriah's mount too. The large ears were pointed forward. She lifted her head, trying to see past the front of their train. "Ah. There is a grove of trees. Perhaps it is time for a break."

Moriah smiled. "I do hope so. My body is not used to this type of activity."

Hannah laughed. "I guess we will just have to toughen up!"

Laman had indeed called a halt. He and Lemuel stopped their camels just outside the oasis and were directing everyone else to move past them into the cover of the trees.

For the next hour, Hannah and her family enjoyed both the cool waters of the spring as they watered their stock and themselves, as well as the welcome shade of the trees, which sheltered them from the fiercest rays of the midday sun.

The trees were date palms, and though some had been mostly picked over, there were others still heavy with ripe fruit.

The girls happily stripped handfuls of the rich produce, placing them carefully into their baskets. Then they joined the rest of the party gathered near their mother's wagon and helped serve everyone with cheese and bread brought from home and tasty dates supplied by the Lord.

Far too short a time later, Nephi got up and said something to Laman. Laman scowled darkly at his younger brother, but then sighed and got to his feet, announcing that they needed to once more be on the move.

Everyone packed up and Hannah's mother and her brothers' wives and children crawled back into the wagon. Then the rest of the group mounted up and they all followed Laman and Lemuel back out into the desert.

The afternoon wore on. And on.

Tired of riding, Hannah and Moriah slipped off their donkeys and walked for a time beside them. Hannah noticed that other members of their train were doing the same thing. Despite the heat reflecting up from the sand beneath her leather-sandaled feet, she found it quite refreshing to stretch her legs and move about.

She took a drink from the waterskin tied to her saddlebow, finding it warm and tasting distinctly of animal hide. "Ugh," she told Moriah, "I am already tired of this."

Moriah laughed. "You need to toughen up."

Hannah made a face at her sister. "Do not use my words against me!"

They got back on their donkeys and continued on. The train wound around through some low hills, and Hannah was grateful to note that the sandy track they had been following had given way to a much more hospitable medium—one that supported a fair growth of grasses.

In the distance, she could see another grove of trees. "Maybe that is where we are heading tonight," she said excitedly, pointing.

Moriah followed her finger. "Perhaps." She squinted. "But I think it is already inhabited." Sure enough, they could see a flock of sheep and several camels among the trees.

The animals in front of the sisters came to a halt and Hannah could see Laman and Lemuel, weapons prominently displayed, moving ahead of the train toward the small grove.

Nephi and Sam, also with their swords and bows out, moved up to the front.

Hannah and her sisters slid off their mounts and walked around in circles. The animals seemed to sense that there was water close by and were eager to keep going, tugging at their reins and keeping their eyes, and ears, pointed toward the oasis.

Finally, Laman and Lemuel returned. "We will be welcomed here tonight," they announced loudly. "Abd-al-Ibrahim and those who travel with him are happy to offer us their hospitality on behalf of their master."

Hannah did not bother to get back on her donkey, choosing instead to lead it the short distance to the oasis.

The place was larger than it had first appeared. Not only were there date trees there, but also a patch of wild grapes that had nearly overtaken an ancient and unproductive almond grove. There was even some grass to supplement that which was carried by the pack animals for their camels, sheep, and small herd of cattle.

The men who had taken the place for the night had already pitched their tents around a fire and were in the process of stripping the ripest fruit for their evening meal and watering their camels and small flock of sheep. They stepped back, however, when Hannah's family appeared and, smiling, encouraged them to use what they needed.

Hannah and her two younger sisters had been assigned the task of gathering dried camel dung to build a fire. It was soon obvious that this oasis was very well used. There seemed to be no end of suitable droppings.

The men pitched their tents and secured the animals.

Soon both parties under the trees had a warm fire going and were happily absorbed in eating and drinking.

One of the men from the other camp approached their fire, hands out to show that he carried only a wineskin and a basket of grapes.

Laman got to his feet and acknowledged the man's presence. The man handed him the basket of fruit and the two clasped each other's wrists. Then Laman indicated that the man should join them at their fire.

Hannah stared at the stranger. He was dressed much the same as the men in her group, though his tunic was more flowing and lighter in color—almost white. And his headcloth was far larger, almost covering his tunic.

He sat down beside their fire and crossed his legs comfortably, seeming unconscious of the fact that every eye in the camp was on him and that all conversation had ceased.

Finally, Ishmael cleared his throat. "Welcome, stranger," he said. "Where are you bound?"

The man smiled. "My friends and I are traveling to Jerusalem." He nodded toward the peacefully grazing sheep near his camp. "We are bringing animals that our master will use to improve his bloodlines."

Laman joined the conversation. "This, we can appreciate."

There followed a discussion of pedigrees and animal husbandry that Hannah neither understood nor was interested in. But, knowing that the "law of the guest" dictated that she remain silent during the conversation, she propped herself back on her elbows and took the opportunity of studying the stars.

"Hannah."

She looked up. Her mother was beckoning to her from the other side of the fire. Hannah sighed and got to her feet, feeling every single one of the muscles she had used in her long ride.

The women were preparing beds for everyone. The children had long been comfortably installed in Zedekiah's and Berachah's tents and were asleep. Bedding was brought from the wagon and carried to the other tents. Soon, there was also a comfortable space for her parents and for her sisters and herself.

As the men continued their talk, Hannah helped tidy away the meal, took her turn washing up, and did a last check of their flock and herd. She spoke quietly to her father, who had taken first watch, and then finally approached the tent she shared with her sisters. They had long since settled and no sound emanated from the tent.

Unwilling to go in and shut out the soft, beautiful evening, she sat down just outside. The darkness was absolute. The moon had not yet peeped over the horizon, and the only light was that shed by the myriad stars.

Hannah could hear the rustling and chewing of the nearby animals as they grazed or settled for sleep.

From far away over the dry land came the sound of a great cat's roar, but the noise aroused little fear in her. Their camp was well guarded and that cry had been far away, reaching her only because of the clear night air.

Suddenly, she heard another sound. Nearer. She sat up, straining to analyze and locate. She caught her breath. It was the sound of two feet trying to be noiseless in the rocky soil. And they were coming toward her.

Hannah shrank back against the dark material of her tent, praying the thick shadows would hide her.

The footsteps drew closer and Hannah held her breath. Someone passed by her in the darkness—so close that she could hear them breathing—and moved on.

She remained undiscovered. She slowly let out the breath she had been holding, then berated herself for feeling afraid. Why had she been worried? She knew everyone in the camp—most of them were kin.

The footsteps stopped. Again, Hannah's attention sharpened. They had not faded away. They had stopped. The person was just on the other side of Hannah's tent.

There was a scratching against the cloth wall. Then whispering.

Hannah frowned. Who had been so careful about approaching her tent? And who were they now talking to? Slowly, carefully, she hitched herself along the wall toward the sounds.

She seemed to be able to see a bit better now. Glancing toward the east, she saw the pale flush of gold that heralded the rising of the moon. She edged along, still careful not to make a sound. Finally, she was close enough to poke her head around the corner.

She paused a moment, took a deep, sustaining breath, and leaned forward.

At that exact moment, a figure that had been kneeling beside the tent wall glanced toward her. Laman!

She sucked in a breath and Laman leaped to his feet and disappeared into the night, uncaring now of how much noise he made.

Hannah sat back on her heels. Laman? Here?

Hannah shook her head. She prayed that they would marry soon. Secret midnight meetings would do no one any good.

At that moment, the moon poked above the horizon and cast a long, welcome gleam across the countryside. Its golden glow illuminated the figure of a man a short distance away from the camp on the highest point of land. A man who was on his knees.

Nephi.

Hannah froze at the sight, unable to take her eyes off him.

Nephi had spread a prayer cloth on the rough ground and had his head down and his hands clasped, obviously in an attitude of fervent entreaty.

As she watched, he lifted his head and looked to the heavens, his expression one of utter peace and content. He got to his feet and put on shoes sitting nearby. Then he lifted and shook the prayer mat. Folding it neatly, he tucked it under his arm and disappeared behind one of the other tents.

Hannah sat back on her heels. She had always understood it, but now, she knew it. Nephi would be a prophet of the Lord.

Her body tingled with the realization, and she hugged her arms around herself. Almost without thinking, she got to her feet and moved to the place where Nephi had been praying. Carefully, she removed her sandals and then moved to the exact spot where Nephi had been kneeling.

For several moments, she looked up at the millions and millions of tiny pinpricks of light that formed the heavens. "Beloved Lord?" she whispered finally. "Canst thou see me?"

For a while, she stood there in the light, staring up into the heavens.

She thought about the man she had witnessed in this very spot in fervent supplication to One he both knew and loved. Then her thoughts turned to Nephi's elder brother skulking about the campsite on an unauthorized visit to a young woman to whom he was not yet married. The two brothers could not be more different. The one was concerned only with the Lord's will and the other, only with his own.

She stood there for a few moments longer, then turned and walked back toward her tent.

CHAPTER 13

The other camp, being so much smaller than that of the household of Ishmael, had long been gone by the time Hannah's caravan moved out the next morning.

As their train of animals began to move, Hannah glanced toward the highest point of land, the place where she had seen Nephi praying the night before. It seemed almost a sacred place to her.

She turned to look over her shoulder at the tall young man seated on the camel at the very back of their caravan and sighed.

"You'll give your heart far less pain if you limit your glances to your own intended, my treasure." Moriah had ridden up beside her. "Less pain for you. Less pain for the others in your family."

Hannah blinked. Then nodded. She turned to look at the young man seated on another camel beside Nephi.

Sam. Stalwart, dependable, loyal, faithful, wonderful Sam. She knew his litany of good qualities by heart. Was he as colorless as he seemed? Or was it just that, when standing in the shadow of his younger brother, he appeared so?

She knew he would make a good husband. He would be kind. And, just as important, he would be a faithful man of the Lord.

She shook her head and corrected herself. He would be her husband. He would be kind to her. He would lead her family in paths of truth and righteousness.

Unaccountably, her heart seemed to soften within her. She was suddenly looking at Sam with new eyes. For the first time, she noticed that his hair was lighter than Nephi's, a dark, almost walnut brown. And he was not a short man, only when compared to his brother. She had stood next to him as he took his place at breakfast and had been vaguely surprised at his height.

She now remembered the kind smile she had briefly responded to before her eyes again had sought out Nephi.

Sam. How had she not noticed?

Almost as though he had heard, his eyes were suddenly turned toward her. His wonderful smile lit his face and she felt her own lips curve in response.

Sam.

Throughout the day, Hannah found her mind more and more taken with thoughts of him. She began to notice things he said and things he did. Kindnesses that were second nature to him, services he performed without any thought of reward or even acknowledgement. She watched as he hurried to help the women down from the wagon when the caravan broke for their midday rest.

She saw his endless patience with the babies and Thaddeus, his gentleness with the animals and their response. When one of the camels was being cantankerous—as they often were—it was nearly always Sam who was called upon to sort out the animal.

When the men were called upon to exercise their priesthood, it was Sam who responded almost as often as Nephi. And when his youngest brother spoke with the unusual but unmistakable authority of the Lord, Sam was his closest adherent and staunchest ally.

How had she missed it?

That evening, as the tents were pitched in yet another oasis—this one quite large and with two other encampments already in possession—she was very much aware of Sam, helping here and there about the compound, carrying bedding, hauling feed, watering stock, and even holding tiny Naomi when her mother was dealing with Thaddeus.

At the fire as the men took their meal, her fingers touched his as she handed him his trencher. It was as though an electric shock went up her arm. She felt her face getting hot and she was grateful for the covering darkness and the red glow of the fire to hide her blushes.

Later that evening, as the camp was tidied for the night and the guard was set, she noticed that Sam had drawn first watch.

A few minutes later, she took a waterskin over to him. "I brought this for you," she said hesitantly.

He smiled and reached for it. "How unendingly kind you are, sister Hannah," he said softly.

It was the first time she had heard him say her name. She shivered.

"Are you cold, treasured one?"

"I—um—" Hannah stammered. She could think of nothing more to say. She turned and fled to her tent.

Behind her, she heard his soft chuckle.

She dove into her tent and buried her head under her pillow.

Hannah woke with a start. She had no idea how long she had been asleep. The dark was still thick and deep, so she knew it could not have been long. For a moment, she wondered what had awakened her.

Then she heard the panicked bleating of the sheep.

A predator?

Hannah stiffened.

Men were shouting, perhaps preparing to defend their flocks from some animal?

Then she realized that, somewhere in the din outside, she could hear someone screaming.

A woman screaming.

The thick darkness seemed to close over Hannah, making it hard to breathe. Driving it back, she thrust out her chin and threw back her coverlet, then crawled quickly on her hands and knees to the entrance to the tent and frantically worked the ties to the door. Behind her, she could hear her sisters start to stir.

"What's happening?" Amanna had awakened. "Moriah! Uzziel! Something is wrong! What is wrong?!"

"I do not know, Amanna," Moriah's quiet voice came out of the darkness. "It could be nothing. We must stay calm."

"It is not nothing!" Uzziel was awake. "Listen. I can hear someone screaming! And look at that light! Something is on fire!"

Indeed, the interior of the tent had suddenly brightened as something outside began to burn. Hannah could clearly see her sisters silhouetted against the south wall.

Moriah was vainly trying to keep the others still and quiet.

Hannah took a deep breath and forced herself to calm down. Then she attacked the fastenings to their tent slowly and methodically. Finally, the doorway parted and she was able to see outside.

She gasped and clapped a hand over her mouth.

One of the tents from the camp nearest theirs was completely engulfed in flames. Hannah could see a woman and two young children against the light. All around them Hannah could see the figures of men locked in a deadly struggle.

Swords winked and flashed in the firelight.

She heard something whiz through the air and she saw one of the men go down.

Without thinking, she slipped outside.

"Hannah! What are you doing?" Moriah screamed. "Hannah! Come back at once!"

But Hannah ignored her, ignored the shouting and screaming about her as she dashed the short distance from her tent to the flaming one. She snatched the smaller child and thrust the baby into the woman's arms. Then she grabbed the hand of the woman and the elder child and started to pull them toward her tent.

For a moment, the woman resisted. Then, seeing the relatively peaceful campsite ahead of her, she suddenly lifted her tunic and started to sprint.

Hannah saw another man go down. This time, she could see the arrow that seemed to have sprouted from his chest.

A horse suddenly appeared before them with a masked rider. Hannah and the woman slid to a stop and the woman screamed loudly. The young child in the woman's arms began to cry. The man's sword was out and, although Hannah could not be positive in the firelight, she thought it was covered in blood.

The man smiled down on the two women staring dumbly up at him and raised the sword.

Hannah dove against the woman, bringing her and the elder child down in a heap on the rocky soil.

She felt the sword part the air behind her as she fell. Then she was on her feet again, facing their foe, who was now laughing and starting to climb down off his horse.

Frantically, Hannah looked around for something to use as a weapon. The only thing she could see in the uncertain light was a stone, lying innocently in the dirt. She grabbed it and turned back, waiting for the man to approach.

In the meantime, the woman had regained her feet. She backed slowly away from the raider, clutching her younger child and pushing the elder behind her.

But the man's eyes, dark holes in the cloth of his mask, were on Hannah. She could see white, laughing teeth. His intent was obvious. Get rid of these women and children, who posed no real threat, then get on with the work of raiding the rest of the camp.

Hannah looked toward her tent. She could see one of her sisters in the doorway. Anava. The girl's face looked white and frightened in the ghastly light.

Hannah felt her face harden as she thrust her chin forward. Her grip on her stone tightened. How dare this man threaten innocent women and children! How dare he frighten her sisters!

Before he could take one step more, she swung her arm with all her might and released the stone. It was not a large stone, but it flew with deadly accuracy, striking the man just below his eye. Hannah blinked. When she and her brothers had hunted grouse in the brush around their home, her rocks had always gone wide. This was the first real strike she had ever made.

The man fell to his knees, and Hannah felt a brief thrill of victory.

But he was not as incapacitated as she at first thought. With a roar of anger, he leapt up. The smile had gone and there was deadly purpose in the man's step now.

Hannah vaguely noted that the woman and children had managed to move a bit farther away. She was facing the raider alone. Turning, she tried to run, but the man was faster, and he grabbed her by the hair. The smile was back as he slowly lifted his sword.

Hannah shut her eyes and waited for the blow.

She felt him start his swing, but then there was a loud clash of metal and she was thrown violently to one side.

Struggling to regain the breath that had been knocked from her, Hannah slowly dragged herself to her feet and tried to move away from the two men now exchanging blows in a fire-lit duel to the death. The raider—

And Sam.

For several minutes, the two faced each other, hammering quick blows with their swords or using them to deflect the other's advance.

Hannah saw another man approaching on the run, his sword bright in the golden light: Nephi coming to his brother's aid.

The raider saw him approaching too, and he shuffled around so that he could face both Sam and this new opponent.

She turned back to the two fighters, clapping her hands over her mouth to stifle a scream as Sam went down on one knee just as the raider swung with wicked intent. The raider's blow skinned past Sam's head, brushing his dark hair. Then Sam sprang up out of his crouch before the man could summon up a defense and buried his sword to the hilt in the raider's belly, just below his chest.

The man stared down stupidly at the hilt protruding from his gut, then looked at the young man who had beaten him. His sword fell from a slack hand, and he slipped to his knees, then fell sideways onto the rocky soil.

Nephi skidded to a stop beside his brother. Both of them looked down at the dead raider. "Well, I guess you did not need me after all," Nephi said, putting a bloody hand on Sam's shoulder.

Sam smiled and replied, "Sometimes I can fight my own battles, and I do not need my baby brother to protect me."

Both of them laughed.

Sam looked toward the other camp. "Are they beating the men back?"

"Yes. The raiders saw only families and easy pickings. They did not count on Laman or Lemuel's arrows or our swords."

"Good."

"Better get your sword, brother," Nephi said, gesturing toward the man lying at their feet.

"Yes." Sam crouched down and slid the long blade out of the body. Then he used the man's clothing to clean his weapon.

"Good idea," Nephi said. He also used the dead man's clothing to wipe his sword.

Hannah watched them numbly. Her eyes were unwillingly drawn to Nephi's sword. Whereas Sam's weapon was serviceable but quite plain, Nephi's was ornate to the point of pretension. The hilt looked like it was solid gold, and Hannah could see the flash of several jewels in the firelight.

A king's sword.

What was it doing in the hands of a sixteen-year-old farmer from the outskirts of Jerusalem?

Sam suddenly turned to her. "Are you all right, sister Hannah?" he asked.

She started and looked at him, tearing her eyes away from the flash of gold and jewels in Nephi's hand.

"I am um—" She felt suddenly lightheaded.

"What are you doing out here, Hannah?" Nephi asked.

"I—well—I saw—"

"She came to help me."

Hannah turned. The woman from the burning tent had returned.

Both men looked at her. "Was that your tent?" Nephi asked.

The woman turned to look, then shuddered, "Yes. The raiders came and my husband and our servant—" She shook her head. Tears had started to flow down her cheeks.

"Your husband is alive," Nephi said. "Or was when we drove off the last of the raiders."

"He's alive?" the woman turned, and, grabbing her elder child's hand, started back toward her camp.

"Sam, do we have any spare tents in our supplies?"

Sam smiled. "We do. Shall I fetch one?"

Nephi's eyes were on the woman and children. "I think our new friends will definitely need it."

Sam nodded and smiled at Hannah. Then he disappeared toward their camp.

"Sister Hannah, may I accompany you back to your tent?"

Hannah smiled. "You may, brother Nephi. And thank you."

The two walked the short distance back to Hannah's tent. As they approached, Hannah could see the other men from their camp, hanging back in the shadows, but with swords drawn or bows out. Laman and Lemuel came forward, each still with an arrow nocked.

"All well, little brother?"

Nephi nodded. "Thanks to your arrows and your aim, the fight was over quite quickly." He turned to glance at the still-burning tent. "I think their only losses will be a few sheep and that tent."

Laman nodded and let the tension off his bow. Lemuel did the same.

"Why did that fool woman dart out there like that?" Lemuel asked. He narrowed his eyes at Hannah. "Is not she the same one that dumped a bowl of bread on my head a few years ago?"

Hannah felt her face grow warm.

"She did what any good person would do, brother," Nephi said calmly. "What you and Lemuel and Sam and I were all doing. What Father Ishmael would have done if we had let him. She helped."

Hannah felt suddenly close to tears.

"You go and rest, Sister Hannah," Nephi said softly. "What you did took great courage and I am proud to know you."

He turned back to his brothers. "And now we need to spend some time thanking our Lord who made our victory sure."

"What did He do?" Laman asked. "I did not see him draw a weapon or run out onto the battlefield."

"No. He was the one who made your aim sure and my sword arm strong."

"Oh, right." Laman laughed.

Lemuel joined him.

"You go ahead, brother," Laman added. "Thank Him for us!"

The two elder brothers turned away.

Hannah heard Nephi sigh. The sound was both sad and discouraged.

She gave him a sympathetic smile, then walked over to her tent.

Her four sisters boiled out like bees from a hive, speaking over each other in their excitement.

"Hannah, we saw you!"

"What were you thinking?!"

"—watching—and when that man swung his sword—!"

"I cannot believe you'd do something so foolish!"

Nephi's voice came from behind Hannah. "My sisters, Hannah was simply trying to help. With the Lord's protection, she has survived, but she has had a bad scare. Maybe what she needs right now is your sympathy and not your questions."

"Thank you, Nephi," Anava said softly, her gentle eyes glowing as she looked at him.

Nephi smiled at her. "It is not me you should thank. Sam had taken care of things before I even made an appearance."

Anava smiled shyly. "Well, I thank you. And you can thank him!"

Nephi nodded and grinned. "I will, gentle one. I will. Now, the five of you try to get some sleep. We have another long day tomorrow."

He turned and disappeared into the shadows.

CHAPTER 14

The men went over early the next morning to collect and bury the bodies of the raiders killed in the skirmish, five in all, and to help the people from the other camp collect their scattered belongings. Their losses were small compared to what they could have been. They had lost only one sheep and the tent, and their servant had been wounded.

Of course, the emotional toll was much higher and harder to calculate. Hannah had walked over to wish the woman a quiet farewell and received a grateful hug from both her and her children and an invitation to stop and visit if she were ever in Nazareth.

Hannah smiled and nodded, then turned away, knowing that, in her present circumstances, the likelihood of her ever traveling to Nazareth was slight indeed.

The rest of the day passed much like the one before. Heat. Dust. Constant movement. More heat. More dust. Too brief rests.

She knew that the trip was beginning to wear on everyone. The children were much more irritable, and the men were shorter with one another. Laman and Lemuel were especially vociferous, especially when Nephi made any sort of suggestion whatsoever.

Hannah did not understand it. Nephi's suggestions were always purely practical, and most of them saved time and effort. But it seemed that any time he opened his mouth, Laman was especially anxious to leap down his throat, with Lemuel following immediately behind.

Their favorite mantra circled around the idea that Nephi was trying to take over, to forget his place as fourth son and usurp his elder brothers' power and stations.

But as far as Hannah could see, all Nephi wanted was to keep everyone safe, happy, and close to the Lord.

All with which she most assuredly agreed.

Things came to an apex just after camp had been set up that night. The oasis they had found was very small—just a pond of spring water and a couple of trees. There were no other caravans, and Hannah and the rest of the women felt quite exposed—especially after the events of the night before.

And to make matters worse, Laman, after a talk with his youngest brother that left him surly and withdrawn, had announced that there would be no fire that night because they did not want to make a beacon of themselves.

Everyone seemed on edge and there were two or three minor explosions between the men as they laid out the camp and pitched the tents.

Shaking his head, Hannah's father passed her mother and herself as they sorted bedding, near ready to distribute. Her mother put a hand on her father's arm.

"What is it, husband?"

He stopped and took a deep breath. "I think everyone is simply tired of the travel. Too much dust and too little luxury."

"What did they expect out here in the wilderness?"

"From what I have been hearing, they expected a little less 'wilderness' in the wilderness."

Hannah's mother laughed softly. "Oh, the young," she said, shaking her head. "I should think it would be us elderly who would most protest these new and uncomfortable conditions."

"Oh, yes, my aged one!"

Hannah's mother giggled.

Her father looked toward the men, scrambling to put up tents against the inexorable waning of the sun. "I am concerned with our young brother Laman," he said softly.

Hannah's mother straightened, a bundle of cloth in her arms. "What about Laman?"

"He has a real problem with his youngest brother. A real problem."

"What seems to be the matter?"

"Well, Laman neglects his priesthood duties, then rages when Nephi reminds him."

"Much like the people of Jerusalem." Hannah's mother handed her bundle to Hannah. "Take these to your tent, my treasure."

"Yes, mother." Hannah started walking, then found an excuse to turn back and fumble a bit more with her bundle.

"Yes. The people of Jerusalem did not want to be reminded of their duties to the Lord, either," Hannah's father was saying. He shook his head. "Why is it that they will not do anything, and then when they are prodded, they simply get angry?"

"Have not we discussed this before?"

Her father smiled. "Frequently. But now we can study the whole marvel at close range—within our own family."

"My heart sings."

He laughed. "Wife, you never fail to put the sun into my day."

He touched her hand, and then walked away.

Hannah's mother watched him go. Then, without turning, she said, "Hannah. Those bedclothes."

Hannah ducked her head and scurried to obey.

Hannah was pulling the bread from a bag and piling it on a platter when Anava came running into the compound. "Oh, Hannah! Where are Mother and Father?"

"I am not—" Hannah looked up and saw her sister's expression. "What is it, Anava? What is the matter?"

"Laman! He and Lemuel have Nephi tied up! And they say they are going to kill him!"

"What?" Hannah shot to her feet. "Where are they?"

"Over there!" Anava pointed. "Near the spring!"

"Find Mother and Father!" Hannah started running in the direction Anava indicated. Several other people were also hastening toward the same place. Hannah arrived at the same time as Sam.

Laman was addressing those who were already there. Lemuel stood just a pace behind him, and behind them, face down in the dust of the desert and bound hand and foot, was Nephi.

Hannah started forward, but Laman moved to stand in front of her. "Careful, little sister. You do not want to get involved."

Hannah looked at him, lifting her chin. "What do you mean not get involved? Here is your brother, Nephi. Someone has attacked him and tied him and—"

"I have done this, little sister," Laman said, rather grandly. "I have had enough of his prattle and his endless advice and criticism. Who does he think he is? Is he the elder brother? Is he the future leader of this people?"

Hannah stepped back, staring at the great black-haired man in astonishment. "You would do this to your own brother?"

Laman laughed. "Is this not the way? Because he is my brother, does that mean he can say and do whatever he likes and need never suffer punishment?" He looked around at the silent group. "And seek to rule over me, his eldest brother? When has that ever been the case?"

"When King David was chosen over his elder brothers to rule over Israel," Hannah said. "When Jacob received the birthright over Esau. When Isaac was selected over his elder brother, Ishmael."

"Enough!" Laman roared. "Silence, woman! Or you shall suffer the same fate as our brother!"

Hannah clamped her lips shut and stepped back, but the mulish expression remained on her face.

"Our little brother tried to rebuke me—me, his elder brother—for having a—how did he say it—a hard heart? As if I am incapable of feeling love!" He glanced at Uzziel, who stood proudly at the very front of the gathering. "He also scolded me for forgetting an encounter with an angel. And how do I know it was really an angel? Lemuel was there and he agrees with me. It was merely an interfering passerby who overstepped his authority. And speaking of forgetting, has our oh-so-perfect little brother told you about the man he murdered and robbed?" Laman nudged Nephi's body with a toe. "Go on, little brother. Tell them how you came to possess the finest sword in all of Israel!" He turned back to the crowd. "Tell them how you came across an innocent man lying drunk in the street and how you used his own sword to cut off the man's head!"

There was a collective gasp among the people.

Laman smiled. "You killed him," he said softly. "Then you stole his clothes and his sword and even went so far as to steal his servant."

Hannah looked from the one brother to the other. What was the truth? Could this Nephi that she had placed so high on a pedestal really be the murderer and robber that Laman described? There was the sword to explain. She had seen it up close. She had thought it certainly a finer sword than a normal Jerusalem farmer would carry.

"So before you lecture me, your elder brother, perhaps, Nephi, you should clean your own front step. There's a bit of blood spilled on it, I think."

Hannah looked at Sam.

He sighed and shook his head. "All is not as it appears, sister Hannah," he whispered.

"Something to add, Sam?" Laman was riding high now. "Maybe you want to join our brother here in the dirt?"

"I think even if your younger brother has, in your opinion, overstepped his authority, he should still be treated with respect." Hannah's father had joined the group.

Hannah looked over at him. Her mother stood beside him.

"Father Ishmael, this is a disagreement between brothers." Laman's light had dimmed a bit. "It is for the eldest brother to pronounce judgment. You are not yet a member of our family. I suggest that you and yours return to your tents and let us handle this."

"I think you are making a mistake, young Laman," Ishmael said quietly.

"Well, let us put it to a vote, shall we?" Laman asked. "If you people want to do what my youngest brother suggests—stay out here in the desert, following an unseen, unknown Lord instead of returning to life and comfort in Jerusalem, if you are so convinced that I am mishandling justice, let us do what you are so fond of doing. Let us vote." He looked over the crowd. "All in favor of putting this little upstart in his place, raise your hands."

Hannah looked around. Uzziel, Lemuel, both of her brothers, and, when directed by their husbands, both of her sisters-by-marriage, put up their hands. Hannah gaped at them. Father Lehi's daughters would also oppose him?

"You mean, we could go back to our home?" Amanna asked. "We could have our things? And our beds?"

Laman nodded.

"Then I vote too," she said, raising her hand.

Uzziel looked at her little sister approvingly.

Laman did not call for a dissenting vote. Instead, he smiled in an ugly way and raised both of his hands. "There. We've had a vote. Now we can decide just how to rid ourselves of the upstart."

"Just kill him, Laman," Lemuel said. "He's a murderer. Eye for an eye."

Laman nodded. "That has the ring of real justice to it."

"You cannot kill your own brother!" Hannah said. "He's—he's—your brother!"

"Who is a liar and a thief and a murderer! Any of which is punishable by death!" Laman took a step forward. "And did not I warn you, woman, to hold your tongue?"

Just then, everyone gasped and took a step back.

At first, Laman thought they were shrinking from him and he smiled again. "Well—"

He got no further.

Standing beside him, unfettered and free, was Nephi.

CHAPTER 15

Laman blinked and looked accusingly at Lemuel, who violently shook his head. "I did not do it, brother!" he assured.

"Who—who did this?!" Laman's face was mottled with red splotches, and there was a bit of spittle on his lips. "You will answer to me!" He turned to grab Nephi, but his youngest brother held up his hand and, for some reason, Laman stopped.

"No one released me," Nephi said quietly, "but the Lord of Israel, whom I serve."

The night passed peacefully, and when morning came, the camp was struck quickly—with minimal discussion and no voiced differences of opinion.

Finally, when they were assembled and nearly ready for the call to leave, Laman suddenly stood before everyone and held up his hands. Lemuel moved to stand a pace behind.

"I have something to say," Laman announced. "Something that needs to be said." He looked at Nephi. "Brother, I have laid hands on you in violence and I have no defense. I was hungry and tired from the days of travel and lack of sleep, but these are not excuses and I do not offer them as such. I acted in a cruel and violent manner—aberrant for a man of the Lord or a son of Lehi. I offer you my apology and ask for your forgiveness."

He sank to his knees and held out his hand to his youngest brother. Lemuel looked at his eldest brother then he, too, knelt down and held out a hand.

Without hesitation, Nephi grasped the outstretched hands. "With all my heart, I forgive you, brothers."

Laman nodded. "I thank you."

"And I," Lemuel added.

"But there is one other to whom you must ask forgiveness," Nephi said. He knelt down beside them.

Laman looked at him, and then nodded again and bowed his head. "Lord, I ask thee to look upon this poor, weak man before thee and give him thy forgiveness for his shortcomings and wrongdoings."

The prayer went on and Hannah found herself more and more aware of the righteous man behind the unrighteous, gruff exterior. By the time Laman closed his prayer, Hannah could feel tears on her face. Lemuel followed him, again voicing a prayer surprising in its humility and depth.

Hannah stared at him in wonder. She had not heard the man say more than a few words, and those usually echoing something his elder brother had said. To hear him actually supplicate the Lord in such a manner was both hopeful and encouraging.

Nephi added his voice to those of his brothers, then the three rose to their feet. Sam joined them and the four embraced.

Then Laman took a deep breath. Smiling, he looked at the rest of the group. "Forgiven and forgotten. Shall we get under way?"

The mood was definitely lighter as they started out as a happy group, speaking cheerfully to each other when they passed.

But as the day wore on, everyone seemed to tire.

Hannah felt gritty and stained with travel. Even her teeth seemed coated in grime. It was as though she had been traveling for months, not three days.

Just before it was time to break for their midday rest, Hannah saw Sam, who had been manning the perimeter, ride hurriedly toward Nephi. The two of them discussed something for a few moments, then Nephi jerked his head toward Laman.

Nodding, Sam urged his camel toward the front of the line.

As he passed, though he nodded and smiled at her, Hannah could see the concern behind his smiling eyes. Something was bothering him.

Beside her, Amanna and Anava were chattering happily. Not wanting to alarm them, she said nothing. She looked over at Moriah and realized that she had seen the same thing. The two of them exchanged a look.

They watched as Sam rode up beside Laman. For some minutes, the two of them spoke quietly. Lemuel, who had been riding beside Laman, suddenly turned his camel and left the caravan, moving toward a high dune on their left.

Laman nodded at Sam and turned his camel so he was facing the caravan. "My family," he called, "it is time for our midday break. Let us move into this bit of shelter here to our right." He indicated a flat piece of land a short distance away, partially surrounded by a series of small hills. "Father Ishmael, if you would lead the way."

Hannah's father looked at Laman and nodded, then he moved his camel past Laman and Sam and entered the area, followed immediately by the rest of the caravan.

Hannah and Moriah stopped their mounts just inside the perimeter and turned to watch as Nephi and Sam helped Hannah's brothers bring the flock and herd past them.

Then the three brothers arranged their camels across the wide opening to the rudimentary shelter and turned them to face outward. The camp settled for its usual break, food and drink was passed around, and the small children were given some time to recover from their enforced inactivity. Only Hannah and Moriah seemed to sense anything out of the ordinary.

Later, the two sisters lay under a hastily erected sun screen and attempted to sleep as the sun burned high overhead. But the three men nearby who remained mounted in the heat of the day made it difficult for Hannah to let go and drift away.

She was intensely curious and not just a little concerned.

Finally, she saw Lemuel ride back and join his brothers. The four of them moved their camels close together and spoke quietly. Then Laman turned to the group. "Time to continue on everyone!"

In a short time, the caravan was once more on the move.

Hannah kept her eyes on Laman and Lemuel leading the way. Perhaps it was her own heightened imagination, but they seemed much more attentive than usual—constantly looking about.

She turned and looked toward the rear. Sam was following as usual, but he seemed to be very interested in their surroundings. Nephi was nowhere to be seen.

Hannah assumed that it was his turn to ride the perimeter.

That night, when they camped—again at a small oasis capable of watering and sheltering only one camp—Hannah was aware that the men seemed even less inclined to talk than they had been the night before, but this time, the feeling was totally different. This time, there was no avoiding each other's eyes. Instead there seemed to be much silent communication going on with all of the menfolk.

They set the watch even before they sat down to their meal, and this night there was again no fire.

The night passed without incident, and Hannah was grateful to see the dependable light of another sun. She roused her sisters and started to fold up her bedding.

Soon they were gathered with the others, enjoying the morning meal of dried fruit and cheese washed down with the cool, but slightly gritty, water from the spring.

Today the brothers seemed to be a little more relaxed.

In no time, the caravan was again assembled and winding its way across the dry land.

Hannah looked to the rear. Once again, Sam rode there alone. She glanced around, then spotted Nephi and his camel off to the right, making a wide circuit around their train. Taking a deep breath, Hannah made a decision, and then pulled up her little donkey and waited for the flock of sheep and the herd of cattle to pass with Berachah and Zedekiah. Then she rode over to Sam.

Sam looked down at her from the great height of his camel and smiled. "A lovely morning, my sister Hannah," he said quietly.

"It is, brother Sam," Hannah said.

"And what brings you back to this end of the caravan?"

Hannah was silent for a moment, summoning up her courage. It had taken everything she had to do what she had just done. Now she had to find further courage to actually carry on a conversation with Sam. "I—I—"

Sam's smile widened. "Go on."

"I was wondering what everyone was so worried about yesterday." The words came out in a rush, and Hannah felt her face grow hot.

Sam frowned slightly. "What makes you think something was wrong?"

"I could tell," Hannah said simply. "I saw you talk to Nephi, then to Laman. I know Laman placed us deliberately in the protection of those hills and Lemuel kept watch. And then last night we had no fire for the second night and a guard set before we even gathered to eat."

Sam sobered. "There is not much you miss, sister Hannah."

"Are we in danger?"

Sam sighed. "Sister Hannah, we are always in danger in this place. There are marauding bands that prey on caravans. Women and children are especially vulnerable. And valuable." He fell silent and looked around. Then he sighed again, seeming to come to a decision. "Yesterday, I saw a small group of riders off to the north. They did not seem aware of us, separated as we were by the hills, but we thought there was enough possibility of danger to—take precautions. When we broke for our midday rest, it was as much to keep from raising dust as to give the people and animals a break. The riders, by the grace of the Lord, kept moving west, undoubtedly to prey on a less-blessed caravan, and missed us entirely. But we were taking no chances and stayed vigilant."

Hannah nodded, "And you kept this from us." It was more a statement than a question.

"Yes, sister. We felt it would be best if we simply allowed you to go on in peace."

"But I could feel that something was wrong."

Sam smiled again. "That is because you are you, sister Hannah."

"Moriah knew too."

Sam looked forward to where Hannah's sisters rode. "There are many special women in Father Ishmael's family."

Hannah felt her face redden again. "Well, I should go back. Moriah and the others will wonder where I got to."

Sam nodded. "I am sorry for the world in which we live, sister Hannah. I would wish only peace and prosperity to you for all of your days."

Hannah smiled. "In company with the sons of Father Lehi, I think those blessings are more possible."

A shadow seemed to pass over Sam's face. Then he smiled. "We will do our best, sister Hannah."

Hannah nodded. Kicking her donkey, she rode past the cattle and sheep until she was once more with her sisters.

"Why were you talking with Sam?" Moriah asked.

"Oh, I just had a question for him."

Moriah looked at her. "A single girl talking alone with a single man?"

"Morrie, there was the whole camp spread out around us."

"No. There was not. There was the camp all walking along ahead of you—"

Hannah sighed. "I wanted to know what was happening yesterday and last night."

"Did he tell you?"

She nodded. "He said there were riders."

Moriah caught her breath. "Riders?"

"Yes. A small group of them heading back that way," Hannah pointed off in the distance.

"Did they see us?"

"Sam said not, but the brothers were watchful throughout the rest of the day and night."

Moriah nodded. "Well, I am glad I am crossing the desert with such careful people." She glanced back. "I feel, when I am with them that the Lord of Israel rides with us."

Hannah smiled. "As do I."

CHAPTER 16

The long trip finally drew to a close, suddenly and without warning.

They simply rode around a small hill, through a slender opening between two more hills, downward along a narrow canyon and there they were, in a lovely valley, green and growing, with laden fruit trees and a clear river of water.

To Hannah, after the dust and heat of the desert, it looked like paradise.

Tents had been pitched beside the water and she could see a few people moving about.

As they drew closer, Laman let out a great shout. The people stopped and looked, then began to rush toward them, shouting with joy.

Hannah smiled. Father Lehi and Mother Sariah usually so dignified, were laughing out loud as they grasped each of their sons in a warm hug. Then they turned to those whom their sons had brought.

"Brother Ishmael," Father Lehi said, grasping Hannah's father's hand. "It is with profound gratitude and joy that I welcome you to the

Valley of Lemuel. Your sacrifice in coming and continuing the Lord's work will be noted in the books of heaven throughout the ages."

Hannah's father smiled. "When the Lord commands—" he said simply.

Father Lehi returned the smile.

Little, round Mother Sariah had enclosed Hannah's tall mother in a tender embrace and the two women, so alike in faith but so different in shape and size, exchanged warm greetings. Then Mother Sariah took her friend's hand. "Well," she said, "we should get everyone settled. We have tents prepared and there is food for all."

"Those are welcome words indeed, Mother," Laman said.

The rest of the group voiced their hearty agreement.

The next few hours were a blur of activity. First, warm, fresh food—the first in three days—and making the acquaintance of a man named Zoram, a quiet, kindly-looking young man. Then they settled their belongings into the tents provided by Father Lehi.

Finally, just as darkness descended, the girls were taken to a bend in the river and, in the deep cover provided by bushes along each side, encouraged to bathe and refresh themselves.

For Hannah, floating free and unencumbered in the clear, cool water, it was as though she truly had entered paradise. She and her sisters scrubbed and splashed and played for nearly an hour before they finally, reluctantly, pulled themselves out onto the sandy shore, dried themselves, and donned fresh clothing.

Hannah and Moriah gathered the soiled clothing into a bundle and left it beside the water to wash the next day. Then the girls walked together back to camp.

A small fire had been lit on one side of the compound, and Father Lehi was supervising the ceremonial sacrifice of a young lamb.

Hannah slipped into a space near Moriah and watched as the flames devoured the specifically chosen, unblemished animal.

Lehi sank to his knees before the fire and prayed, "Great Lord, all powerful and all wise, we thank you," he said. "Thank you for the safe travel of our sons, for their successful journey, and for the continued faith of our good friends and family." His prayer continued, brimming with love for the Lord and His goodness in bringing them out of Jerusalem and sparing them. He spoke of continuing to dedicate his life to Him, then concluded with a vow to continue building up the Lord's kingdom on the earth.

When he finished speaking, he remained kneeling for a few moments with his head bowed.

Finally, he got to his feet and turned to the rest of the company. "Our sacrifice is acceptable to the Lord."

Hannah smiled.

Father Lehi pulled off the cap he wore and set it and his prayer shawl reverently aside. Then he joined the rest of the company seated around a larger fire in the center of the compound.

Someone started plucking the strings of a lyre in a lively rhythm and the sound, together with the feeling of being clean, the warm fire, the faces of those most dear, and the thought of being able to sit still for a time, combined to infuse Hannah with a shot of pure joy that shone to her very soul. She jumped to her feet and began to dance.

Her two younger sisters joined her, and then the rest of the young people did too. For several minutes, the group danced about with the sheer joy of being alive and healthy and safe. Then, exhausted by the exercise after so many days of traveling, Hannah sank to the soft grass beside the fire and fanned herself with one hand. The younger girls danced a few minutes more, then they, too, succumbed to fatigue and sat beside Hannah.

Talk went on as the stars appeared, one by one. Finally, the moon, quite lopsided now, peeped over the rim of the valley.

"Time to retire," Father Lehi said. "The fire is dying down and we have many things of importance to discuss tomorrow."

Hannah felt a tingle of excitement. What things would be discussed?

The night passed peacefully. The calming babble of the river water and the soft breezes through the trees had both served to lull Hannah to an immediate sleep. She awoke from a dreamless rest to the light of the sun on her tent and the sound of birds and cheerful conversation from the compound just outside.

She looked around. Her younger sisters were just stirring. Moriah was up and nearly dressed for the day.

Uzziel was nowhere to be seen.

"Come, girls," Hannah heard her mother's voice say. "Your father needs his wash water!"

Hannah giggled happily. Nothing else could have made her feel more at home than those few words.

She threw back her coverlet and stretched, then bounced to her feet. "I think I can get dressed before you!" she challenged the twins.

Anava leaped to her feet. "Never!" she cried.

The two girls laughed as they frantically pulled on outer tunics and scrambled to find shoes and head cloths.

Both collided in their doorway and rolled out of the tent onto the soft grass outside.

Hannah looked up. "Ummm—we're here, Mother!"

Moriah stepped over them demurely. "And I, Mother."

Hannah's mother rolled her eyes. "There is the water, my doves. Do you think you can carry it safely?"

Hannah laughed and got to her feet. "We shall try, Mother. We shall try."

The three of them, Hannah carrying the water, Moriah the tray of soaps and ointments, and Anava the stack of neatly folded cloths, made their way to their father's tent.

"We are here, Father!" Moriah called. "May we enter?"

"Come, my treasures!" their father replied.

Moriah lifted one side of the tent doorway and held it while her sisters passed through.

Hannah smiled. It was almost as though they had never left their home.

The rest of the day passed like an idyllic dream. There were chores—a joy to do when one was not eating dust with every breath; duties, also much more easily accomplished with the softer winds and ready water; and the heady release of knowing one did not need to keep moving or be on the constant lookout for trouble.

Every time her father or Father Lehi came into view, Hannah looked up excitedly, expecting to be called into a general meeting to address those things that were topmost in everyone's minds. Well, at least in her and her sisters' minds.

But the day went past without even a hint of some greater purpose or the promised discussion.

And the next day.

And the next.

Before long, those things that Hannah had anticipated with such impatience began to fade in importance as her life absorbed this new rhythm.

Nephi had turned one of the three-walled shelters near the center of the camp into a sort of workshop. He spent hours covering thin parchment sheets with precise writing.

Early in the morning of the fourth day, Hannah stopped beside him. "Brother Nephi, what is it you are working on so intensely?" she asked.

Nephi looked up at her and smiled. "I am writing the things of the Lord." He looked down. "Writing to persuade men to come unto the Lord of Abraham and be saved."

Hannah was amazed. Nephi was just sixteen—only a few months older than she, and already he was showing that he had the makings of a great spiritual leader.

She looked around the small structure and saw Nephi's sword in its holster, hanging from a hook in the wall. She walked over and touched it.

"Brother Nephi, I would ask you—"

He looked up and saw what had absorbed her attention. "What would you like to know, sister Hannah?"

"This sword. I would know—" she took a deep breath. "I would know how you came by it."

Nephi carefully set down the tool he had been using. Then he looked at her and nodded. "It is something you need to know, my sister. But it is not an easy story to tell."

"I would hear it."

He nodded again. "Very well." He got up and motioned toward the only stool. "Would you sit?"

Hannah started toward it.

"Wait. Let us find places near the fire pit. It is yet early. There are few about. Better that we talk there."

Hannah preceded him, finding a place near the newly rekindled fire.

Nephi sat down opposite her. "You know of our family's flight into the wilderness?"

She nodded and added, "And of the Lord's command to return to Jerusalem."

"Not once, but twice," Nephi said.

Again, she nodded.

He sighed. "Well, on that first trip back, my brothers and I were to go to the house of Laban and receive from him a book, the scriptures and the record of our family. The Lord did not want us to start our journeys without His word and the record of our people."

"But you did not get it?"

Another voice spoke, "Oh, we did, but at great cost."

Hannah looked up. Sam had joined them.

"May I tell the story, brother?"

Nephi smiled at him. "I'd be grateful."

Sam took a seat beside his younger brother and looked across at Hannah. "Laman went first to talk to Laban, but was rejected. Still determined, we went to our home and retrieved the gold and precious things left there. These we took to Laban in an effort to bargain for the record. Our gold was acceptable to him. The bargain was not. He kept our wealth and sent his servants to kill us."

Hannah caught her breath.

"We escaped by hiding without the city." Sam made a face. "Our elder brothers were quite ready to give up, and equally ready to force Nephi and me to agree with them." Sam smiled. "Only a visit from an angel convinced them that, maybe, it would be possible to try one last time. For that final effort, Nephi went alone, not knowing how he would accomplish the task, but knowing that the Lord would lead him."

"I should probably tell it from here," Nephi said.

Sam nodded.

"In an alley near Laban's house, I stumbled over a body, a man who had drunk himself senseless with wine."

"The drunk man!" Hannah whispered.

"I realized it was Laban, the very man I was going to meet." Nephi looked at her. "The Lord had delivered him into my hands."

Hannah frowned. "But he was drunk. How did the Lord deliver—?"

Sam broke in, "The Lord's work will be done. Do you think it is coincidence that Laban celebrated stealing our wealth with strong drink?" He looked at Hannah. "There are no coincidences, sister Hannah. It was important that we receive the record from Laban. Therefore, the Lord set in motion a series of events that delivered Laban—and by him, the record—into our hands."

Hannah looked at Nephi and said, "You killed him."

Nephi was still for a moment. Finally, he nodded. "I did. The Lord told me it was better that one man die than that an entire nation should dwindle and perish in unbelief." He snorted softly. "I did not want to do it. I did not like it. I still do not. Never before had I shed the blood of a man." Again he looked at Hannah. "But the Lord commanded it. Much the same as he commanded King Saul to destroy the Amalekites that the righteous might prosper."

Hannah was silent for a moment.

"So now you know how a farmer came by his 'king's' sword," Sam said.

"You killed him." Hannah was looking at Nephi.

"I did."

She folded trembling hands together and added, "But only because the Lord commanded it."

"There could be no other possible reason." Nephi looked away. "Sometimes I think of it still, but the Spirit comforts me and reassures me."

Hannah looked at Sam. "And you believe this?"

Sam smiled. "I know it, sister Hannah. I know my brother. He would never do something like this on his own. He would give his life rather than take the life of another." He looked at her. "You know him. You know what he is capable of."

Hannah nodded, "I do." She got up. "I will think on this. Thank you for telling me." She walked toward her tent.

She glanced back at the two brothers seated beside the fire. They were watching her.

Later, when Hannah walked past Nephi's little shelter, he was again busy with his parchment and stylus.

Father Lehi had joined him and was filling other sheets with writings of his own.

Hannah stopped. "Do you believe, Father Lehi?"

Both Father Lehi and Nephi looked up. The elderly man studied her for a moment. "I know what you ask, young Hannah. Did the Lord command my son to do what he did that dark night in Jerusalem?"

Hannah's eyes widened and she caught her breath. "Yes," she said. "Only the Spirit could have told you that."

"I believe, my daughter," Father Lehi said. "The Lord's work must go forward, and sometimes He does what He needs to do."

Later, as she ground grain for bread, Hannah watched the two of them as they continued their scribing. Father and son. How alike they were in love for their Lord! She smiled and nodded, suddenly sure. Only a commandment from the Lord would have forced Nephi to such an action.

Her faith was whole once more.

Hannah and the twins were carding wool, getting ready to spin.

Nephi walked past them, across the compound to his father's tent. There, he did not even wait for an invitation but flipped the door back and strode inside.

"Father," he said. "Something has happened!"

Hannah almost quit breathing.

"What is it, my son?"

"Father I saw it! I saw the tree of life!"

The two spoke at some length. Then, "I must write this—" Nephi charged out of the tent and across the compound to his little shelter, where he immediately sat on his little stool and took up one of the sheets of parchment.

For the rest of the day, without even taking time to eat, he remained hunched over his work, carefully scribing symbols on his piece of animal hide.

He even continued working by lamplight.

Hannah and the rest of the company had gathered around a bright fire when she felt someone sit next to her. Startled, she looked up and realized that Nephi had abandoned his work for the day. "Brother Nephi. I did not think to see you here tonight," she said.

Nephi smiled. "My too, too mortal eyes have abandoned me with the failing light."

Father Lehi looked at him. "My son, is it time for talk?"

Nephi smiled. "It is."

Until long into the night, he spoke of a vision of a tree that dispensed divine fruit, of believers and non-believers, and of the Son of God who would come to earth and change everything.

Hannah drank up his words like manna from heaven.

The next morning, when she emerged from her tent, Nephi was already at work with his sheets and his stylus.

On the fifth day after their arrival, Hannah's world changed forever.

CHAPTER 17

Hannah seated herself across from her father and Father Lehi, wondering why they had called her into Father Lehi's tent.

Her father smiled at her encouragingly and she returned the smile.

Father Lehi cleared his throat. "Hannah, child, your father tells me that he and your mother chose to name you after the Hannah of old—the great and humble servant of the Lord. Hannah, who, when finally given the gift of a child, returned him back to the Lord as His servant. A woman of rare strength and courage. A woman of faith." He smiled. "He tells me that you have never failed to live up to your namesake, that you, of all his daughters, recognize the words of the Lord when you hear them. He says that you, alone, have a thirst for knowledge and truth and that you have the mettle to go after these things, to seek them."

He looked at Hannah's father. "We have need of those qualities—that faith and courage—at this time."

Hannah stared at him, then at her father, her heart hammering heavily in her chest.

Again, Father Lehi spoke. "We have had to change our plans somewhat." He cleared his throat again, obviously uncomfortable.

Hannah jumped at the sound, then looked at her father, who nodded gravely.

She turned back. "Y-yes, Father Lehi?"

He sighed. "I know that you had been proposed for Sam."

Hannah felt her eyes widen. Were they worried about Sam? Was something wrong with him? With her?

Her father took up the conversation. "But, due to new circumstances we have decided, as your father and future father-by-marriage, that we need to change that."

Hannah could hear buzzing in her head and a wave of dizziness washed over her.

"My treasure, we are going to marry you to—" For some reason, her father paused on the name, drawing out the suspense, "—Lemuel."

Hannah blinked. Lemuel? She had hardly even spoken to Lemuel. Ever. She had dumped bread on his head!

"My treasure, are you listening?" Her father's voice seemed to come to her from a long distance.

She looked at him.

"Hannah!" Her father looked alarmed. "My treasure, are you all right?"

"I—I—" she could not manage any more than that. Her mouth did not seem to want to work.

Her father drew her to him and wrapped her in his arms.

"I know that this will come as a surprise to you, Hannah," Father Lehi was speaking again. His voice sounded hollow, like he was speaking from a great distance.

Numbly, she turned her head till she could see him.

"But we have our reasons for doing things this way. Laman is already betrothed to Uzziel. Nothing we can do will change that. But Lemuel needs a strong wife who will be an unending support to him in his priesthood duties, who will encourage him along paths of righteousness. He needs a wife who will cross with him into paradise." He was looking at her. "Can you be this wife?"

"My treasure." Her father sat back but still with his hands on her shoulders. "This family needs you to a be help meet to Lemuel. Can you do this?"

"I—I—" Suddenly, inexplicably, Hannah recalled the prayer uttered by Lemuel several mornings before, on his knees in front of the whole camp. The humble, sweet prayer of the truly repentant. Her mind cleared. A single tear made its way down one smooth cheek. She took a deep breath. "I—can."

Her father's face cleared in a great smile. "My daughter, you have made me very happy."

"I know that you will all think this an unusual way of doing things," Father Lehi said. "But then, this is an unusual situation."

The members of both families had gathered in the center of the compound, seating themselves on rugs around the cold fireplace in a great circle. Father Lehi was standing to one side and all eyes were on him.

Hannah's heart was thumping with a thousand different feelings—most of which she could not even name. Terror. Excitement. Dread.

"Because of the position we are in, far from our homes and embarked upon a new, Lord-directed path, the customs and traditions of our homeland must be—changed somewhat." Father Lehi looked around. "I know that some of this will not be unexpected. But some—" He looked at Hannah's father, who nodded gravely.

"First and most importantly, the marriages of our children." Again he looked at Hannah's father. Again a nod. "We are ready to proceed," Lehi said as he looked down at Laman. "Laman, please stand."

Laman sprang to his feet.

"Laman, you and Uzziel—" Father Lehi nodded at her and she also rose, "—have long been betrothed. Today, your marriage will finally be accomplished."

Laman and Uzziel looked at each other and smiled.

"If you would move over here behind me, please," Father Lehi indicated. They moved and took hands. "Now Lemuel."

Lemuel stood and looked at Moriah, who was keeping her head down.

"We have discussed the wife for you, my son, the wife who would encourage you in your faithfulness to your Lord and your religion. We have decided that Hannah will be the one."

There were several gasps in the circle and Hannah felt more than saw Lemuel turn to look at her. She did not dare take her eyes from Father Lehi for fear of bursting into nervous tears.

He nodded at her and she rose slowly to her feet. "Hannah will be the fine help meet who will stand by you, my second-born son. She will support you and encourage you in the Lord's work." He nodded and smiled at Hannah. "She has rare strength and wisdom."

Hannah stumbled as she moved to join Lemuel. When he took her hand, his felt hot and dry. Hers was icy.

They looked at each other for the first time as an affianced couple.

Hannah took a deep breath, calming herself, and then smiled at him.

He blinked, then managed a small smile.

Hannah looked toward the others in the circle and found everyone's eyes on her. Her mother's expression was grave. Doubtful.

Mother Sariah's was joyful, her smile wide and happy.

Hannah clung to that expression. Her own heart felt like lead in her chest.

Father Lehi was looking again at the group. "Sam, my son who has the ear of the Lord," he said.

Sam stood up, his stricken eyes on Hannah.

Hannah felt a tear run down her cheek. The thought of marriage to him had been a trifle unreal. Now she realized that it was what her heart had been expecting. Maybe even yearning for. She looked away.

"Sam, my son, we have chosen Amanna for you."

Amanna bounced to her feet and over to Sam. Taking his hand, she smiled at him and pulled him to the lineup of future husbands and wives.

"And Nephi, my strength."

Nephi stood and smiled at his father.

"Nephi, Father Ishmael and I have decided that you shall marry gentle Anava."

Nephi's smile widened. "I thank you, Father. And you, Father Ishmael." He bowed slightly to the one, then the other. "I shall endeavor to deserve her. Anava and I will be very happy together." He held out his hand and Anava jumped up to grab it, holding it with both of hers and smiling broadly at him.

Again, Hannah's heart gave a sad little thump.

"One last thing," Father Lehi said. "There is the matter of our sweet Moriah."

Hannah saw her sister raise startled eyes to Father Lehi.

"Moriah, our own Zoram has asked for your hand. Will you give it to him?"

Moriah looked at the quiet young man who had risen and was looking at her with questioning eyes. Then she smiled and got to her feet. "Yes, Father Lehi," she said. "I will marry Zoram."

Father Lehi smiled. "Then it is done." He looked around at the five couples. "Now, there are some things we still can do. I need you all to return to your tents and ready yourselves for the marriage. We will assemble at sunset."

A pair of hours later, after much hauling of water, applying of lotions and unguents, fussing over the exact braiding of hair, and donning their finest tunics and headscarves, the sisters were ready.

Only Uzziel expressed disappointment that she would wear neither jewel nor coin when she presented herself to her Laman.

Hannah looked around, wondering briefly how any rich jewelry could enhance her beautiful sisters more. All of them were alight with anticipation and excitement. Almost, she could enjoy the day for their sakes alone.

But there was her own marriage to a stranger that she needed to understand and accept.

And right now, she was struggling mightily. She shook her head. Her attraction to the righteousness and strength of Nephi had been immediate. And for a while, she had entertained the notion that, somehow, she would be his. But when her eyes had been opened to the goodness that was Sam, she had welcomed the thought of marriage to him.

And now, all of that had changed. In one statement, Father Lehi and her father had stripped away her gentle, girlish dreams and replaced them with stark reality.

She was marrying a stranger. A stranger she had known of for many years, but a stranger just the same.

She tried to comfort herself with the thought that she was marrying a brother of Sam and Nephi, but it helped little.

In fact, the only thing that kept her from running crazed across the countryside was the memory of her future husband kneeling in the dust with the words of a humble, tender prayer falling from his lips.

"Hannah, my treasure? Are you happy?"

Hannah looked up. Moriah was standing before her, a vision in her soft tunic and headscarf, a slight frown of concern marring the perfect features.

Hannah managed a smile. "I am well, Morrie," she replied. "Very well." She tipped her head and looked at Moriah. "So. Zoram."

Moriah flushed. "He is a kind and gentle soul, devoted to Nephi."

"That speaks well of him, for Nephi will one day be the prophet."

"Human voices could not have told you that, Hannah, dear, but heavenly ones."

Hannah nodded. "But you must know it too."

"Yes. I do." Moriah sighed and smiled happily. "And I know my husband will follow him steadfastly down paths of righteousness."

Hannah smiled, wondering as she did so whether her own husband would do the same. She straightened her shoulders and lifted her head. She would simply have to encourage it. Build on the man she knew was under the Laman-following exterior.

From outside, someone sang out, "The bridegroom cometh!"

The twins squealed with excitement and, grasping each other's hands, stood at the door. Uzziel and Moriah came next. Then Hannah.

Someone flipped the tent flap open and the girls emerged, a bouquet of colors, to take the arms of the men waiting outside.

Father Lehi stood with his sons and smiled as the couples assembled. "Please come with me."

The five couples, arm in arm, followed in a line behind their prophet and father. He led them to a green space outside of the campsite, near the river, where soft grass was almost completely surrounded by towering trees. In the center, someone had erected an altar of stones and formed a small perimeter with several lit lamps. The gentle sounds of trickling water, wind in the trees, and birdsong provided a musical backdrop.

The sun slipped toward the western rim of their valley as they assembled, throwing the entire area into soft shadow.

The rest of the family spread themselves in a semicircle around the altar, just outside the lamp-lit perimeter.

One by one, each of the couples removed their shoes and knelt at the altar and, one by one, Father Lehi pronounced the words that would tie them forever.

In a dream-like state, Hannah knelt across from Lemuel and looked into his dark eyes. She heard very little of what Father Lehi said, but did manage to respond when necessary.

Finally it was done and she, still in the dream—now Lemuel's new wife—stood with her husband as the rest of the ordinances were performed.

Then, just as the sun had dipped below the western rim of their valley, Father Lehi clapped his hands. "And now, we celebrate!"

Hannah remained in the dream for the rest of the evening. People came and went. Congratulations were offered, responses given, food consumed, but she tasted nothing. Felt nothing.

It was as though some other part of her, the rational part, was beating at the inside of her skull and screaming at her to think, to feel, to do something!

But she had separated herself from that rational part and was carrying on without it.

Finally, the long evening drew to a close and Hannah found herself, for the first time, in her husband's tent. Hovering in the doorway, she glanced around.

The tent was divided into two spaces by the addition of a curtain down the center. There was a single pallet in the center of each space, both neatly made, with a coverlet folded down invitingly. A couple of trunks, obviously meant for personal items, were pushed against the far wall of each compartment.

A pair of large shoes were placed beside one of the trunks, and a coat was flung across it. She took that as a sign that the other side was for her use. Slipping past the barrier, she moved to the trunk and flipped the lid back. She had guessed right. Her clothing was there, all tidily packed for her.

Automatically, she readied herself for bed. Then, with a coverlet thrown about her shoulders, she squatted on her pallet to await her husband's presence.

She could hear snatches of other conversations outside. Murmurs. Giggles.

Then a conversation in whispers came from just outside her tent.

"But I do not know what to do!"

"You will figure it out—as have men throughout the ages before you!"

"But—"

"Lemuel! I cannot hold your hand through everything. I have my own bride. One who has been waiting a lot longer than yours!"

The conversation ceased and Hannah heard the sound of footsteps moving away from her tent. Then she heard a deep sigh and someone moving closer.

"My bride, I am here."

Hannah rose to her feet and approached the door just as Lemuel pulled the flap open and stepped inside.

"My husband," Hannah said, bowing her head.

"My wife," Lemuel replied, also bowing his.

"Humbly I give myself to you, husband."

He reached out and grasped her cold hand in his. "I shall endeavor to be a good husband for you."

Hannah nodded as he dropped the flap and drew her into her portion of the tent.

She stopped beside her pallet and gripped his arm. "Husband, let us talk a little."

Lemuel turned to look at her. "Talk?" He sounded alarmed. "What would you have us talk about?"

"Us. Our goals and dreams."

"Oh. Well—" he squatted down on her pallet. "So—talk."

Hannah sighed and sat beside him. "Husband, what are your dreams? Your goals?"

"I—uh—I am not certain."

"You do not have dreams? Goals?"

"I have them. It is just hard to put them into words."

She smiled at him. "Try."

"Well—I would like to be a hunter."

Hannah blinked. "Really?"

"Yes!" Lemuel seemed to light up. "I have always wanted to learn to pass unnoticed through the countryside, to be able to provide for my family by using my wits and my bow."

"That is admirable, my husband."

"The power one feels when taking that fatal shot, when bringing that animal down."

"I imagine it to be very—erm—satisfying."

Lemuel became quite animated. "It is!" He smiled dreamily. "I remember my very first kill. A large rodent of the marshland. Laman said it was a perfect heart shot. He was so proud of me." He looked at Hannah. "He had been training me for some time and said I was his very best student."

"How old were you?"

"Six. Young to be so proficient with the bow." He sighed. "But Laman said I was not too young to learn."

"He could not have been very old at the time."

Lemuel smiled. "He was eight. I thought he was vastly older and wiser than me. One of the servants had been teaching him, and he was so generous to pass that teaching along to me."

"Generous."

"Laman is generous. He shares his wisdom always."

"Wisdom."

Lemuel looked at her. "I know that you do not share my admiration for my elder brother. But know this, wife, he is my greatest mentor, and I will always—always—follow his leadership and share in his knowledge. It is of utmost importance to me."

Hannah shivered. She put her hand on Lemuel's arm. "But what of your faith, Lemuel? Is that important to you as well?"

"My faith?" Lemuel seemed puzzled.

"Do you have faith in your Lord? Do you know He exists?"

He blinked. "I guess so. Father has always talked of Him and Nephi talks of nothing else."

"Your father is a prophet, Lemuel. Does that mean something to you?"

Lemuel shrugged. "I know that he believes . . . " His voice faded away.

"But do you believe?"

"I—" Lemuel frowned thoughtfully. Then he looked at Hannah. "I guess I do."

Hannah smiled at him. "You do?"

"Well, I have never really thought about it before. But deep down, there has always been the—assurance, I guess, that there is a Being watching over me. That He is there. Caring."

"That is sufficient for me," Hannah said, smiling. "I want our marriage to be based on principles of righteousness, on the knowledge that the Lord lives, that He directs and cares for us, and that my husband—" She again put her hand on Lemuel's arm. "—will lead our family in the paths of righteousness."

"Your husband can do that," Lemuel said softly. "If you will walk alongside."

"Happily!" For the first time, Hannah felt joy in her marriage. She leaned close and kissed Lemuel's bearded cheek. "Thank you, husband."

He smiled. "And now, it is time for the marriage bed."

Hannah felt her face redden. "Yes."

Lemuel, too, was flushing. "We—um—we will have to learn together."

Hannah looked down. "Yes."

"Will you walk alongside?"

She smiled. "Yes."

CHAPTER 18

The next morning, after breakfast, the sisters gathered at the river for their daily ritual of washing and laundry.

The twins were full of their first night in the marriage bed and were whispering and giggling together.

Uzziel, too, was extremely satisfied with her married state and willing to tell anyone who brought up the topic.

Moriah and Hannah kept their conversations firmly away from such talk, content to let the conversation go on around them.

"And when he took me in his arms—" Uzziel was getting a little too personal.

Hannah had had enough. "Uzziel, some things simply are not meant to be shared outside of the marriage bed!" she scolded.

Uzziel drew herself up and stared at her little sister. "Well, I answer only to Laman now," she said, twisting her lips into a sneer. "You and others who would try to direct my life have no say."

"Are you telling us that our parents no longer hold any authority over you?" Hannah was surprised. She thought Uzziel's obvious disdain for figures of authority would take a bit longer to surface.

"I am saying exactly that," Uzziel said, her mouth curving into a smile. "I only answer to my husband!"

Hannah thought about that for a moment and asked, "And what if Laman does something he should not?"

Uzziel snorted. "He is my lord and master," she declared stoutly. "It is for me to support him in all of his decisions."

Hannah shivered.

For the next several days, Hannah's routine varied little. She found that being a married woman did little to change her daily plan. She now cared for her husband's personal belongings as well as his needs, but except for his nighttime visits and their marital conversations, her duties were little changed from those she had known since she could remember.

Her sisters, too, seemed to adapt well to the married state. Anava developed some sort of fever a few days after the marriage, but, with her mother's and Mother Sariah's help, she was soon healthy and glowing.

Hannah noted that neither she nor her sisters were as closely supervised as they once were. In fact, no one commented when she sat with Moriah and the twins to hear Lehi or Nephi speak of their visions, as they did almost daily. The two great men seemed in constant communication with the Lord and had many teachings to share.

Brother Sam, as well as Zoram, was nearly always present for these discussions, and both often expressed their own growing testimonies of the Lord and His goodness. Nephi's mother and Hannah's own parents, too, would join in, and Hannah knew great joy when so many members of her family were gathered together.

But one thing was lacking: her new husband's presence. Lemuel claimed hunting and providing for his family as his excuse to be absent from Nephi and Lehi's great messages, and this, along with his obvious admiration for Laman, was the blight that marred Hannah's happiness. She and Lemuel got along surprisingly well, even affectionately, except when Laman was around.

She was growing to dread seeing Laman.

About a month after the marriages, Father Lehi, upon rising, found something strange just outside the door of his tent.

His cry of astonishment brought everyone running.

Hannah emerged from her tent and joined the group gathered near Father Lehi. "What is it?" she whispered loudly to Moriah, who had only just preceded her.

"I have no idea," her sister whispered back. "Something Father Lehi found on the ground outside his tent."

Just then, someone shifted and Hannah caught a brief glimpse of a bright brass ball in Father Lehi's hand.

She stared at it in the moment before her vision was again obscured. "It is some sort of ball," she told Moriah.

"A ball? That is what everyone is so excited about?"

"I wonder where it came from."

Just then, her brother, Zedekiah, turned to look at his sisters. "It is a large brass ball, something none of us has ever seen before, though I would not be surprised to find that Nephi and his handy little tools had something to do with it. It has two little pointers inside and some sort of writing that only Father Lehi can read."

Hannah caught her breath. "Only the prophet of the Lord can read it?" She turned to Moriah. "Then there is no doubt about its origins!"

Moriah nodded and craned her neck, trying to see over the people in front of her.

Finally, done with her inability to see what was going on, Hannah took Moriah's hand and pulled her forward through the crowd.

"Wait! Hannah, that is my foot you are treading on!"

"Hannah! Careful there!"

Finally, the two girls were standing at the front—a couple of handbreadths from the ball Zedekiah had described, only Zedekiah had not done it justice.

It was glorious, its brass shining like new in the early morning sunlight. It was round like a ball and seemed hollow like a ball, but there all similarity ended. It had a pointer on top and windows cut into the surface, which allowed the viewer to peer right into the center.

Hannah shuffled around behind Father Lehi and managed to peer past him to see the two little sticks inside, both of which were spinning lazily as though they were quite uncertain which way they wanted to point.

Father Lehi moved the ball closer to his face and examined it carefully.

Then he looked at the group. "This is a director ball from the great God Himself. It will direct us according to the faith and attention which we give it."

Near her, Hannah could hear Laman muttering something. Lemuel laughed.

Their father looked at them. "Something you wish to share, son?"

"I told him I thought your little brass ball looked like something our little brother would craft," Laman spoke up. "Lemuel merely appreciated the joke."

Zedekiah joined in. "Exactly what I was saying."

Father Lehi lowered the ball and looked at his eldest son. "Laman, I would warn you that it is folly to sneer at the things of the Lord."

"Yes, Father, you are always warning us."

Again, Lemuel laughed.

Father Lehi's eyes flashed, but he kept his voice tightly controlled. "My family, this ball, this Liahona, has been given us by a just and caring Lord, who would have us never lose our direction in the wilderness."

"Lose our direction?" Hannah said. "But are we not already here? Is this not the place where our Lord would have us settle?"

Father Lehi smiled at her. "No, my dear. This was merely a place to rest for a while." He lifted his head. "And now is as good a time as any to make the announcement."

Hannah's heart froze.

Father Lehi smiled at her, then looked out over the group. "We have been commanded to move on. Our Lord has promised us a land that is green and flowing with milk and with honey, a rich land that we may inherit to preserve the teachings of our forefathers and our posterity, where we may dedicate ourselves to pleasing Him. This land is far, far away to the east, away from the wickedness of Jerusalem and the horror of the great Babylon. We will gather what we can and, in the coming days, we will leave this place and move forward." He smiled. "Will you all join me in a prayer of thanksgiving and hope?"

As he bowed his head, Hannah glanced sideways to where Laman and Lemuel were standing. Neither was participating in the prayer, but they were instead exchanging looks and gestures.

She sighed. Obviously, not everyone was excited about moving on.

CHAPTER 19

Less than a week later, they were all once again in a caravan, making their way out of the canyon and into the dusty, scrubby grasslands interspersed with rocky outcroppings and large hills that covered the land for miles.

Father Lehi had explained that, unlike their outward journey to the Valley of Lemuel, they would not be able to always stay in the borders near the Red Sea, but instead would be heading east and southeast, trusting in the Lord to bring them to places of water and game.

For the first few days, according to the brass ball, they did travel east, with occasional diversions to go around hills and other natural formations. Hannah's fellow travelers seemed cheerful and excited over every new feature in this unknown landscape. They were traveling with the Lord, and the feeling was euphoric.

Up until this time, they had been able to hunt for their food, having no problem finding sufficient game to feed them all. And, though they were unable to light fires due to lack of wood or dung or because of the threat of raiders, the animals they killed were somehow rendered edible, even without cooking.

Hannah called it a miracle, as did the majority of their group. Laman dismissed it as a different type of animal common out here in the desert and as usual, despite Hannah's coaxing, Lemuel agreed.

They were fed and strengthened in their daily toil, in their setups and takedowns, in their eating and drinking and finding forage for their animals. The great brass ball directed them to the more fertile parts of the wilderness, and though Father Lehi had said they would be leaving the borders of the Red Sea, they were still quite close and taking advantage of the comparative abundance in this part of the land.

All seemed as it was meant to be. All was peace. Then, several days after starting out, something changed.

Their caravan had camped in a quiet spot. Laman and Lemuel, usually the archers in the group, had both lost the use of their bows. Hannah did not understand exactly what had happened, only that they no longer had any spring. Only Nephi's bow—crafted of fine steel—had remained usable. But on this day, as he had sighted on a lone gazelle on a mountaintop, his bow had snapped in two just as the arrow had left the string. Shards of the bow had scraped up his chin and one side of his face, and the arrow, which had gone far wide of its mark, disappeared over the cliff. The brothers had come home bloodied, empty handed, and completely discouraged.

The camp, especially the children, suffered for the lack of food.

Complaints were voluble, most particularly those of Laman, Lemuel, and Hannah's brothers.

Once again, Father Lehi was cursed for dragging everyone out into this land that even the Lord Himself had forgotten.

Hannah was holding her brother's son, Thaddeus, rocking him as he cried from hunger, and trying to get him to take sips of water instead. The small boy could not be distracted and was wailing brokenheartedly.

Father Lehi sat beside her and watched the small boy for a few moments. Then he burst out, "Why did the Lord send us out here? To watch our children die in the desert?" He looked over toward one of the tents. "And brother Ishmael's illness is not improved by lack of food."

Hannah's father had been feeling poorly for most of the day. Hannah's mother had attributed it to the heat and lack of water, but now he was suffering from lack of food as well.

Just then, Nephi approached his father. He was carrying a rudimentary bow, fashioned from a long piece of wood, and he carried an arrow made from a short, straight stick. He also had a sling and a small leather pouch he had equipped with a quantity of stones.

"Father, you are the Lord's voice in this wilderness. Where shall I go to find food?"

Father Lehi stared at him. Then his expression collapsed and he bent his head and placed it in his hands. He shoulders shook with silent sobs. Finally he said, "You are right, son." The words were muffled and indistinct. "I am a sinful man!"

Hannah reached out to touch his shoulder and he looked at her, dust and tears streaking his face, and tried to summon up a smile. "Hannah, you are looking at a humbled man."

Nephi knelt beside Father Lehi. "Father, consult the ball. Tell me where I ought to go."

Father Lehi nodded and got to his feet. "One moment, my son." He disappeared inside his tent.

A span of minutes later, he was back, carrying the ball. He had dried his face, but his eyes were still red-rimmed and shadowed.

By this time, the rest of the camp had assembled, all of them looking sad and wretched and a few still voicing their opinion of wandering without food in the wilderness.

Father Lehi held up a hand. "I have spoken with my Lord," he said softly. "And I have repented of discourse against Him." He took a deep breath. "I will consult the ball." He looked down at it for a moment. Some of the color left his face and he looked a bit sickly. Then he held out the ball so his other sons and Hannah's brothers could look into it. They grew silent and, one by one, stared at the ground.

Nephi leaned forward and he too studied the ball. He put a hand on his father's shoulder. "We must—all of us—remember this lesson, Father," he said quietly. "The ball will direct us only according to the faith and diligence we give it."

"Yes, son," Father Lehi said quietly.

"Where do I go to find food?"

Father Lehi looked again at the ball. "It says you must go back into that mountain from whence you came and look again. The Lord will deliver food into your hand."

Nephi nodded, strung the bow over his shoulder, and, carrying the arrow, walked purposely from the camp.

After he left, Father Lehi stood up. "The rest of us need to spend some time in repentance and speaking to the Lord." He turned and walked slowly toward the outer edge of the camp.

"Well, maybe he does—" Laman started to say, jerking his head in his father's direction.

"Did you not read what the ball said?" Sam asked. "Did it mean nothing to you?"

Laman was again silenced. He, with Uzziel in close attendance, turned and started toward his tent.

Hannah looked at Lemuel. "Husband, we need to pray," she said.

Lemuel had been watching his elder brother walk away. He turned to her and, to her surprise, nodded. The two of them also retired to their tent.

That evening when Nephi returned bearing not one, but two fat deer, the celebrating was notable for being much quieter than the complaining had been earlier. Hannah looked around at the people gathered in the center of the camp.

All were happily filled but decidedly subdued, and, with the exception of the small children who were satisfied merely to be fed, all looked just slightly guilty.

She and Lemuel had spent the intervening time alternately praying and talking.

It was amazing to her how much more communicative her normally taciturn husband was when weak with hunger.

When Nephi had reappeared with his catch, his father had been the first to greet him, having carried on a long conversation with the Lord while waiting at the edge of camp.

It seemed that the time between Nephi's leave-taking and his return had been an opportunity for the rest of his family to humble themselves and leave their arrogant attitudes in their tents.

Again, the camp followed the Lord. Again, they consulted His prophet and listened to what he said. Again, the Liahona directed them to food and safety.

Hannah knew joy in her husband, Lemuel, as it seemed he had shaken off Laman's influence, at least for a time, and was intent on walking with the Lord.

The only concern that marred this time was the continued ill health of her father. His strength seemed to ebb from him day by day, and he was finally reduced to riding in the wagon with Mother Sariah and the young mothers and children, where he slept most of the daylight away.

One morning, Anava, too, awakened feeling rather ill and, for the first few hours, the entire camp kept careful watch for fear that some dread disease had decided to stalk their caravan. Throughout the morning hours, Anava was entirely unable to sit on her donkey, so instead she also found a spot in which to lie with her father and the others in the wagon.

By midday, to the relief of the rest of the camp, she was feeling better and once more able to ride with her sisters.

That evening, after a quiet consultation with her mother, she announced to Nephi that he was going to be a father.

After that, it seemed as though an epidemic of babies accompanied their caravan, with nearly every newly wedded woman submitting.

Only Hannah remained unencumbered.

Now while the men talked in the evenings, the women gathered and had their own conversations around their bodies and the changes each was undergoing, as well as the hope expressed that maybe their child would be the long-awaited Messiah and what they would do if this were so.

"It must be one of us," Amanna declared. "We are the only ones left!"

Hannah shook her head. "Have you not been listening, my sister? There will be many left. They will be smitten and scattered, but they will again be gathered. Have you not listened to our Father Lehi or to your brother-by-marriage, Nephi?"

Amanna shrugged. "What if it is me?"

Hannah sighed. Sometimes, she felt like a lone voice crying in the wilderness.

As the weeks progressed and their pregnancies did too, the women found it much more difficult to endure the rough conditions necessitated by their travel across the mostly barren waste.

At times, they had to make wide detours to avoid dangerous valleys and high mountains. At others, their caravan threaded its way through narrow passages, praying with every step that their passage would not close off in front of them. At times they did not know if they could go on for one more step.

But then there were days when they happened upon unexpected expanses of water. Those were the idyllic days, when they pitched their tents, watered their stock, and spent hours in the water, luxuriating in its soft feel on their dry, sun-parched skin.

They were just two days out from such a haven, encamped in a place called Nehom, when their caravan encountered its first real disaster.

CHAPTER 20

Hannah's father had been ill for several weeks, almost since they left the Valley of Lemuel. Her mother and Mother Sariah had cared for him in his weakness, and he constantly assured everyone who inquired that he was, indeed, improving in both health and strength. So though Hannah worried, it was not excessive.

Thus, in the very early morning hours, when the sun was merely a rosy stain on the eastern horizon, Hannah was taken by surprise to hear the piercing shriek of grief that emanated from her father's tent.

The death wail.

Hannah's heart stopped, and despite her belief in her father's reassurances, she knew instantly what had happened.

Immediately the cry was followed by other soul-numbing cries and moans and, somewhere, the wail of a child.

Gasping for breath and letting out little whimpers of anguish, Hannah stumbled to the door of her tent, then waited impatiently while Lemuel fumbled with the ties. Once freed, and totally heedless of the fact that she wore only her under tunic, she ran across the central space and dove into her father's tent.

Her mother, kneeling beside her father's mat, had thrown her arms around her head and was rocking back and forth, wailing loudly. Her tunic was torn at the neck and she had rubbed dirt into her hair. "Oh, my husband! My husband! Would that the Lord had taken me instead of thee!"

Hannah's father was lying peacefully on his pallet, his hands composed on his breast and his eyes closed as though in sleep. Hannah leaned over him and placed her cheek against his.

The beloved skin was cold to the touch.

She was vaguely aware that several other people had come into her father's tent behind her, but she had no wish to glance around to see who it was. White-faced, she sank to her knees and, with tears pouring down her face, starting wailing for her father.

Soon the small room was filled with people in the act of mourning. Tears poured like rain. Hannah recognized her sister Uzziel's voice behind her as she loudly declared her grief and incredulity.

Someone placed a hanky across her father's face, shielding him from their view and their grief.

For much of the day, they alternately wept and wailed.

Finally, as sunset neared, someone handed Father Lehi a sturdy wooden chest. He threw the lid back, exposing white linen bandages and pots of herbs and spices.

Hannah caught her breath and shivered as the finality of the situation washed over her.

The time had come to dress her father for his last journey to meet his Lord.

The womenfolk were ushered outside while Hannah's brothers and Father Lehi remained to perform this one final service to father, cousin, and friend.

Laman and his brothers disappeared in the direction of a small, rare grove of trees a short distance away.

The tears continued unabated as the women sat just outside the tent, trying in vain to comfort each other.

Little Thaddeus crawled up on his mother's knee and stared up into her face. Then he put his curly-haired head on her breast and cuddled close.

The two babies were crying and the servants brought them over to their mothers and grandmothers. A small measure of comfort was found in shushing their unhappy cries.

Finally, Zedekiah appeared in the doorway and nodded.

Laman, who had been standing a little way off, returned the nod, then beckoned to someone just outside of Hannah's sight. Lemuel, Sam, and Nephi came around the tent, carrying a bier.

Hannah stared. Where had they found that?

The four men followed Zedekiah into Ishmael's tent. A short time later, Zedekiah, Berachah, Nephi, and Sam emerged with the bier on their shoulders. Hannah's father had been carefully arranged atop it.

It was time.

The men moved forward toward a rocky formation to the east. The women fell in behind, still keening and wailing vociferously as they walked. Hannah and her sisters supported their mother. The rest of the company followed them.

Hannah noticed several things as they walked: the men's sandaled feet in the sparse grass and dry ground, raising little puffs of dust with every step; a lone bird flying past, glistening a deep red-white in the waning sun's rays, its lonely cry bouncing back to them from the stone cliffs; Rachel, holding the hand of her small son; the line of women, many of them leaning on each other as they walked and the dust of the trail marking the hems of their tunics; and her father, riding silently and serenely atop his bier—ready and willing to meet the Lord.

Hannah felt a fresh flood of tears and, unable to focus on the uneven terrain, she tripped and fell to her knees.

A strong hand appeared and helped her to her feet. Looking around, she saw that it was her husband, Lemuel, who had come to her aid. She gave him a watery smile of gratitude, and then walked the rest of the way with her hand in his.

As they neared the rocky outcropping, Hannah noticed a dark shadow at its base. A cave. This, then, was to be her father's final resting place.

The men moved closer until they were standing immediately beside the tower of rock.

The cave was small, hardly more than the height of a man, and the ground before it was rocky and uneven. This was not to be easily done.

The four men made their way slowly and carefully, testing each footstep before they took it. Finally, they stood next to the opening in the cliff face.

Stooping, they each took a corner of the bier and, with much effort, started to slide it into the cave. Realizing what they were about to do, Hannah hurried forward for one last look at the beloved face, falling and striking her knee painfully on one of the rocks. Ignoring the pain, she scrambled to her feet and reached the bier just as the men slid it inside.

Hannah fell to her knees and bowed her head. "Farewell, Father," she said quietly. "Till we meet again at that great, last day."

When the bier disappeared from view, Hannah's mother sank to the ground and gave another great shriek of pain and loss. It seemed to act like a signal to the rest of the company, because everyone knelt and the wailing increased exquisitely in volume.

The men enlisted the help of the others in the crowd, and together, the four sons of Lehi and the two sons of Ishmael managed to push a large stone across the opening of the small cave. The stone was not quite enough to hide the entrance completely, so they stacked smaller stones around and over it, finally obscuring all sign of the entrance.

Then, panting with the effort, they joined the rest of the company seated on the outcroppings and dirt facing the pile of rocks, and they wept for the man too.

After some time, Father Lehi stood and said a final prayer to his good friend and brother, taken too soon, even before he was able to see the vast new land he had glimpsed once in a dream.

Then the company got to their feet and turned toward their camp.

Hannah felt tired and drained. She stumped along on two legs that did not feel as though they would hold her up another second. And her knee hurt.

Finally reaching the camp, she slumped down tiredly on a cushion in the central area and tried to empty her mind.

Soon the entire company was seated around her, most eating bread and drinking wine served them by the few servants.

Numbly, Hannah took a piece of bread, then rolled it and dipped it into her goblet of wine. It was the first thing she had eaten that day, but she found it tasteless and unappetizing.

Across from her, Uzziel was staring into her goblet. Suddenly, she threw the cup to the ground. The purple liquid made a spot of color on the light-colored soil. "I will not take another step!" she shrieked.

All eyes were instantly on her.

"For shame, you, who call yourself a prophet of the Lord! You have forced us to leave our home and all of our possessions! You have forced us to travel day after day in the heat and dust with no food and no water and being heavy with child! And now—" her voice broke and she bowed and put a hand over her eyes.

Laman put a hand on her arm, but she shook it off and straightened.

"And now," she went on, "our father has been taken from us because of these filthy, terrible conditions! And it is your fault!" The last two words were shrieked as she pointed at Father Lehi.

He nodded sadly. "I am sorry for the death of your father—" he began.

Uzziel laughed a trifle hysterically. "You are sorry? You have taken everything from me! Everything!" She sank to the ground and put her face into her hands, sobbing loudly.

"Our father has been taken from us," Amanna said. "We will never see him again. He was fine at home. He was never sick at home. It is this—this—horrible place that killed him!"

"Uzziel! Amanna!" their mother said, her voice weak and shaky. "You know this is what we were meant to do. To follow the prophet—"

"Mother, how can you say such a thing?" Uzziel broke in. "We've followed the prophet. And what has it brought us? Hunger and thirst and fatigue and death!" The tears were streaming down her face. "Our. Father. Is. Dead. And there is nothing—nothing we can do about that." She paused. "Except go home."

Laman got to his feet. "I agree with her, Father. We can stop all of this now. We can go home."

Father Lehi looked suddenly old. He was silent for a moment, then he looked at his eldest son. "We cannot," he said quietly. "Our Lord has commanded that we go on, that we follow Him. Did His instructions tell us to follow until the path became hard? No. He said to follow. Just that—follow. It is not up to us to choose when we obey. It is simply for us to obey."

"Father, that is foolish talk! We obey, yes. But we are not to obey blindly! The Lord does not expect us to simply follow without thinking. So let us think! We are suffering here! Our wives are being forced to travel across this inhospitable place in delicate condition. People are dying, Father. They are dying! It is time that we inform the Lord of our new situation and tell him of our decision."

Father Lehi stood up. "Do you think He does not know our situation, son? Do you think He is unaware of our difficulties and our challenges?"

Nephi stood also. "Laman, who is it that sent the ball? The director?"

Laman spun around and pinned Nephi with his gaze. "This is not your discussion, younger brother," he spat. "This is talk for the elders in the group."

Nephi smiled. "I think if it is a discussion of the group, it is a discussion for the group. If you are deciding my spiritual and physical welfare, I want to be involved in the discourse."

Father Lehi nodded. "Nephi is right, son. We cannot decide anyone's future without allowing him some input."

Laman curled his upper lip. "Like you allowed my input when you decided to drag all of us out here?"

Father Lehi sighed. "That was not me, but our Lord who commanded—"

"I am weary of what the Lord desires of us!" Laman said. "If He would have us survive, then He needs to make survival possible."

"The Lord is strengthening us, brother," Nephi said. "He is refining us as gold—"

"Well, I, for one, do not want to be boiled into a small, cold, golden object!" Laman nodded to Lemuel, and then turned and left.

Uzziel leaped up and ran after him. The two of them disappeared into Laman's tent.

Lemuel got up as well. "Wife," he said and held out his hand to Hannah.

Hannah looked up at him, surprised. Then, sighing, she got to her feet and took the proffered hand.

He pulled her along to Laman's tent as well.

Hannah frowned. Why were they going to Laman's tent?

They ducked inside. Uzziel and Laman had gone into the compartment on the right. Uzziel was seated on a cushion to one side. Laman was pacing back and forth, muttering and waving his arms.

Someone entered the tent behind her and she glanced over her shoulder to see her brothers, looking equally as fierce as Laman.

Lemuel let go of Hannah's hand and approached his brother. "Brother, I am here," he said. "What would you have me do?"

Laman spun around, noting the presence of Lemuel then looking past him to Zedekiah and Berachah. He put his hands on Lemuel's shoulders. "Lemuel," he hissed. "Let us slay our father!"

Hannah caught her breath.

Laman glanced at her briefly before he looked back at Lemuel. "And also our brother Nephi," he continued. "From the days of his youth, he has taken it upon himself to be our ruler and our teacher." He dropped his hands and started pacing again. "He claims the Lord and angels have talked with him, but we know that he lies, thinking to lead us away." He stopped and looked at his small band of supporters. "And after he has led us away, he thinks to make himself a king and a ruler over us."

Hannah stared at him.

The others in the room said nothing, but Hannah could see by their expressions that they were all in agreement.

"So let us free ourselves from those who would suppress our freedom, from those who would rule unrighteously over us."

Laman belted a sheath about his waist and slid a long knife into it.

Hannah leaped to her feet. "Laman!" she yelled. "Brother! You cannot do this!"

Lemuel put his hands on her shoulders and turned her toward him. "Hush, wife. These things do not concern you."

"Do not concern me? Husband, they concern all of us! We cannot kill a prophet of the Lord! We will be just like those people of Jerusalem!"

Lemuel smiled. "We are the people of Jerusalem. The righteous people of Jerusalem, the people who do not allow themselves to be led away by false prophets and cunning arts!"

Hannah stared at him. "But—you think your father is a false—" Her voice trailed off as the breath seemed to leave her.

"Our father is a visionary man," Laman said. He patted the knife. "And it is time to put an end to this foolishness." He left the tent, not bothering to see who followed.

His little group trailed behind, Hannah stumbling along in the rear. It was hard to keep her limbs going when she could not seem to get enough air into her lungs.

The group moved back into the central court, with Laman and Lemuel at the front and the others arranged behind them. Opposite them stood Nephi, Sam, and their father, as well as Zoram, the servant Ebed, and the rest of the women.

Rachel and Talitha had moved off with their children and now stood at the edge of camp behind Father Lehi's group.

Laman stepped forward and patted the knife sheathed at his side. "We've come to make things right," he said.

Nephi stepped forward as well. "And by right, you mean the way you want it."

Laman sneered, "The way that will ensure our wives and our children are safe once more. In their homes in Jerusalem."

"And you are sure this will keep them safe?"

Laman snorted, "At least safer than they are out here!"

Nephi glanced at Laman's knife. "So you think that by killing a prophet of the Lord you will be safer?"

"If we are not forced to follow a visionary man, we will not be forced to follow his visions."

"Even if those visions are what will keep you safe?"

Laman took a deep breath. "Look around, brother. Look over there." He pointed toward the outcropping that was now Hannah's father's crypt. "Is Father Ishmael safe?"

"He is now," Father Lehi said quietly.

Laman looked at him. "Safe?"

"He is with his Lord. He is safe."

"And that is where we plan to send you, Father. Somewhere safe."

Father Lehi shook his head and sighed sadly.

Nephi looked again at the weapon his brother wore. "By violent means, brother?"

"By whatever means it takes, brother."

Nephi moved in front of his father. "Then you had better come to me first."

Laman shrugged. "Whatever you wish." He started forward again, one hand pulling his knife from its sheath.

For a moment, the two brothers faced each other. The one armed with a sharpened steel weapon, the other only with the Spirit.

Laman crouched and swung with the blade, and Hannah gasped, clapping a hand over her mouth.

Nephi leaped out of the way and the blade whipped wickedly through the air just in front of him.

Another swipe. Again Nephi avoided the bright blade by a hairsbreadth.

Laman changed his tactic and tried stabbing with the knife. As he thrust forward, Nephi dodged, and then brought his fist down on Laman's knife hand, knocking the weapon to the ground.

At that moment, a great gust of wind blew through the camp raising a stinging cloud of sand and dirt.

Laman threw his arms protectively over his face.

Hannah glimpsed many others do the same before she drew her head cloth over her eyes and held it there as the tiny grains bit into the skin of her hands.

Then, as abruptly as the wind started, it stopped.

Hannah could hear the sand falling back to the earth like soft rain. Then she heard something else, something that started low, then slowly gained in volume. She lowered her head cloth and looked around.

What was that?

The other people in the caravan were also looking around, various puzzled expressions on their faces.

Then, as the noise increased in volume, Hannah began to recognize words.

"—of the Lord, your God. Think ye to counsel Him? Think ye to correct Him? Who are ye to admonish the Lord of Heaven and of Earth? The Creator of all things?"

Laman and the others were looking around, trying to discover where the voice was coming from. Laman looked uneasy. He had regained his knife and was holding it in front of himself defensively.

Nephi, Father Lehi, and those who stood with them were looking up.

Hannah, too, lifted her eyes heavenward. A golden light seemed to be shining down. A bright, otherworldly light.

The voice was also coming from there.

It went on. "Laman, Lemuel, Zedekiah, Berachah. Think ye to destroy a prophet of the Lord? Think ye that in destroying the word of the Lord ye will destroy the Lord Himself?"

By this time, Laman and his followers had also discovered the source of the voice. One by one they sank to their knees, their eyes looking heavenward.

The knife Laman had held so fiercely fell to the earth, forgotten.

For some minutes, the voice spoke, outlining the mistakes made by Laman and his followers and the consequences of such folly.

Such dire consequences.

Hannah glanced over at Laman. The man was pale and trembling. She looked at her husband. He—in fact all of their group—seemed equally affected.

She looked over toward Nephi, Sam, and Father Lehi. They were still gazing up into heaven, but their expressions were of joy and peace.

If Hannah had not known before, she certainly knew now that Father Lehi was a prophet and that Nephi and possibly Sam were following in the great man's footsteps.

Finally, the speaking ended and the golden light disappeared from the heavens.

For several seconds, no one moved.

Then Laman, leaving his knife behind him on the ground, got shakily to his feet and moved over to where his father and brothers were standing. Once there, he sank to the ground before them and bowed his head. "I have transgressed again, my father, brothers. Please. Please forgive me. I thought to counsel the Lord, to correct Him. My folly astonishes even me."

Father Lehi put a hand on his eldest son's head. "Know you your errors, my son?"

"I do, Father. Seeking my own path and fighting against the Lord's."

His father nodded. "And what do you propose now?"

"To follow the prophet," Laman said quietly. "To do that which my Lord would have me do."

Father Lehi smiled. "It is well," he said, simply. He turned to Nephi. "What say you, my son?"

Nephi smiled as well. "That we have witnessed a miracle, Father." He reached out a hand to his elder brother. "Kneel not before me, Laman. We are brothers!"

Laman got slowly to his feet. "Can you forgive me, Nephi? Again?"

"From a full heart, Laman." Nephi's smile widened and he offered his hand, which Laman gripped firmly. "Let us all learn from this."

"When you fight against the Lord, your God, you are left to kick against the pricks," Father Lehi said. "Good will never come from evil. Never."

Laman nodded. "I understand, Father."

Lemuel moved to stand before his father as well. "Forgive me, Father. Brother," he said.

Father Lehi and Nephi turned to him. Lehi gripped his son's hand. "You are forgiven, Lemuel."

"I will not make the mistake of seeking to advise my Lord," Lemuel said.

"You are wise, my son." Lehi's eyes twinkled. "And it is not I who have revealed this to you, but the Lord which is in heaven."

Lemuel nodded and Hannah joined him.

"Ah. Hannah," Father Lehi said. "Faithful, little Hannah."

Hannah bowed to father Lehi. "Forgive me as well, Father Lehi," she asked.

Father Lehi looked surprised. "Why would you have need of our forgiveness?"

"I—I—was there," Hannah stammered. "I heard what Laman said. I—did not do anything."

"Sweet, faithful Hannah, you may counsel your husband, but when you try to counsel others, you are usually disregarded." He rubbed his fingers over his brow. "I know of this personally."

Hannah looked down and put her hands together. "I feel I need to ask your forgiveness, Father Lehi." She looked at Nephi and added, "Brother Nephi."

Nephi smiled. "No need, sister Hannah, but, if it would ease your mind, I forgive you."

"Thank you; it does!"

The group spent some time in prayer, then retired to their tents.

Hannah looked at her husband once they were safely inside. "Husband, I would not seek to lead you. However, it is the wife's duty to counsel with her spouse."

"As you have told me many times."

"It dismays me when you follow Laman."

"Laman is my brother. I would follow him anywhere."

"Even into darkness?"

Lemuel stiffened. "I have not followed him into darkness!"

"Where were you today, husband?"

He was silent for a moment. Then, "Today was different."

"How?"

"Things got beyond control. The grief. The—the funeral."

"How is this any different than when we were traveling from my home and Laman tied Nephi up with the intention of killing him?"

Lemuel was silent.

"I will say no more, husband. I just ask that you think—and pray—before you follow Laman in his schemes." She smiled at him. "I want to follow you. But I will not follow you into sin and darkness."

Somehow, the contention and confusion that had followed the burial of Ishmael burned off much of the feeling of loss and despair.

With the restoration of peace in the campsite, Ishmael's family once again permitted their pain and anguish at the loss of their husband and father to show. But their distress seemed removed. Lessened.

When they packed up the camp the day after the burial, only Hannah's mother still seemed incapacitated by her loss.

She sat outside her tent and watched, tearless and numb, as her sons and her daughters folded up her husband's tent and, once her personal belongings were safely stowed, divided Ishmael's worldly goods among the people of their caravan.

Finally, the camp was packed.

Hannah looked toward the spot where her mother had been sitting. The elder woman had disappeared. She glanced around the camp at the people now saddling the riding beasts, ready for the onward journey.

Her mother could not be seen.

Growing slightly alarmed, Hannah moved to the far side of the group, looking constantly for the familiar figure.

Nothing.

Then she noticed someone walking toward the rock formation that was now her father's tomb. Lifting the hem of her tunic, Hannah sprinted across the rocky soil.

The person had disappeared before she had covered half of the distance, but Hannah kept on, slowing to a walk only when the base of the outcropping came into view and she could clearly see her mother crouched there.

She approached slowly, not wishing to disturb unduly.

"Husband, what do I do?" her mother was saying. "I need your presence for strength, for wisdom." She placed her head in her hands. "I do not know how to go on without you."

Hannah moved closer and sat down beside her mother on a fold of rock.

Judith gasped and looked up, her tear-stained cheeks and red-rimmed eyes mute testimony to her ongoing grief.

Hannah reached out and took her mother's hand. It felt cool and limp.

"What do I do, treasured one?" her mother asked.

"You go on, Mother," Hannah told her. "That God who guided your husband still guides your prophet and can still guide you. You find your strength in following that prophet."

Her mother sighed. "Yes." She gave just the faintest smile. "But it is not quite the same."

"Mother, nothing is ever the same. This day may look like the last one, but it is not. There are daily changes, daily beginnings and endings." She looked toward the camp and saw Rachel leading Thaddeus toward the wagon. "Did you know that, this morning, little Naomi took her first step? Soon her days of creeping about will be past and her days of walking just starting. An ending and a beginning." She looked at her mother. "We, too, have an ending and a beginning. Yesterday was the last of our days with Father." Her eyes filled with tears. "And today the first of our days without him." Her mother was weeping again. "But there will be good days ahead. Always, there are good days, new teachings, new experiences." She sighed. "It is the way of the Lord, Mother. One cannot learn and grow without the experiences to teach us to learn and grow."

Her mother looked at her. "Where did you get such wisdom, child?"

Hannah smiled and ducked her head. "It is not mine, Mother," she said. "It is the wisdom of the prophet, Lehi, and his son, Nephi. I simply listened."

Her mother patted her hand. "Continue to listen to them, Hannah."

"I intend to, Mother."

Judith looked toward the camp, then got to her feet. "I can see that they are readying themselves to travel."

Hannah looked too. "Yes, they are." She turned back toward the pile of stones that covered her father's crypt. "We must say one final good-bye to Father's earthly remains."

"Yes." Her mother said, touching the large stone with one hand. "Farewell, my husband. Until we meet in glory at the Lord's side."

Hannah smiled. "What a lovely thought."

Her mother stood up. "It is more than a thought, daughter," she said with some of her usual fire. "It is a promise."

Hannah nodded and got to her feet. She took her mother's hand, and the two of them turned and walked toward the assembling caravan.

CHAPTER 21

For several months, the caravan wound its way peacefully through the scrub grasslands, deserts, and the occasional verdant patches that formed the patchwork land.

Though they traveled near the known trade routes and the waters of the great Red Sea, Father Lehi directed them to remain at a distance, thus avoiding most of the travelers and ensuring very little outside contact.

Their caravan became a little world in itself, a quiet place of refuge where the things of the Lord were discussed openly, and the Spirit of the Lord was in constant attendance.

The women grew great with child, but, sustained by the meat on which they lived, they were strong and able to withstand the rigours of travel without difficulty—or complaint.

When everyone had been fed and the caravan readied for the night, there was often music, singing and dancing, long discussions of the Lord and spiritual matters, and the joy of being with those best loved in all the world.

With Laman's new steadfastness in spiritual matters, Lemuel was freed to find his own testimony. He and Hannah had many long discussions about faith, and she knew happiness in the man she had married.

She and Lemuel had grown closer, exploring each other's minds and hearts and discovering many similarities alongside the obvious differences.

Tonight, five months after the death of her father, Hannah and her husband were discussing the reason they had been placed on the earth.

"So why do you think we are here?" Hannah asked.

Lemuel smiled. "To work hard, get rich, and die leaving a great legacy and many, many children."

Hannah sobered and peered at him in the dim light of their tent. The daylight had nearly gone, and because they did not make much fire, their day ended with the going down of the sun. "Is that a rebuke because I am not yet with child?"

Lemuel frowned. "I did not even think of that!" he said.

Hannah looked away. "I know not why the Lord has chosen to punish me in this fashion," she said.

"You sound like her."

"Who?"

"Hannah. The woman you were named for."

Hannah caught her breath and recounted the story of her namesake in her mind: the faithful woman whose womb had been shut up, the prayer of anguish, the answer to her prayer and birth of her son Samuel as requested from the Lord.

Her eyes closed and, quite suddenly, she was pouring out her heart in prayer to the Lord. "Please, Lord. If you remember me, give me a child. Take away my shame and give me a child." Hannah's lips moved with her fervent prayer, but no sound emerged.

"Just like her," Lemuel said. He got up and moved to his own portion of the tent.

"Mother Sariah! It is time!"

Hannah heard her mother's whispered words just outside her tent. She rolled her head and looked at the tent wall, but it was dark.

Not morning then. She frowned into the darkness. How long had she been asleep? And what was it time for? She pushed her coverlet down to her feet and rolled onto her knees. Then she stood up and, as quietly as possible, crept toward the doorway of her tent.

"It is of little use for you to creep around. I am awake." Lemuel's voice sounded tired and annoyed.

"Forgive me, husband," Hannah said. "I heard my mother's voice and I wanted to see if she needed help."

A grunt was her only response.

Hannah quickly worked the fastenings and slipped out into the cool night air, not bothering to find a cover for her under tunic.

She was surprised to see a light in one of the far tents. A light. Something must be happening in—she frowned and counted—two over—second row—Nephi's tent. Lifting her tunic hem, she ran toward it.

In the doorway, she bumped into Nephi.

Quite literally.

Her small form bounced off of his and she landed on her back. Fortunately, they had camped in a place of water and lush vegetation. She landed in the thick, soft grass and only the breath was knocked from her. Life remained.

"Who—sister Hannah!" Nephi reached out a hand and Hannah took it. With one pull, he lifted her to her feet. "I am so sorry, sister. I did not see anyone coming."

Hannah stood, rather shakily, and tried to catch her breath. Finally, she managed to gasp out a weak, "Okay."

Nephi's white teeth showed in the darkness. "Good."

"What—is—"

"What is going on?" He laughed. "I am about to become a father."

"Oh."

Someone appeared in the doorway, a dark shape against the lighter lamplight inside. Mother Sariah. "Nephi, could you—Hannah! Good. I need some water and a bottle of wine and the small bag of salt. The one with my healer kit."

Hannah nodded, then not knowing if Sariah could see her in the darkness said, "Yes, Mother Sariah." She turned and dashed toward the wagon.

In a moment, she was back, carrying a wineskin and a small linen bag of salt.

Nephi had sat down outside his tent and looked as though he was prepared to stay for some time.

Hannah brushed past him and entered the tent. "Here you are, Mother Sariah."

Her mother, who was sitting beside Anava, looked up. "Hannah! I am sorry, my treasure. I did not know you were awake."

"I want to be awake for this," Hannah said. She crossed the tent and knelt beside Anava. "How are you, sister?"

Anava bit her lip. "The pain comes and goes," she said quietly. "Oh. Here it comes again!"

Hannah's mother put her hand on Anava's large, round belly. "They are getting quite strong, gentle one, and the baby has moved well into position. I do not think it will be long now."

Mother Sariah handed Hannah's mother a basin with some water in it. "Here, my sister," she said. "Sponge her face and neck and try to keep her comfortable. It is far too hot in here!"

Hannah realized that Anava's brow was liberally beaded with perspiration, and that her tunic was definitely showing signs of dampness.

Hannah's mother stroked the perspiring brow with the cloth. "Perhaps the best thing would be to remove the tunic now and cover her with only a light sheet."

Mother Sariah nodded and, with Hannah's help, the two women quickly stripped the soggy garment from the laboring girl and draped her in a soft linen sheet.

Anava briefly smiled her thanks, then closed her eyes as another wave of pain washed over her.

Mother Sariah smiled. "They are running together now. I think—"

Anava gasped. "I feel—strange!"

"Like you need to push?" Mother Sariah asked.

"I do not know, I just—" Anava suddenly clamped her mouth shut and her face slowly suffused with color.

"She's pushing!" Hannah's mother said. "Let's get her up."

The two women, with Hannah hovering a short distance away, hooked their arms in Anava's and pulled her up to a squatting position.

"Hannah, help support her!" Mother Sariah took up a position directly in front of Anava, then grasped both of the girl's arms and pressed them behind her own neck. "Here, dearest one, lock your hands together and let me hold you."

Anava nodded and clasped her hands behind her mother-by-marriage's neck and leaned into them.

Hannah's mother moved to collect cloths and prepare for the imminent arrival. She set a small cushion on the floor in front of Anava.

Moving carefully for fear of doing something she should not, Hannah crept nearer and grasped her younger sister's shoulders.

"Good. Now hold her there!"

Anava gasped and moaned slightly as her face again went red.

"That's it, gentle one!" Hannah's mother said. "The baby's coming now!"

"Push, Anava!" Mother Sariah said. "Push!"

Another moan.

"You are doing so well. One more push! I can see the baby's head!"

Anava took a deep breath, then clamped her mouth shut and pushed. Slowly, she turned more and more red.

"Anava, dear, you must breathe!" her mother said.

"Anava!"

But the girl kept on pushing.

"Here's the head! Okay, wait a moment while I—here's the baby!"

There was a sound of snuffling and a weak cry. Then more snuffling and a stronger wail.

Hannah's mother lifted the small, red bundle and wiped the baby's face and nose with a soft cloth. "Anava, you have a daughter!" she said. She laid the baby gently on the cushion, where she started to cry in earnest.

"Nothing wrong with those lungs!" Sariah said. She laughed happily.

Anava smiled. "She's all right? Can I see her?"

"Fine and healthy," Hannah's mother told her. "A beautiful, little girl! But gentle one, you are not quite finished. We must deliver the afterbirth—"

Some moments later, Hannah helped Mother Sariah lower Anava onto her mat and supplied cloths and wash water for cleansing.

Hannah's mother had taken the baby and was performing the same service for Anava's tiny newborn daughter, who continued to wail and protest everything in this strange, new world.

A short time later, Hannah witnessed mother and daughter being introduced for the first time. As the baby suckled, Hannah felt again her yearning to become a mother herself.

Tiny Esther's arrival seemed to act as a signal to the rest of the women in the camp and, before the week was out, three more babies made their arrival, all safely and all in the middle of the night.

Hannah found herself called in to assist with first Uzziel and Laman's daughter, Gaza; then Amana and Sam's son, Heman; and finally, Moriah and Zoram's son, Ezekiel.

Moriah labored longer and her baby needed to be turned before he could be birthed, but soon she, too, was holding her fine, fat boy and Hannah was completely swamped with women, babies—and heartache.

For the next couple of months, during the rites of circumcision and period of purification, the camp remained where it was. Hannah was grateful that the babies decided to arrive in a place of comparative comfort with plenty of water and grazing for the animals.

But all too soon, Father Lehi, upon consulting the brass ball, announced that the Lord needed them to move on.

It was with a pang that Hannah watched their campsite disappear behind them as, once more, they traveled the dusty trail toward their destiny.

CHAPTER 22

The days became weeks, the weeks months, and the months years.

And still they wandered about in the wilderness. Babies came—even to Mother Sariah, in her age. Children grew. People passed—the daughters of Ishmael were called upon to again say their farewells as their beloved mother Judith left to join her husband, and the people followed Father Lehi.

"It has been seven childless years, Morrie," Hannah said firmly, swallowing the lump that seemed a permanent part of her. "It is time. Lemuel needs his heritage."

Moriah put an arm around Hannah's shoulders. "Oh, treasured one."

Father Lehi looked at Hannah questioningly.

She nodded.

He turned back to the couple kneeling at the makeshift altar before him and completed the ordinance that bound them together.

Lemuel got to his feet and reached for Iscah's hand. "I shall endeavor to be a good husband to you, wife," he said.

Iscah smiled shyly. "And I shall provide you with many, many children, husband."

Hannah smiled through her tears.

"To think it has not yet been a year and here you have twin daughters, Hannah! Your family has been truly blessed!"

Hannah nodded and looked over at Iscah, cradling not one, but two swaddled bundles. Lemuel was standing behind her sister wife, a broad smile on his face, accepting congratulations from the family.

"We have," Hannah said quietly. "Very blessed." She gazed at the happy couple and swallowed her own agony. "Very blessed indeed."

Lemuel's visits were fewer, with his new family and his productive wife, but still, each time, Hannah kept a small hope alive that she would, one day, present him with a son.

And then, eight years after they had left the Valley of Lemuel, they reached the place they would call Bountiful.

The caravan wound its way through thick vegetation and tall, laden trees. Hannah noted date and nut palms; orange, lemon, and olive trees; and even some fruits that she did not recognize. Ropes of wild grapes grew abundantly.

Clear streams of water were everywhere, and their pack animals splashed through them happily.

Suddenly, they broke through the undergrowth and came upon an area of deep, white sand, which ended at a great expanse of water.

Hannah slid off her donkey and stared out at the water. Never had she seen so much of it in one place, and it did not behave like the bodies of water she had known. The day was beautiful, with full sunshine and little wind, and yet the waves did not lap up on the beach gently, like the waters of the Red Sea on a calm day. Instead, huge troughs of water with curling white tops crashed down on the sand with a great, hungry, roaring sound.

Several of the children, newly released from their pack animals, were running down toward this new marvel and Hannah found herself, with their mothers, sprinting to get ahead of them and protect them from this strange, new, unknown entity.

Thaddeus, a strapping lad of ten years, was the first to reach the water. He knelt in the sand and, cupping his hand, dipped some water and brought it to his mouth. Then he made a face and spat it out.

"Salt!" he said in a loud, disgusted voice. "The scourge of the Dead Sea!"

Thaddeus had only seen the Dead Sea as a very small child and, in point of fact, Hannah herself had only glimpsed it as they had traveled past in those first breath-snatching days of the beginning of their journey.

But both knew the unproductive properties of such water.

Hannah looked at Father Lehi, who had come up beside them. "This is where the Lord has brought us?" she asked. "To a land with water that is as barren as—I am?" The last two words were spoken in a whisper.

Father Lehi looked at her. "You must never describe yourself as such, daughter Hannah." He looked out to the water. "Your time will come. You will have a son. It is the will of the Lord."

Hannah's heart gave an excited little leap and she stared at Father Lehi. "Are you saying—what are you saying?"

He smiled and looked at her. "That you will be 'barren' no longer." He turned back to the water. "And these waters will not be barren to us, either. These are the waters that will lead us to the promised land."

Hannah felt her eyes widen as she turned to stare at the sun-sparkled waves. "There is a path over these waters?" she asked.

He smiled and nodded. "Most assuredly, my daughter. A path over these waters to the place prepared for us by the Lord."

He turned as Nephi joined them. "We have arrived, my son," he said.

"Is this the place, Father?"

Father Lehi smiled. "It is a place, my son, a place of peace and rest, of preparation."

"Preparation?"

"Here, we will rest and here we will prepare for our greatest journey yet." He nodded toward the water. "Over there."

CHAPTER 23

"Our brother is a fool!"

Hannah looked up from the wool she was carding.

Laman was stomping through the sand toward them in an obvious temper.

Lemuel set down the tool he had been using to engrave a piece of leather. "What is it he has done now, brother?"

"He thinks to build a ship!" Laman threw himself down into the sand beside Lemuel. "A ship! And just how does a farmer who has never even seen a ship propose to build one?"

Lemuel was staring at him. "A ship?" he asked faintly.

"A ship. And do you know what he intends to do with it once he builds it?"

"Cross the great waters," Hannah said.

Both men turned to look at her.

Finally, Laman nodded. "Yes," he said. "He plans to herd all of us aboard his 'farmer's ship' and take us out on the water in it. I do not know about you, but I can think of other ways I would rather die." Laman got to his feet and started pacing again, though the deep sand made walking difficult, and he found it rather hard to maintain his disgruntled demeanour and his pace. "He claims that the Lord has commanded it and that the Lord wants you and me, Lemuel, to help him build it! We are right back to being ordered to do foolish things by our little brother!" He spat into the sand. "He has already made a fire and found some lumps of ore somewhere out there in the mountains," he waved a hand, "and now he is trying to make some tools." He looked at Lemuel. "And he took that piece of leather you were saving and he has made a bellows with it."

"My leather!" Lemuel said.

"So," Laman's voice dropped in volume, "what are we going to do about it?"

Hannah looked at the four men standing together in front of Nephi, arrogance and belligerence in their stance and expressions. She tried to catch Lemuel's eye, but her husband would have none of it. Hannah sighed. He was like a small boy, intent on his way and trying very hard to ignore the voices of reason in his head.

Laman was speaking loudly. "So you need not ask Lemuel or me—or Zedekiah or Berachah—" he nodded toward them "—because none will waste our time with such foolishness!" He lifted his hands and indicated the lush land around them. "Finally, we have come to a land rich in grains and game, flowing with milk and honey, and now you have decided we must leave? Well, it will not happen!" He folded his arms across his chest.

Nephi sighed deeply and, pulling off the heavy leather gloves he had been wearing to pour molten metal into a form fashioned from a block of sandstone, he sat down tiredly on another large stone.

Laman laughed. "Well, finally you see as I see. We knew that you could not construct a ship, for we knew that you were lacking in judgment. How could you accomplish so great a work?" He looked around, collecting everyone's attention, and then turned back to Nephi. "You are like our father, led away by the foolish imaginations of his heart."

Nephi lifted his head and gazed silently at Laman for a moment.

Laman seemed to take it as a signal to carry on with his criticism. He opened his mouth to speak further, but Nephi came suddenly to his feet and stood straight and tall before his elder brother.

Confused, Laman backed off a pace or two.

Nephi reminded them of the times the Lord saved and chastised and preserved the Israelites during their escape from Egypt and during their forty years in the desert.

He turned back to Laman and emphasized his points with a finger and thumb pointed toward his elder brother's chest. "According to His word He did destroy them; and according to His word He did lead them; and according to His word He did do all things for them; and there was not any thing done save it were by His word."

He sighed and looked away. "And you are like unto them," He said as he jerked his head toward the west. "You are swift to do iniquity but slow to remember the Lord your God. Why is it that ye can be so hard in your hearts?"

Nephi dropped his arms to his sides and leaned back against the stone.

As Nephi seemed to weaken, Laman moved forward. "Enough talk!" he said. "And now I say we take our younger brother and throw him into the waters." He turned and smiled at the others. "Let us help him start his journey!"

But behind him, Nephi had straightened.

Laman started visibly as Nephi's next words rolled out of him like thunder, "In the name of the Almighty God, I command you that ye touch me not, for I am filled with the power of God, even unto the consuming of my flesh; and whoso shall lay his hands upon me shall wither even as a dried reed!"

Laman stumbled back from him. Lemuel caught him when he might have fallen, and they stared at their younger brother in silence.

"Murmur no more against your father, nor withhold your labor from me, for the Lord has commanded me that *I should build a ship*!"

Hannah looked at the men who had been standing with such assurance before Nephi only a few minutes before. They looked pale and shaken. Without a word, they turned and left.

Nephi sank to his knees in the sand and bowed his head.

Knowing it was most certainly time for her departure, Hannah turned and hurried after her husband.

For the next few days, the work seemed to progress smoothly. Nephi had drawn out the Lord's instructions on a piece of hide and fastened it to a framework nearby. His brothers and brothers-from-marriage had been using the tools he had fashioned in cutting and hauling timbers, which they then stacked to one side.

Nephi continued to molten metal and craft further tools. Soon he had a goodly number—enough for the entire company—and the sounds of pounding and sawing and shaving of wood became common.

Before long, there were enough timbers laid out on the ground that Hannah could actually see the shape of the ship in them. She knew that the tangible forming of the ship's body would take many months—maybe years—but what progress had been made was thrilling to her.

About a week after the work had commenced, it was Hannah's turn to bring the men their afternoon drink. She brought a brimming bucket to the ship site and, one by one, she toted it to each man and waited while he took a dipperful of the clear, cold water.

As she stood beside Lemuel, waiting for him to finish, she noticed Laman walk toward Nephi, who was standing, looking over the ship's plans.

"Brother!" Laman said.

Nephi lifted his head. "Yes?"

Laman stopped where he was, looking suddenly anxious. "I—I had a q-question."

Nephi sighed and indicated that Laman should come closer. "Yes, my brother? What can I do for you?"

Lemuel handed the dipper back and Hannah carried her bucket over to Sam.

"Yes. That will be fine," Nephi said behind her. "Just keep on bringing them this size or as near as you can find."

Hannah glanced around. Laman was looking relieved as he skittered across the clearing toward the trees.

"My brothers," Nephi called out.

Laman stopped and everyone turned to look.

"We cannot continue to work in this manner," Nephi said. "I cannot have you running from me like frightened quail every time I speak."

"Well, you are the one with the power!" someone said.

"The Lord's power, my brother. The Lord's power." He looked around the group. "I would have your aid in preparing this great vessel for the Lord, but I cannot have you all quaking whenever you have a question."

"You told us what would happen if we were to touch you, brother," Zedekiah said. "I would not risk it!"

"Our Lord will no longer have you consumed by his power. Instead—" Nephi stretched forth his hand and all of the men present cried out and fell to the ground.

Hannah ran to Lemuel and dropped to her knees. "Husband! Are you—"

Shaking his head dizzily, he sat up and looked at her. "I have not been consumed, wife." He looked at Nephi. "I know that the Lord is with him, for what I felt was the Lord's power."

Hannah sank back on her heels.

The men struggled to sit, to kneel. Then all started crawling toward Nephi.

Laman was the first to reach him. He bowed his face to the sand.

"No, brother," Nephi said.

Laman looked up.

"I am your brother, Laman, your *younger* brother. Arise. Worship the Lord!"

From that day forward, the work progressed steadily on the great ship. Slowly, there on the shore of the great waters, it grew in size.

The workmanship was different than anything that Hannah had seen before. Not being expert in such things, she at first dismissed it as "how things were done."

But one afternoon, she was sitting under a tree near the beach with Anava and her tiny seventh daughter, Bathsheba. The two sisters were tearing apart some of the camel-hair tents and fashioning the heavy material into sails for the almost-completed ship rising majestically below them.

"It is truly a beautiful ship," Hannah said.

Anava nodded, her eyes also on the vessel. "Father Lehi was talking to Nephi about his strange way of working the timbers."

"Strange?"

"Mmm—Yes. Father Lehi said he had never seen things done in that way before."

"I thought they looked different."

"Well, they are." Anava smiled. "What do I know of such things? I just assumed that was how they were done."

"I, as well," Hannah said.

"Nephi told Father Lehi that was how the Lord wished them done. Then Father Lehi said that was good enough for him." She looked again at the great hulk below them. "But that did not explain how strange the ship looks."

Hannah looked too. "Strange?"

Anava nodded. "Do you not remember what ships back home looked like?"

"The only ships I ever saw were those made to sail the Red Sea." Hannah peered past the craft to the waters beyond. "If these waters are wider, perhaps the ship needs to be different. Stronger? Bigger? Wider?"

Anava laughed. "I do hope the waters are not too wide." She sobered. "Our time here in Bountiful has been pleasurable indeed, but I would have this journey finished."

Hannah patted her sister's arm and smiled. "It will be, gentle one. Soon you and your family will be safely settled in the promised land and you will forget all the hardships of reaching the place."

"I will pray for that, treasured one."

CHAPTER 24

And finally, it was launching day.

The family assembled on the shore and stared up at the great ship.

"It is so big!" Thaddeus stated, his fourteen-year-old eyes large as saucers.

Laman and Lemuel said nothing, but Hannah, looking into her husband's eyes, could see the doubt there.

She sighed. His faith was still lacking.

Nephi led them all in a prayer of praise, thanksgiving, and entreaty. Then he looked around at everyone. "It will take all of us who have the ability, so everyone take a pole or a rope!"

Nephi indicated the neat coils in the sand and the pile to one side.

Soon, everyone with any amount of strength had equipped themselves. The stronger of the men had each hefted a rope and waded into the shallow waters.

Nephi and Sam convinced many of the camels to do likewise.

"When I call!" Nephi shouted. He bowed his head for a moment, then raised it and shouted, "Now!"

At once, everyone either pushed or pulled.

Sam shouted, "Ki! Ki! Ki!" to the camels and the taciturn animals pressed forward into their makeshift harnesses.

For several seconds, nothing happened. Then Hannah, up to her knees in the surf, felt her rope give. She pulled harder. It gave again.

The ship was rolling along the great logs upon which it had been built.

Pulling steadily, Hannah and the others beside her began to move further out into the water. Soon it was up to her waist and the ship had nearly reached the edge of the beach.

Finally, the water was too deep for her to proceed, so she dropped her rope and turned back toward shore.

The craft was moving steadily into the water. First the forward part—the bow, Hannah reminded herself—dipped below the waves. By this point, the water was too deep even for the camels, and Sam was directing them back toward the beach. Only those at the back—the stern—were able to do much. They continued to push with their long poles until the boat finally slid far enough into the water that they had waded in past the point of comfort.

They, too, turned back.

Hannah saw that Nephi had fastened a great, long rope between the boat and a massive rock on the shore and that now, he was playing it out as the ship slid further and further into the water. It pulled tight and the stern slid slightly sideways as all forward movement stopped. Then the ship bobbed slowly up and down in the constant waves.

Floating.

Hannah felt a slow smile appear on her face. Nephi had done it. Nephi and the Lord.

For a moment, everyone simply stared at the craft they had worked so long to build as it floated lightly in the blue water.

Then a mighty cheer went up, echoing off the nearby cliffs and startling a cloud of white birds.

Hannah sloshed over to Lemuel and received a rare hug. Then she joined in the happy splashing and laughter that had broken out among the rest of the family.

They had finished their task. Nephi had proven himself both a prophet and a leader.

Still smiling, Hannah glanced back at her husband.

Lemuel had joined Laman on the beach and the two of them were staring steadily and soberly at the ship.

Well, maybe not a prophet and leader to everyone.

The men spent the next few days constructing a framework that they could then set in the waves to make reaching the boat a simple matter of walking out over the water. Once finished, the ship would be tied tightly to it and loading could actually begin.

While they were thus engaged, the rest of the camp was assembling provisions and preparing them for storage. Meats and fruits were dried and packed into crates, cheeses wrapped and stowed, seeds of all kinds—sorted and dried during each successive season—carefully arranged in chests, and barrels of water and casks of honey rolled up onto the beach. Every provision they could possibly need during the voyage and after their future arrival in the promised land was gathered, ready for stowing in the bottom of the great ship.

The framework, or wharf, as Father Lehi called it, was finished and installed. After a few test runs with people and barrels, Nephi pronounced it solid and began directing the stowing of the assembled necessities.

In a remarkably short time, all was prepared.

Now the last and most important step: to encourage the family, which now numbered many dozens of persons, to get on board a strange-looking boat built by a farmer with the promise that if they did, they would then be crossing waters so deep and wide that one could not see the other side—even on the clearest day and from the highest point of land.

Hannah watched as her sisters—Anava and Uzziel with their brood of girls, Amanna with her mix of sons and daughters, and Moriah and her five sons—all stepped confidently and happily up the ramp and onto the great ship. For the first seconds after boarding, the children, a bit hesitant about walking on the lightly moving deck, huddled close. Finally one, then another started to move away from the group. Soon, all of them were running about the deck, shrieking and laughing excitedly as they dodged the other people coming on board.

At first, all seemed confused, but as families settled in their assigned places below the main deck and personal belongings were stowed, things calmed remarkably.

The ship had been built with three main decks: the top deck, where all of the business of sailing took place; the one beneath that, where the people were housed in small, wood-walled cubicles with doors for privacy created from the final remnants of their old camel-hair tents; and a third beneath that, a windowless space for the storage of household goods and any live animals not crated in the open air.

Beneath that lower deck was a space that Nephi—for reasons unclear to Hannah, but which included the unfamiliar term "ballast"—had ordered filled with stones.

Hannah visited her tiny space on the middle deck, an area closest to the stairway, and deposited her few belongings. She helped Iscah get herself and her four daughters settled in another cubicle further down along the wall, then she walked back up onto the main deck and moved to the bow of the ship where Nephi and Father Lehi were standing.

"I feel that we are meant to leave tonight," Nephi was saying, "once the sun sets."

Father Lehi nodded.

"Please consult the ball, Father."

Father Lehi nodded again and looked down at the ball held carefully in his hands. For several seconds, he studied it. Then he looked back at Nephi. "The Lord so directs, let it be as you say." He tenderly deposited the ball into a leather-lined box at his feet and smiled at his son.

Nephi nodded and moved away.

Hannah watched him walk to the beach and disappear into the trees.

She turned back to Father Lehi and was surprised to find his grave eyes on her. "What is it, Father Lehi?"

He smiled. "Nothing, my daughter. Just realizing, again, what a stalwart and faithful young woman you are."

Hannah smiled and pointed to a gray streak in her dark hair. "Not so young any more, Father Lehi."

He reached out a hand and gently touched her shoulder. "Still young, my daughter. With great things in your future."

Hannah looked at him. "Great things?" Her voice came out breathy and faint. She coughed.

He nodded and smiled. "Great things." He patted her shoulder, then hefted the box holding the ball, turned, and made his way across the deck to the open hatch and disappeared below.

The sunset was glorious. A crimson and orange ball of fire dipped into the trees and set the sky alight. Puffy, white clouds were stained a deep and brilliant red. The forest instantly turned a deeper green, the skies a richer blue.

It was as though all the heavens and the earth were creating a show to wish them a spectacular farewell.

Hannah—together with nearly everyone in their company who was not pulling on a rope—watched as the land they had walked on, the land that had supported all of them and everyone they had ever known since birth, slowly receded from their sight.

No few tears were being shed.

Hannah moved through the group and walked to the front of the ship, the part of the vessel currently pointed into the great waters, the Irriantum.

The unknown.

She braced herself against the sturdy rail and looked out over the water. The last small point of land to her left passed from her sight, and the great ship rocked slightly to the right as it reached a place where only water surrounded it.

For a moment, Hannah felt her heart speed up as her soul filled with fear. There was no land around her! She was adrift on an expanse of water that only the Lord knew.

She caught her breath.

The Lord knew.

All was well.

CHAPTER 25

For two weeks, the ship sailed peacefully, driven forward by the breath of the Lord as the men spent their time learning about directing such a great craft. They scrambled about, studying how the ropes worked the sails—at times actually climbing up the masts to manipulate the great sheets of coarse cloth by hand. They constantly consulted the brass ball and became familiar with the rudder that directed the great ship, the proper handling of the great water barrels and other storage that must be tied down at all times, and the multitude of other processes that went into safely crossing the great waters, or Irriantum.

They were a happy, excited lot, anxious to explore and control this strange, new, watery world on which they bobbed like a chip of wood. When they were not engaged in actual toil, they were at the rail, looking out over the sun-sparkled waves and watching the water curl away from the ship's bow.

At least these were the stories that Anava and Moriah brought down to Hannah as she lay in utter misery on her pallet in the hold.

Others in the company had found themselves dizzy and disoriented by the movement of the ship, but they had completely recovered after a day or two.

Hannah had not been as fortunate.

Never in her life had she been so ill. The constant rocking of the vessel, soothing to some, brought her nothing but wretchedness. All desire for food had been forgotten and, in her anguish, she thought often of death as a blessed and welcome release.

Very occasionally, she was able to swallow a bit of water and a bite or two of sustenance, but those moments were all too few.

She marked the passing of the hours by the progression of the patch of sunlight from the small single window high up in the wall or by the periodic movement of the other members of the company across her opened doorway.

And she existed in utter despair.

One evening, after the children had been put to bed and happily lulled to sleep by the rocking of their home on the waters, the adults on the deck of the vessel began to sing.

At first, it was a pleasant and welcome change to the unending, miserable sameness of her days. Hannah rolled on her mat and sighed deeply. Singing. She remembered singing. Some time in her long-gone, healthy past life. She smiled ruefully at herself and pulled the light blanket over her frame, snuggling into its warmth.

For some time, the singing continued. At first, it was pleasant to listen to and soothing to Hannah's aching body. Then, slowly, it became louder, more shrill, and punctuated by great bursts of laughter.

Mother Sariah appeared, her face looking rather pinched in the dim light below the deck. She saw Hannah looking at her and slowly made her way to her daughter-by-marriage's side.

"How do you feel, my daughter?" Mother Sariah asked.

Hannah shrugged. "Miserable, Mother Sariah. But I was able to keep a little food down tonight."

Her mother-by-marriage nodded. "This will pass, my dear. You may not think so, but—"

A loud burst of laughter from the upper deck stopped her. She looked up toward the sound, then shook her head. "It can come to no good," she muttered.

"What is it, Mother Sariah?"

The older woman looked at her and immediately replaced concern with a bright smile. "Nothing, dear. Just merrymaking."

"It sounds like they are very merry."

Then came another shout of laughter and speech that sounded slurred and strange.

Mother Sariah looked toward the source of the sounds. "Very merry indeed. Perhaps too much so." She turned and Hannah could hear her slow steps as she moved out of sight along the line of cubicles to her own. A child immediately stirred and cried out for her. The footsteps continued into the small room, followed by the sounds of a gentle, murmuring voice.

"Good evening, my sister." Moriah had stopped in Hannah's doorway.

"What is happening, gentle one?" Hannah asked her. She looked up toward the outer deck. "The singing seems—"

Moriah looked up too, and then turned to Hannah. "Coarse? Harsh? Unworthy of a company of people following their Lord?" she said.

"Well—yes."

Moriah sighed. "Well, you would be right. They are acting unworthy. They have been pouring strong drink down their throats for hours. Laman just told Father Lehi to quit preaching at everyone and trying to get them to attribute everything to the Lord."

Hannah caught her breath and bit her lip.

Moriah went on. "He said the ship had been built by him and his brothers and that he had not seen the Lord lift a single hammer or pound a single peg. He called Father Lehi an old, useless man who should have remained in Jerusalem calling righteous people to repentance."

Hannah put a hand to her head. "Pure foolishness."

Moriah nodded. "With all they have witnessed, with all we have endured, they still think they are more clever than the Lord."

"This cannot end well."

"The boat seems to be pitching more," Hannah said.

Moriah set down the tray of food and checked Hannah's water-skin. "It is. A storm has come up and the wind and waves are growing quite vicious." She stepped back to the opened curtains of Hannah's cubicle and looked toward the stairs. Then she peered up and down the line of cubicle walls, came back to Hannah's pallet, and squatted down beside her. She leaned close to Hannah's ear. "Mother Sariah told me not to tell you, but I feel you should know," she whispered. "Trapped down here like you are—" She paused and lifted her head, looking again toward the stairs.

"What?" Hannah's heart seemed to freeze in her breast. She lifted herself up on one elbow. "What is wrong?"

Moriah sighed again. "It is Laman and your Lemuel and Uzziel and our brothers. They have lost their minds and tied Nephi to a mast with strong cords."

"What?" Hannah sat up, but then put a hand to her head and moaned. Then, more quietly, she asked, "They have tied Nephi to a mast?"

Moriah nodded. "They have tied him so tightly he cannot even move."

Hannah put a hand over her mouth and stared at her sister in shock.

"He was trying to talk to them and they started shouting that he was the younger brother and could not presume to rule over them. They all grabbed him and forced him to the deck. Then they tied him and lifted him up to the mast." She looked upward. "He is tied there now and has been for hours."

Hannah threw back the coverlet and attempted, weakly, to get to her feet.

"Sister, what are you doing?"

"I must go and speak to my husband," Hannah said. "I must make him see the truth."

Moriah put a hand on her arm. "Sister, he will not listen. He only listens to Laman."

Hannah nodded and sank back onto her mat. "As it has always been." She looked at Moriah. "Where is Father Lehi? Your Zoram? Have they tried to talk to them?"

Moriah shuffled the food around on Hannah's tray. "They treat him so badly," she said, her voice sinking to a whisper. "Father Lehi."

Hannah had to lean forward to hear her sister's words over the moaning sound of the wind about the vessel. She felt the blood leave her face. "Badly?"

"Oh, Hannah, they say such vile things to him. Their father!"

"Their prophet!" Hannah said.

"Here, my dear," a new voice said. "You will feel better."

Both sisters looked around as Mother Sariah and Father Lehi descended the stairs. Mother Sariah was holding little Joseph, who was clinging to her tightly; and Jacob, only a year older than his little brother, had a hold of his mother's tunic. Without looking around, they disappeared in the direction of their cubicle.

Hannah struggled to her knees and finally to her feet.

"Hannah! You must stay in your bed!"

"I must help!"

"Hannah!"

Hannah shook her head at her sister and turned away.

Moriah frowned sadly, but remained where she was.

Hannah managed to make her slow way along the wall, silently cursing her weakness.

The boat seemed to be pitching even more, and many of the smaller children and their mothers, most of them soaked and dripping, were finding their way to the hold and the comparative dryness and safety of four walls.

Amanna was herding her children and Anava's daughters before her toward their family's compartments.

"Where is Anava?" Hannah asked.

Amanna put her hands on her hips. "Hannah! What are you doing up?"

"I—I need to—"

"What? What is so important that you would crawl from your bed in this storm?" Her younger sister stopped at the bottom of the stairs.

"I have something I need to do." She looked toward the stairs. "Someone only I can talk to."

Amanna looked at her for a long moment, then finally nodded and stepped back, but continued watching unhappily as Hannah climbed the stairs on her hands and knees.

The higher she climbed, the heavier the rain became, and by the time she reached the top step, she was thoroughly soaked. Shivering mightily, she stopped to look around as she caught her breath.

The sky overhead was black, and great streaks of golden lightning shot through it almost constantly. The sound of rolling thunder, crashing waves, sheeting rain, and flapping sails created a cacophony of sound that was deafening. As Hannah paused there at the opening to the lower part of the ship, several more of the older children passed her hurriedly on their way down. Most of them looked at her in surprise, and a few offered their aid in taking her with them, but she shook her head.

The wind was blowing so strongly and the rain so blindingly that Hannah, already in a weakened condition from her days of illness, did not dare get to her feet but instead began to crawl across the deck.

In the center of the ship, between the two great masts, several barrels of water had been lashed, ready for use or for filling if the rains came. The sheets of rain had already filled them and they were overflowing in great torrents of water.

Hannah passed the foremast, making her way to the barrels. Then she slowly pulled herself upright.

Standing there, she was able to look about the entire deck, gray and colorless in the pouring rain.

But she needed to look only a few feet to see her brother-by-marriage, Nephi, lashed to the hindmost mast and completely at the mercy of the elements and the cruel ropes that held him hand and foot.

Anava was a little way off, desperately clinging to part of the rigging as she tried to maintain her footing on the slippery deck. She was screaming something, but the elements were dashing away her words the instant they left her lips.

She was obviously trying to speak to the four men who stood between her and her husband: Laman, Lemuel, Zedekiah, and Berachah. Most had turned their backs to her in favor of watching Nephi. Only Berachah seemed to be listening and was looking at his younger sister with something akin to sympathy in his eyes. Finally, he too shook his head and turned away.

Hannah dropped again to her hands and knees and slowly crept across the deck until she reached Anava. She reached out and tugged on her younger sister's soaked and dripping tunic.

Startled, Anava looked down. Her lips formed the word "Hannah" but no sound reached her sister's ears.

Hannah grabbed some of the same rigging that Anava was holding and pulled herself to her feet.

"Oh, Hannah!" Anava shouted into her ear. "You should not be here!"

"There is nowhere else I should be, sister!" Hannah shouted back. The sisters clung together as Hannah turned to look at Nephi.

He had obviously been there for some time. Hannah could see that his hands and his feet were already swollen and purpled because of the tight cords bound about them. His head hung down and swayed with every toss of the ship. He looked dead.

"Is he—?" She could not bring herself to say the words.

"He lives," Anava said. "But with no thanks to his brothers. Or ours."

Just then, Nephi lifted his head and looked at his tormentors, his mouth moving as he shouted something.

Laman stepped forward and slapped him across the cheek.

Nephi's head snapped back against the thick, wooden mast behind him and, for a moment, hung down once more. Then he slowly lifted it.

Blood trickled from the corner of this mouth. Slashed by the rain, it formed a thin, reddish rivulet down his chin and throat and across his chest. He merely looked at Laman, who shouted something to Hannah's husband and the others.

All of them laughed.

Hannah let go of the ropes she had been holding and let herself fall to the deck. Then, slowly, she made her way the few feet to the men, who jumped and moved aside as she brushed into them.

She sat down on the deck in front of Nephi and faced the others. "Lemuel, what are you doing?" she shouted.

Lemuel looked away.

Hannah stared at him, not believing that he would simply turn away from her. How could he do this? "Lemuel you must speak to me!" Hannah paused a moment to breathe and renew her strength, then tried again. "Lemuel! I am your wife! You must—"

Laman interrupted. "When does a man answer to a woman?" he shouted.

All pretence of patience and serenity vanished in an instant as a wave of anger swept over Hannah. "When that man is in league with the devil!" she screamed at Laman. "And when his wife and help meet desires to speak to him!"

Laman laughed, the sound rising over the wind about them. "You always were trouble, sister. And I think we have better to do than listen to a dried-up, childless crone such as yourself!"

Hannah felt her breath leave her body at the insult. She looked at her husband, but Lemuel looked steadfastly away. She set her jaw and turned back to Laman. "You are killing a prophet of the Lord!" She looked at Lemuel. "You must stop this, Lemuel!"

"*I* will stop this!" Laman said. He reached down and picked Hannah up.

"Laman! Stop!" she screamed into his ear.

He merely laughed, the sound echoing weirdly about the rain-slashed ship. "Lemuel! Take care of your woman!"

Lemuel came and Laman threw her over his brother's shoulder like a sack of meal. Then, weaving around the deck, Lemuel walked to the black hole that led to the lower reaches of the ship.

As he walked, Hannah squirmed violently, trying to free herself. But Lemuel, so much bigger and stronger, maintained his strong, sure grip.

When he neared the stairwell, Hannah suddenly saw someone out of the corner of her eye. Twisting about, she was shocked to see Sam, sprawled face up on the deck, his one cheek split open across the bone and oozing blood. His eyes were closed and Hannah caught her breath. The man kneeling next to him and applying a cloth to his wound looked up at her.

Zoram.

Her brother-by-marriage continued to look at her and nodded. He would look after Sam.

Ignoring the two men on the deck completely, Lemuel gripped the rope support that had been fastened to the stairwell and managed to carry her down into the hold. There, he swung her off his shoulder and dropped her to the floor. "Do not interfere again, woman!" he said. Turning, he started to make his way back up the stairs.

Hannah gripped his tunic. "Lemuel. A prophet of the Lord! You have to think about this! You cannot—"

But he slipped the cloth from her weakened fingers and was gone. Once outside, he dropped the heavy wooden door over the stairwell, shutting them in completely.

Hannah collapsed into a little sodden heap at the bottom of the stairs, sobbing uncontrollably.

Moriah and Amanna came and helped her back to her pallet. They removed her wet things and helped her into dry ones, then covered her and sat down beside her.

Hannah shivered uncontrollably for some time. Finally, as the shivering lessened, she was able to speak to her sisters. "Thank you," she whispered. Then she sat up. "Sam! Zoram!"

"They are fine," Moriah patted her hand. "They came down while we were looking after you."

"Sam tried to talk to his brothers," Amanna said.

Hannah looked at her. "Is he—?"

"Laman hit him and he has a cut over his cheek," Amanna pointed to her own face. "But Mother is caring for him and he is feeling mostly sorrow," she looked down, "As the rest of us are."

Hannah looked up toward the upper deck. "Do they realize what they are doing?"

Moriah shrugged. "Who knows what they know any more? They have lost their minds."

Hannah thought of the people gathered in the hold of the ship, totally dependent on the outcome of the drama unfolding above them.

"They are killing a prophet of the Lord," Hannah whispered. "And us with him."

CHAPTER 26

For three more days, the storm lashed the ship.

The same ship that had seemed so enormous and strong while standing in the calm bay at Bountiful now seemed a mere chip of wood dashed atop the surface of waters gone mad, sliding down, down, and down until it seemed as though it would embed itself into the very floor of the great waters, then surging up and up, finally breaking through the waves themselves for a brief glimpse of sky and air, then down and down once more.

The erratic movements made it impossible to do anything more than lie on one's bed, pray, and try to hold on. Pallets slid back and forth. Goods, even those that had started out firmly tied down, rolled everywhere, threatening lives and extremities.

A barrel broke through the wall of Moriah's cubicle and landed on her son's leg, breaking it and causing the boy no end to his agony as his mother tried in vain to hold it and her son steady in the constantly canted and heaving ship.

The wetness had permeated everything and there was not a dry piece of cloth anywhere to be found. No lamps could be lit and the days passed in a gray half-light, the nights in complete and utter blackness.

Food preparation was impossible, and the children and everyone else in the ship were fed ground grains, fruit, and cheese only when they could be found in the mess and confusion.

The youngest children cried constantly and Hannah and the other women despaired of ever seeing them happy or comfortable again. Mother Sariah and Father Lehi were so low that they would not accept any nourishment, as inconsistent as it was, and Mother Sariah had no strength to feed or care for her little Joseph and Jacob.

After a day, Anava had finally been convinced to leave her husband's side and was brought, shivering and nearly incoherent, to her pallet, where her elder daughters, weeping and exclaiming, tended to her.

Occasionally, one of the four men guarding Nephi would stumble to the hold, but he would be met with stony silence and no offer of help or aid. Even Uzziel, captive as she was by her affection for Laman, could not face her husband when he ventured below. Finally, the men stopped coming, remaining on the top deck with their co-conspirators and their guilt.

On the fourth day the storm raged on with even more ferocity. Even crawling about on hands and knees was treacherous. The women and children in the lower deck had given up hope—too weak by this point to do anything more than pray—and were waiting for the final plunge that would signal their doom but also mean the end of their suffering.

And then, all at once, the ship stopped moving.

In the calm that followed, people blinked into the dim light and looked around. No one ventured off their pallets for several minutes, expecting, at any moment, that the pitching and heaving would resume again.

Finally, some of the elder boys got cautiously to their feet. As the boat remained calm, they grinned and began to move about.

Others began getting to their feet. Soon people were moving about and beginning to pick their way through the mess of scattered household goods and belongings toward the stairway.

Moriah's eldest, Ezekiel, and Thaddeus were the first to climb the stairs. The two of them pushed the heavy door back and it landed with a loud thump on the deck.

Hannah lifted her head just as a beam of sunlight shone down to the lower floor from the sky above.

Now everyone was making their way toward the stairs.

Even Hannah, weakened as she was, slid off her mat and crawled toward that beam of sunlight, that promise of warmth and life.

Moriah and Zoram helped her stand and slowly climb the stairs.

Once on deck, Hannah looked up at a rapidly clearing sky. The black storm clouds were disappearing toward one horizon, and the sunlight, golden and glorious, was shining steadily. The soaked wood of the ship was already steaming in some places.

The sails that had not been tied up were hanging limply in dripping shreds from their frames. The animal pens had disappeared, as had most of the barrels and many of the goods that had been lashed on the top deck.

Hannah continued to look around, her eyes going to where she had last seen her husband and the other men. Her lips parted in a gasp.

All were now kneeling on the deck in a partial circle around Nephi. Also on his knees, hair matted to his scraped and bloody head, and clothing ripped and torn by the elements, their younger brother was pouring out his heart in earnest prayer.

Hannah looked at his hands, swollen and bleeding from his days of being tied to the mast. He had clasped them together about the brass ball, and Hannah could see the blood dripping off them, running down the side of the ball and pooling onto the wet deck below.

Everyone had gathered near Hannah by this point, all watching the scene before them silently.

After some time, Nephi rose shakily to his feet and handed the ball to Sam, who had hurried forward as soon as he saw his younger brother move.

The rest of the group closed in around them, offering quiet words of love and sympathy.

Anava and her daughters crowded close and threw their arms around their husband and father. He held them close and shared in their tears.

Then, unwilling to release each other, the family moved as a group toward the stairwell and their own space. Everyone else let them go.

It was some minutes before the rest of the men kneeling on the deck stood up. Zedekiah and Berachah were the first to move, then Laman and Lemuel.

No one spoke to them as they, too, made their way toward the stairs. The others merely parted and let them pass.

It took many days to clean up and tidy the ship after the storm. There were goods to sort and dry, foodstuffs to gather and either toss over the side or store, ropes and sails to mend, scrapes and bruises to treat and, in the case of Moriah's small son, bones to splint and wrap.

Everyone was eager to help, but most especially Laman, Lemuel, Zedekiah, and Berachah. The four men could not seem to do enough to make things right. They took upon themselves the repair of the sails and any other job that could have been considered even slightly dangerous, waited until everyone else had eaten before they ate, and cleaned out the lower deck where the last of the animals had ridden out the storm.

Hannah, still suffering and ill, watched her husband with a slight smile on her face. His repentance had even carried to her and, for the first time in months, he was attentive and considerate of her needs, stopping by when he had a few moments of leisure to engage her in conversation, to ask her opinions, to treat her as a wife.

She felt as if her forgiveness flowed out of her like sunlight.

The boat had settled into a calming rhythm that Hannah discovered was soothing. But still her illness raged on.

Finally, a week after the storm and in complete despair of ever feeling well, she made her way to Mother Sariah's compartment.

"Mother Sariah, may I speak with you? I have a question to ask."

"Come in, dear."

Hannah pushed aside the curtain and stepped into the small space. Sariah, still not wholly well, was cuddling with her two little boys on her pallet.

"Mother Sariah, I—" Hannah hesitated to speak further with the little boys in the room.

Mother Sariah smiled. "Wait here for me, boys," She said, sliding carefully to one side of her mat and getting to her feet.

"I am so sorry to disturb—"

"Nonsense!" Mother Sariah said, sounding, for the first time in days, like herself. "Come with me, dear, and we will talk."

The two women ducked back through the curtain in the doorway and out into the storage space.

"Over here." Mother Sariah took Hannah's arm and guided her to the far side of the deck, where many of the crates and barrels had once again been lashed.

Mother Sariah stopped. "Now, what is it you wanted to talk about?"

Hannah took a deep breath. "The waters have calmed, but I am still so ill, Mother Sariah."

The elder woman smiled and she patted Hannah's arm. "I am sorry to seem to make light of your condition, my dear, but I am afraid it will be some time before you will start feeling better."

Hannah felt her heart sink into her sandals. "But why—?" she asked faintly.

Mother Sariah touched her forehead to Hannah's. "Because, my dear, you are with child."

The words were spoken so calmly that, at first, Hannah did not take them in. "With—?" Then she caught her breath and looked at her mother-by-marriage with wide eyes. "With child?" Her voice had grown quite small.

Mother Sariah smiled again. "Most definitely, my daughter," she said, smoothing Hannah's dark hair. "It is strange how those who have helped the most babies into this world seldom recognize when they, themselves, have been caught."

Hannah suddenly needed to sit down.

Mother Sariah smiled. "You probably need a moment. I will go back to my room. When you are ready, or if you have any other questions or concerns, please come to me."

Hannah nodded and sank to the floor. She slid her hand over her stomach and thought about the tiny life that now rested there. How could this be? After the years and years when she had hoped and prayed? How could this have happened now?

She pushed herself to her feet, swaying slightly at the unaccustomed exertion. She must tell Lemuel!

As quickly as she could, Hannah walked to the stairway. Then, not wishing to risk her delicate balance, she dropped to her hands and knees and climbed the stairs.

Once on the upper deck, she stood and looked around for her husband.

Everyone was busily involved in something. Floors and other surfaces were being scrubbed, snapped and splintered timbers being repaired or replaced, and tattered sails taken down, assessed, and assigned to the needle wielders or to the refuse.

And while they worked, there was a constant pleasant hum of talking and laughter.

Hannah paused for a few minutes and simply took in the sight and sound. She smiled. This was family. This was how family was supposed to be.

"Hannah!"

She turned.

Lemuel was coming toward her, a load of wood in his arms. "Should you be up here? Are you feeling better?"

She smiled at him. "I am not feeling much better, I am sorry to say. Well, not—" her voice trailed away.

He frowned. "Then what—why—?"

She put her hand on his arm. "Lemuel, I have something to tell you."

He set down the wood and, taking her arm, led her to the right side of the boat where there was a little less activity. "What is wrong?"

Hannah paused, studying his face. A face she had grown accustomed to seeing. A face that, at times, she was very fond of.

"Hannah, what is it?"

"Lemuel. Where is my wood?" Laman's voice. Laman was coming toward them.

Hannah's heart started to hammer in her chest.

Lemuel had turned and was watching his elder brother.

"Husband!" she said.

His eyes turned to her, but kept straying back toward his brother.

"Husband, I am to have a child. Our child. I am with child."

Now she had his attention.

He looked at her. "A child?"

She nodded and smiled. "That is why I have been so ill. Not because of the boat, but because I am with child."

Lemuel stared at her. Then, quite suddenly, he treated her to one of his rare smiles and took her hand. "A child!"

"Who are you calling a child?" Laman had reached them. "Lemuel, I need that wood."

Lemuel turned to his brother. "Hannah is with child."

Laman's dark eyebrows went up. He blinked, then looked at her. "Truth?"

"Truth," Hannah said, clutching Lemuel's hand a little tighter.

Lemuel smiled happily. "Finally, I will have a child by my wife!"

"Huh." Laman shrugged and stooped to pick up the wood Lemuel had dropped on the deck.

"You say that like it was not important!" Lemuel was staring at Laman.

Laman looked at him, surprised. He straightened. "Of course it is important. But you have four other children by your other wife. I cannot understand why this is so important to you now."

"Because it is!" Lemuel put his arm around Hannah's shoulders. "My wife is with child," he said levelly. "She is going to present me with another child. Her first. It is important."

Laman shrugged again. "Well, join us when you can. We are working on the main sail if you have forgotten."

Lemuel scowled at Laman as his brother walked away. Then he turned back to Hannah. "Do you know when the babe will be born?"

Hannah shook her head. "I came to you as soon as I found out." She turned away. "I will speak of this further."

"And I will be here." Lemuel released her hand and sighed. "Helping Laman."

Hannah smiled and started to move back toward the stairwell, but the sun was shining brightly and its warmth seemed to seep into every pore. Instead of returning to the lower deck, she veered off and sat down on a large coil of rope. From there, she was able to observe much of the activity here on the upper deck.

Someone was shaking her shoulder. "Hmmm?" she mumbled sleepily.

"Sister Hannah."

"What?" Her eyes had not yet opened.

"Sister Hannah."

She cracked an eyelid and peeped upward. A large, dark shadow was looming over her.

Hannah gasped and shrank back against—against—she looked around. How had she gotten up on the deck? And, more importantly, what was she doing sleeping atop a big coil of rope?

The shadow reached out a hand and grasped hers. "Careful now, sister."

Hannah finally recognized Nephi. Her heartbeat slowly returned to normal.

He grinned at her. "I hate to be prosaic, but is Lemuel right? Are you with child?"

Hannah smiled. "I am."

"Then we must celebrate this!"

Hannah was horrified. "Oh no, brother Nephi! We must treat this as if any of the other women had made the announcement!"

"Sister Hannah, every other woman *has* made this announcement!" He smiled at her. "This is a special time." He placed a large, warm hand on her head. "When, at last, our sister has such a dream fulfilled."

Hannah smiled back at him. "It has been my greatest dream."

"I know."

There was a passage of days where Hannah's great news was the main subject of every conversation, but soon all was as it had been, and family members stopped popping up unexpectedly to chat with her about the anticipated birth.

Iscah, her husband's second wife, was not as enthusiastic as the others, and would glare silently at Hannah whenever the two were in the same place, which was often, as Hannah had long ago volunteered her aid with one after the other of Iscah's four daughters.

Finally, Hannah grew tired of the silent simmer and confronted her sister wife with her hands on her slender hips. "Iscah, why do you glare? Would you have me be childless?"

Iscah colored richly. "No, sister," she said finally.

"Then why the heated looks? Why are you not happy for me?" Hannah took Iscah's cheery little fourth daughter, placed the tot on her own knee, and bounced her up and down. "Iscah, sister, you have four. I have none. Would you deny me this joy?"

Iscah looked around at her three elder daughters, all happily engaged in grinding grains across the deck with their grandmother. Her face reddened still more. She shook her head.

Hannah put a hand on Iscah's plump shoulder. "Rejoice for me, Iscah, for I have rejoiced for you."

Iscah nodded. "I will, sister."

The days flowed into weeks, the weeks, months. All passed like the waters of the great Irriantum, sunlit and sparkling, while the family worked together, prayed together, and stayed together.

Nephi and Lehi were constantly in communication with their spiritual and physical guides, and the ship made steady progress on the spangled waters.

Occasionally, they would stop at an island that chanced in their way to collect water, gather food, and hunt game. These short idylls became much-anticipated breaks from the sameness of a gently heaving deck and the necessarily close confines of shipboard life.

Hannah could not remember a happier time in her entire life.

Lemuel spent much time with her, even seeming to prefer her company over that of his elder brother—something Hannah had never seen in almost twelve years of marriage.

Now there were afternoons spent talking quietly in Hannah's cubicle, learning things about the other that should have been learned in their early days together.

"I guess I've always idolized him," Lemuel had been speaking of Laman.

"Well, he is your elder brother," Hannah said. "It is understandable."

"Maybe. I just knew that he was everything I was not. Strong. Forceful. Knowledgeable."

"But you are something he is not."

He looked at her. "What?"

She smiled. "Spiritual."

"Me?"

Hannah nodded.

He smiled slightly. "When we were younger, Laman used to ridicule Nephi for his spirituality. And now, when Laman is speaking, he makes other things seem more important than spirituality." He looked away.

"More important than—" Hannah sat up, indignant. "How can you even say—" she swayed a bit and laid her head back on her pallet. "Oooo—"

Lemuel smiled. "The child will not allow your outrage." He nodded toward her growing belly. "Perhaps it only permits expressions of happiness and joy."

Hannah smiled and slid her hand over her belly. "Perhaps."

Perched comfortably on the deck in a little nest created by her husband, Hannah was able to spend many hours drinking up the sunshine as she carded wool or spun thread or performed one of the multitude of tasks that still must be done, even when one's home was a tiny cork skipping along a vast waterway.

That morning Lemuel had helped her lower her swollen body to her nest of blankets, set her basket beside her, then disappeared in search of Nephi to discuss the day's work. For a time, she was happily absorbed in her knitting. Then she felt as though someone's eyes were on her. Lifting her head, she found Laman watching.

Hannah felt her eyebrows go up in astonishment. Her eldest brother-by-marriage noticed her seldom, seeming to prefer the idea that she did not exist.

She nodded to him and saw his forehead pucker in question. Then, even more surprising, he set down the rope he had been twisting and came over to her.

"Sister Hannah," he said as he approached. "Are you comfortable? What brings you to the outer deck?"

She looked at him, confused. Seldom did Laman make conversation, and *never* to her. "I just wanted a bit of air," she said finally. "As you know, it gets rather stuffy between decks."

"Ah. Of course." Laman looked pointedly at her swollen belly. "And you are well? Lemuel's child is well?"

Hannah patted her belly. "The child moves often and Mother Sariah is pleased."

Laman nodded. "It is well."

"Brother? Was there something you needed?" Lemuel asked.

Laman swung around. "Ah. Brother. I did not see you there."

"No," Lemuel said. "Was there something you needed?"

Laman smiled. "Just a moment to visit with your bride."

Hannah took in a sharp breath. Bride?

"And now you can see she is fine and healthy?" Lemuel folded his arms.

"Yes. She says the child moves often."

Lemuel nodded.

"Well, I had best return to work," Laman nodded to the two of them and strode back to the rope he had been tying.

Hannah watched him go. That had been odd.

Lemuel, too, was watching his elder brother. "That was strange," he said, echoing her thoughts. He turned back to Hannah. "Did he say or do anything that offended or frightened you?"

Hannah shook her head. "He merely inquired after the child."

"Ah," Lemuel frowned. "Well, I'd better—" He, too, moved off.

Hannah went back to her knitting, occasionally lifting her head to study her eldest brother-by-marriage.

CHAPTER 27

As the baby grew, Hannah often found her sleep disturbed and, once she was awake, it was nearly impossible for her to again find that blissful state of unconsciousness, sometimes for hours. On such nights, she usually succumbed just shortly before the rest of the boat began to stir and ended up sleeping far past the breakfast hour.

One morning, Hannah awoke late from such a disturbed rest and felt immediately the change in the boat's movements—quiet, hardly moving. She frowned, and then lay still and listened. Not a sound penetrated to the second deck and her cubicle. Not a footstep. Not a word. Had everyone disappeared? Had the ship stopped?

She rolled off her pallet and struggled to her feet, then carefully pulled on her outer tunic. As a precaution, in case they were, indeed, softly afloat in the lagoon of yet another island, she picked up her sandals, then made her careful way to the upper deck.

It was nearly deserted. Only Mother Sariah was visible, seated on a bench, looking out across the water.

Hannah joined her, sighing in relief as she lowered herself down beside her mother-by-marriage.

"It is beautiful, is it not?" Mother Sariah waved a hand.

Hannah nodded, then gasped as she caught her first glimpse of the great mound of green that shot halfway to the sky and filled the horizon.

"Is it—are we—?"

Mother Sariah smiled. "It is beautiful, but it is not the promised land. It is another island."

"Oh."

Some of the islands the family had come across had been barren and nearly lifeless. Some, like this, blue and green and growing. Each time they happened on the beautiful, life-filled lands, Hannah and everyone else on board prayed that this, finally, was their goal. Their promised land. But each time, they had been disappointed.

Mother Sariah laughed at Hannah's expression. "Do not be sad, my daughter. We will be there soon enough."

Hannah nodded, unconsciously rubbing her hands over her belly. "I know. It has been such a long time."

"But a happy, safe time."

Hannah nodded again. She looked over the sparkling water toward the land. In the clear air, it looked close enough to touch. "It looks so near."

"It does. The waters are very, very deep here. Nephi was able to bring the ship in much closer than usual. It is only the work of a very few minutes to make the crossing."

"Is that why everyone is gone over?"

Mother Sariah nodded. "It seemed a good opportunity. The small boat can only carry a few of the family at a time, but with the distance so short, many trips could be accomplished with little trouble."

Hannah shaded her eyes and looked toward the island. She could see several figures on the shore.

"Mother! Are you ready—sister Hannah! You have joined us!"

Hannah looked down. A small boat, with Nephi pulling on the oars, was coming around the forward end of the ship. He pulled in close and rested the oars in the clear water. "Are you ready to come over, Mother?"

Sariah smiled. "Is there room for me on your island?"

Nephi laughed. "You are not that big." He turned to Hannah. "My sister, would you like to visit the island? It is a beautiful place."

Suddenly, there was nothing that Hannah wished to do more. She rose to her feet. "If you think your small boat will carry me."

Nephi laughed again. "Come."

The two women moved over to the rope ladder fastened to the side of the ship. Hannah watched as Sariah fell to her knees and then inched her lower body over the edge, feeling for the rungs as she did so. Soon, the elderly woman was seated in the boat beside her son.

She looked up at Hannah. "Come, my daughter. It is safe."

Hannah tried to copy her mother-by-marriage's actions, but her bulk made it difficult to bend and maneuver.

Soon, however, she, too, was seated in the small boat. She heaved a grateful sigh.

Nephi laughed and started pulling on the oars.

In a remarkably short time, he had drawn the small boat up onto the sand of the shore. He waited there while several of the young men came to help their aunt and grandmother onto dry land.

It had been weeks since Hannah stood on something that did not move under her feet and, for a few minutes, she felt dizzy and disoriented. Leaning heavily on the arm of Moriah's eldest son, Ezekiel, she negotiated the few hundred paces between the water and a thick line of trees. Then, exhausted by the unaccustomed activity, she sank down into the soft, warm sand beneath the trees with a sigh of content. From there, she happily watched the rest of the family.

Water barrels, filled with clear water from a nearby stream, were being rolled to the water's edge to await eventual transport to the ship.

Two wild goats had been trapped by the more enterprising of the grandsons and were trussed tightly near the barrels. Shouts from young men still tracking more of the animals echoed through the trees.

Hannah could hear other family members as they enjoyed this unexpected break from the small sameness that was life aboard a ship. Squeals of excitement came from the children and adults alike as they discovered strange birds and animals and an abundance of flowers and fruit.

Lemuel emerged from the trees, rolling yet another large barrel. He saw her sitting there and abandoned his task to come over. "Are you well, wife?"

Hannah smiled and shifted her weight. "Yes, husband."

He nodded and looked around. "This is a remarkable place: streams of clear water, fruit trees, truly a land flowing with milk and honey."

"But not the promised land?"

He shook his head sadly. "So says Nephi." He frowned. "Laman is of the opinion—" he stopped.

Hannah looked at him. "Yes?"

"Nothing." He turned. "I—umm—need to continue with my work."

Hannah watched him cross the sand to the barrel, then continue to roll it toward the water.

Feeling oddly restless, she twitched her legs, then drew her knees up and tried to pull them under her chin.

She laughed softly as she was reminded, rather forcefully, that her knees were going to get nowhere near her chin. There was too much baby in the way.

Just then, a wrenching pain tore through her. She caught her breath, and then, as the pain continued, cried out.

Immediately, several of the people on the beach looked in her direction.

Anava's second daughter hurried over. "Mother Hannah. Are you all right?"

Hannah looked up at her. "I have pain—" she managed to grit out, gesturing to her stomach. "Here." She winced.

"I'll fetch Mother!" The girl disappeared into the trees.

A few moments later, Hannah was surrounded by her mother-by-marriage and three of her sisters.

The elder woman knelt in front of her. "What is it, dear?"

"I have pain!" Hannah said. "Here."

Mother Sariah nodded. "It is time," she said. She looked across the narrow strip of water to the ship. "And I think Hannah will be much more comfortable here on land than she would be on the water." She turned back to Hannah. "Am I right, daughter?"

Hannah nodded, but then winced as another pain started.

"Moriah, find one of the men to take you to the ship. Then bring my healer's kit and the large bag I had stocked ready for Hannah's confinement."

Moriah hurried off.

"Anava, get some help to move Hannah—"

"I can walk," Hannah said. "In just a moment—" The pain eased and she gripped Mother Sariah's hand and struggled to stand.

Once she was on her feet she had little difficulty following Mother Sariah further into the trees.

Her mother-by-marriage led her to a deep, swiftly flowing stream. Trees and other vegetation lined it, creating many quiet, even private, spaces.

Sariah chose one and directed Hannah to a corner deeply lined in thick grass. Flowering bushes grew all around and, with the huge trees forming a canopy overhead, shaped it into a comfortable, fragrant bower. She spread a blanket and helped Hannah sit down.

Hannah lay back and sighed.

She was finally going to be a mother. Her happiness was complete.

CHAPTER 28

Twenty-four hours later, Mother Sariah placed a squalling baby into the arms of a perspiration-soaked, matted-haired, exhausted Hannah.

Instantly, her pain and weariness were forgotten as she looked down at the small, red-faced, dark-haired boy.

"Hello," she whispered. "I am your mother. It is so nice to be able to finally meet you!"

The baby stopped crying for a moment and seemed to be looking up into her eyes. In that instant, Hannah gave away her heart forever and knew that, no matter what this child needed throughout his life, she would move the heavens and the earth to see that he had it.

It was at that moment that Hannah knew real love.

"See if you can get him to suckle," Mother Sariah said.

Nodding, Hannah went through the motions she had witnessed thousands of times, but which suddenly seemed new and unfamiliar to her.

Her tiny son was eager, however, and latched on without much encouragement.

Hannah heard Mother Sariah sigh in relief.

Turning, she was surprised to see a look of fear—or worry?—in her mother-by-marriage's face. "What is it?" she asked.

The elder woman sighed again. "Nothing, favored one. Just—we need to get the bleeding stopped."

She started kneading Hannah's abdomen. "Keep him suckling, dear."

"Find me some moss," Mother Sariah directed her other daughters. "You know the kind."

Hannah was beginning to feel light-headed. She turned a head that felt as though it could float off into the treetops. "Mother Sariah, I am feeling—"

Everything went dark.

A shaft of light. There. In the distance.

Hannah moved toward it. She looked down, but could not see her baby son, nor her feet in the darkness. It was as though she was floating alone somewhere between heaven and earth.

The light broadened, grew brighter.

Now she could see her feet. Bare. And the ground she walked on. Grassy. Soft.

She glanced around. The darkness was lifting and Hannah realized she was moving toward the center of a broad, lush meadow toward a figure dressed in white that stood there.

Hannah hesitated. Should she continue?

But the pull to move closer was strong and she gave in to it.

The person, a man, was watching her. And suddenly, she knew who he was. "Father!" The last few paces were accomplished at a run. Hannah felt her father's arms close about her and she relaxed against the familiar chest and breathed in the welcome scent. "Father," she whispered.

For some moments, she remained in his warm embrace, rejoicing in something she never thought she would feel again.

Wait.

She straightened and leaned back to look up at him. "Father?"

He cupped her chin in a gentle hand and smiled into her eyes. "My daughter," he said. "My favored one."

"Father, where—" She looked around. "Father, where are we?"

His smiled widened. "We are together, favored one."

She smiled back. "But together—where?" She looked around. "Is Mother here?"

He smiled. "She is. But she is allowing us to have a few minutes to speak." He took a deep breath. "We are between the heavens and the earth, my daughter."

"Am I dead?"

"No, my dear. But you do have a choice to make. Come. Sit with me."

Her father led her to a spot in the meadow where a couple of logs had been rolled. They formed comfortable seating for both of them.

Ishmael sat, and Hannah sat close beside him and reached for his hand. "What is it, Father?"

He smiled. "I see so much of your mother in you," he said. "The same eyes, the same sense of purpose and determination." He looked up into the soft sky. "You have accomplished so much, daughter. But your journey on earth is not yet finished. There is more—much more that you have yet to do before you will be taken home."

Hannah frowned. "But you—you were taken before—"

"Do not fool yourself with imagining that our wilderness journey in any way shortened my days upon the earth."

"But the hardships. The dirt. The toil."

"All lengthened my days, rather than shortened them."

"Oh."

He smiled again and squeezed her hand. "Now to you—"

Hannah caught her breath. "Yes?"

"You have been given a special little boy."

Hannah smiled. "Yes."

"Samuel."

"Samuel?"

"Named as was the son of that *other* Hannah. A precious spirit, a name to stand for good or ill as he is taught and raised."

"He will be taught the gospel, Father," Hannah said. "His name will be had for good."

"It is well. Know this, however, that there are forces that oppose you—the forces of evil."

"They are always about us, Father. I will not be moved."

He smiled. "It is well." He turned away for a moment, then back to her. "Your husband—"

Hannah looked up at him. "My husband?"

"He can be easily led. His elder brother, Laman, is an influence over him."

"He has seemed closer to me in the past few months."

"And that is good. But, should Lemuel ever fall again under the power of Laman, there will be little anyone can do to bring him back to the path laid out for him and other righteous men. He, like his brother, will finish out his days in wanton and evil acts, leading his posterity—and your Samuel—astray to the end of time. " He looked at her. "The regrets from a life lived thus will be indescribable."

Hannah was silent for a moment as fear washed over her. "Is there no hope?"

Ishmael smiled. "There is always hope, favored one. Father Lehi and I gave you to Lemuel for this exact purpose, so that you could be a guide and a help meet for him."

"He does not always listen to me."

"What man ever did what he was told by his good wife?"

"But—"

He smiled again. "The things you say, the advice you offer, all are heard by your husband, daughter. All are taken in. Now it is up to him if he listens." He squeezed her hand again. "But know that at the end of time, if you have done all you can, his stain will not become yours."

Hannah felt a tear roll down one cheek. "And our son?"

"Until the time he decides finally that his chosen path is one that leads away from the Lord, you can be a strong voice in your son's life. Keep him from making that decision. Do all you can do."

Hannah nodded. "I will."

He put his hand on her shoulder. "I am placing a lot of responsibility on these slender shoulders, but I know I am not mistaken in you. You will succeed." He smiled. "One last piece of advice and I'll let your mother come to you." He placed a gentle finger under her chin and lifted her face until her eyes met his. "Hannah, my treasure, do not be that person who, at the end of her life, looks back in astonishment and regret at how far she has traveled away from the Lord. Rather, be that person who looks up and sees Him standing before her."

"I will, Father."

"It is well."

"Hannah!"

Hannah turned. Her mother, luminous in a white dress, was standing beside her.

"Mother!"

The two embraced.

"I have time only for a few words, my dear girl," her mother said into her ear. She held Hannah away and looked at her. "And then it will be time for you to go back. You have much to do."

"It is so good to see you and Father," Hannah said, reaching out to grasp one hand of each of her parents. She smiled. "I never thought I would be able to do this again!"

"We were never very far from you, my treasure," her mother said. "We've walked with you throughout much of your journey."

Hannah sighed happily.

"And now we have mere moments and there is much to say."

Hannah looked from her mother to her father expectantly.

Her mother touched her head gently. "Oh, dear girl, the things you will witness! The establishment of our people in the promised land, the building up of God's church, I envy you these first great steps into the Lord's world!" She put an arm around Hannah's shoulders. "Now I know your father has told you all you need to hear, but this one last thing I wanted to say." She smiled. "You are our favored one, so named from the day of your birth. And the Lord has saved you for a special purpose, to bring your son to salvation. Your *son*. Remember what I say this day. It is important—when you have a great choice to make."

Hannah nodded, a slight frown of confusion between her dark brows. "I will, Mother. I will always look after Samuel. Always."

Her mother smiled again. "Your son."

Hannah blinked. "Yes. My son."

"It is well."

A moment later Hannah opened her eyes to trees and flowers. Confused, she looked around. "Father? Mother?"

Mother Sariah's tear-streaked face appeared beside her and she embraced Hannah warmly. "Oh, favored one, you have returned!"

"Mother Sariah! I have! And it was so wonderful. And I talked to Mother and Father!"

Her mother-by-marriage frowned. "But, we thought you were—"

"Oh, Mother Sariah! I was with my parents. And Father told me—" She saw the older woman's expression. "Wait. What are you saying?"

"I thought you were dying, favored one," Mother Sariah said quietly.

"Dying?"

"You had lost so much blood."

"My baby! Is he—?"

"He is fine. Healthy. We will bring him to you now that you—"

"Are not dying."

"Well—yes." Mother Sariah nodded at someone and Hannah turned her head.

Lemuel was standing there, holding a tightly swaddled bundle. He looked at her, relief and wonderment in his eyes. "You have returned to me, and you have given me a son, wife."

Hannah smiled.

His mother took the baby from him and carried him to Hannah.

Hannah looked down at the perfect little face: the nose, the tiny little mouth, the dark brows and hair. "Hello again," she said softly.

The baby had been bathed and rubbed with salt. A light powder still coated his cheeks and chin. He stirred and smacked his lips.

"Hello, Samuel."

"Samuel?" Lemuel had crossed the space and now stood beside her. "I would have him named for *his* father, as is custom."

Hannah looked up at her husband and nodded, then she turned back to her son. "But Samuel has been so decreed by his grandfather."

"Father never chooses the names of our children."

"Not your father," Hannah smiled. "Mine."

She could feel Lemuel's eyes on her, but he said nothing. Finally, he reached out a finger and touched the baby's hand. "Samuel," he said.

CHAPTER 29

The decision was made to continue on the island throughout Hannah's confinement, and the days passed like idyllic pearls pulled along a radiant string.

Hannah was visited, in her confinement, by all of her sisters and sisters-by-marriage.

Moriah and Anava seldom left her alone, cooing and exclaiming over the baby, offering advice and sisterly wisdom, comparing experiences in which she could—finally—join.

Even Uzziel unbent enough to make an appearance, strolling into Hannah's bower in the later afternoon, four days after Samuel's birth. She bent over the baby and gently touched the fine, soft hair.

"He is beautiful, my sister," she said.

"I thank you, he is," Hannah agreed. "The Lord has blessed me."

"In your age."

Hannah nodded. "In my age."

Uzziel sighed. "Our Lord is a being of humor."

Hannah frowned. "I do not know—"

"I have borne daughters to Laman. Many daughters. Our Lord has not seen fit to bless us with a son." She looked at Hannah. "And now you, who have waited so long for your first, are blessed with that which has been denied me."

Hannah did not know what to say.

Uzziel wandered about the bower for a moment. "It is much more beautiful here than in my space."

"Oh?"

"You have flowering bushes all about and trees overhead. And the stream right there."

"I understood that there was room for everyone under the trees and beside the waters."

Uzziel shrugged. "Laman has settled his family further upstream, near a wide meadow. He must see to a distance or he feels shut in."

Hannah nodded. "That cannot be comfortable."

"No." Uzziel moved back to Hannah's side and looked again at her sleeping baby. "I wonder what it would be like to bear a son."

"Much like bearing a daughter, I would guess."

"Well, perhaps with this child I shall know." Uzziel put her hand on her abdomen.

"Uzziel, are you with child?"

Uzziel nodded.

"But that is wonderful! You must be overjoyed."

"Laman and I have rejoiced at our blessings," Uzziel said in a flat tone.

Hannah frowned slightly. "Are you not excited for this baby?"

Uzziel looked at her. "I have done this before many times. Laman would have me bear a son."

"But it is not what you would want?"

"What is a woman except to bear her husband's children?"

"A companion? A help meet? I thought you and Laman were of one purpose and one mind."

"Of one purpose?" Uzziel laughed. "Only if that includes bearing a son who will one day rule—" she stopped.

Hannah looked at her. "Prophecy declares that Nephi will rule, Uzziel," she said quietly.

"Only if Laman does not repent!" Uzziel said sharply. "And he has!" She put a hand on her belly again. "And this son will ensure that Laman's line will continue to rule after him!" She started toward the opening in the trees. "Congratulations on the birth of your son," she mumbled as she left.

Samuel's circumcision was performed with utmost exactness, and when the time came in the ordinance, Lemuel adhered to her wishes and pronounced that his name truly would be Samuel.

In their soft surroundings, even Samuel's discomfort following his circumcision seemed of shorter duration.

Everyone took advantage of the much fruit and game with which the island and surrounding waters flourished and re-stocked the ship's stores.

Fish were caught, salted, and dried. Meat from wild goats, sheep, and cattle, as well as nuts and fruits, were also preserved. They even discovered several beehives.

The ship received long-needed repairs.

Everyone was busy and happy, but none so much as Hannah and Lemuel. Lemuel had done much to make her as comfortable in her small bower as possible, bringing in blankets and foodstuffs and even crafting a bed for the baby out of reeds.

For the first time in her twelve-year marriage, Hannah felt like a wife.

As the time for her confinement drew to a close, there was a noticeable stirring among the family members, whispers that some would have them stay here in this idyllic place. Settle here between the mountains and the sea.

Father Lehi called a council on Samuel's thirty-third day and Hannah, proudly carrying her son, joined in.

"Well, I think our travels have finished!" Laman was saying loudly. He waved a hand, indicating the lush growth around them. "This looks like a promised land to me!"

"It is a beautiful land," Nephi agreed. "But it is not the land our Lord is sending us to."

"And we're back to receiving orders from our 'little' brother again." Laman looked at Lemuel, but his younger brother refused to make eye contact. Laman frowned heavily.

"It matters not what we want," Father Lehi said. "It matters what the Lord wants."

Laman rolled his eyes. "And you are the person to tell us, of course."

Father Lehi tipped his grey head to one side and regarded his eldest son. "Of course."

Laman blinked and looked once more toward Lemuel, who still refused to make eye contact. Then he sat down.

For the next hour, Nephi led a discussion of what would be needed to get the newly preserved foodstuffs, newly captured animals, and other necessities on board the ship. Then he offered a prayer and people drifted away.

Hannah went back to her bower.

A few minutes later, Lemuel joined her. He lay down beside her on the soft grass and leaned back on one elbow.

Hannah watched him as she rocked Samuel.

Lemuel took a deep breath. "I know what Laman is feeling," he said finally.

Hannah nodded. "I do too."

Lemuel was startled. "You do?"

She nodded. "I, too, find this place a paradise." She smiled rather sadly. "It is the first place where I have been truly happy in—oh, a very long time."

"Truly?"

"Truly."

Lemuel's eyes were on her. "I have not been a good husband."

Hannah said nothing.

"Your silence says everything." He looked away. "I know I have not. I have cared more of what my elder brother thinks than what my Lord thinks." He turned back to her. "Or my wife."

"Laman has a forceful character."

"He does that, but I could have been my own man, directed my own life."

Hannah smiled. "We all must reach that shore at some time in our lives."

"Well, I am late to it."

"But what matters is reaching it."

Lemuel smiled and said, "And now we are talking about leaving another shore."

Hannah laughed. "But we know that, through our Lord, we will reach one that is better."

Lemuel lay back in the grass and looked up through the trees. "How can it be better than this?"

She smiled. "I've wondered the same."

Lemuel turned his head to look at her. "Have you always been this wise?"

"Wise? You think I am wise?" Hannah blinked.

"I have not always recognized it—or wanted to recognize it. But now I am fairly certain it has always been there." He took a deep breath and turned back to the trees. "And I am fairly certain I should be listening."

Three days later, the ship was again sailing smoothly across the waves.

For the first time, Hannah was able to enjoy the gentle, rocking motion as she strolled the deck with Samuel safely wrapped against her body.

Her sisters and their daughters were busily grinding grains for the day's bread, and the men and boys were hoisting a new sail the women had made while on the island.

Hannah smiled.

Somehow, their ship had sailed all this way without the benefit of its largest sail, which shredded during the great wickedness and the resulting storm.

The tattered remains had hung from the main mast this entire time, a reminder of the costs of wickedness.

Now, seeing the shreds of the old in a crumpled heap on the deck and the fresh, new sail replacing it, Hannah felt as though evil had been rooted out, that the family was, finally, washed clean of the taint of past sins.

Uzziel was seated, supposedly spinning yarn, but in reality, watching the men. She had not returned to Hannah's bower on the island after that one visit.

Hannah walked over and sat beside her. "Good morning, my sister," she said brightly.

Uzziel nodded. "Good morning." She bent her head to her spinning.

"What a glorious sight," Hannah went on.

"Glorious?" Uzziel looked up. "Oh, the sail. Yes. It is beautiful."

"But it is what it represents that I am speaking of."

Uzziel looked at her. "Represents?" she asked.

"Yes. Past sins are done away and a new, clean life is ahead."

Uzziel said nothing, but turned to stare at the sail.

"Would you not agree?" Hannah said. She indicated the pile of shredded canvas on the deck. "Here are past sins, ready to be swept clean. And there is new life, ready—"

"Oh, please stop!" Uzziel said. "That is what makes it so hard for some to repent! Because others will never—ever—let them forget!" She got up and quickly crossed the deck, disappearing into the opening to the next level.

Two months later, Hannah was in her cubicle bathing Samuel. The baby had grown remarkably and was brown and fat from exposure to the sun and Hannah's rich milk. He was gurgling and blowing bubbles and practicing his smiles for his mother.

"Oh you are such a sweet boy!" Hannah exclaimed happily. "The cleverest, best boy ever!"

"Hmmm, you may find there are mothers plenty around this world that would refute your claims."

Hannah turned her head. "Morrie!" She smiled.

Her eldest sister returned her smile and stepped gracefully into her cubicle. "I have one or two handsome, clever boys in my own family whose names I would put forward."

Hannah laughed. "Nonetheless, I stand by my claim."

Moriah put an arm about her and gave her a gentle squeeze. "And so you should, sister!"

"How goes the day outside?"

Moriah lifted her eyes toward the upper deck. "It is another beautiful day! The sun shines. The breezes fill the sails. The waters curl away from the front of the ship."

"As it was yesterday," Hannah said.

"And the day before that. And the day before that." Moriah smiled again. "Do not mistake my words. We have been greatly blessed throughout this trip—"

Hannah broke in. "After the storm."

"After the storm," Moriah nodded, "and during it."

"Truth."

"But I would have the travel done. Our sojourn on the island of Samuel's birth reminded all of us that we are people of the earth, not people of the water." Moriah sighed. "I would have the promised land suddenly appear on the horizon and hear the welcome words, 'Land! Land before us!'"

"It will happen," Hannah said. "In the Lord's time, it will happen."

Just then, the two of them heard the pounding of many feet on the deck over their heads.

Both raised their heads and stared upward. "What do you suppose—?" Hannah asked.

But Moriah had left the cubicle.

Hannah could see her sister pause at the bottom of the stairway. She cocked her head, listening. Then she laughed and turned back to Hannah. "Someone is shouting, 'Land!'" she said.

Hannah picked up her son and followed her sister up the stairs.

All over the deck, people were dancing and shouting and laughing and hugging each other. Hannah exchanged a smile with Lemuel, busy with the ship's sails, then she moved among the happy crowd, finally joining the silent group at the front of the ship. She peered with them over the rail toward the dark blot on the horizon. The dark blot that was slowly resolving itself into a long line of green.

"Is it true?" she whispered to Anava.

Her younger sister looked at her with tear-drenched eyes. "It is true," Anava said and turned back toward the amazing sight. "At last we are here. The promised land."

CHAPTER 30

The initial exuberance died away, and it was a quiet group that stood the remainder of the morning and watched as the narrow strip of green became something vastly more substantial: mountains, beaches, trees, and finally, bushes and flowers.

Overhead, sea birds wheeled and dove, emitting their eerie cry and watching with curiosity the strange craft that had just floated into their world.

Nephi and Father Lehi, both kneeling next to the rail, were dividing their watch between the nearing shore and the golden ball and calling out instructions to Laman, who was manning the steering mechanism, and to Lemuel and Sam, who were directing placement of the sails.

When the land seemed almost close enough to touch, Nephi ordered the ship to turn to the left, and they followed the coastline for a while.

Unable to tear her eyes from this place that would soon be her new home, Hannah found a seat in a pile of rope where she could keep watching.

The work of sailing went on around her unheeded as the land slipped past.

Beyond the wide, sandy beach, she saw green forests and the occasional meadow of thick grasses with a bounty of flowering shrubs interspersed between. There were trees heavy with fruit and the occasional break in the vegetation that indicated a fresh-water stream.

It looked at once wild and untamed but rich and promising.

Finally, Nephi took one last look at the golden director, spoke briefly with his father, and stood up and nodded at Laman, Lemuel, and Sam.

The ship was directed closer to shore, then grandsons were swarming up the poles and gathering and binding the sails.

Hannah vaguely heard the splash of the anchor and felt the gradual slowing of the ship. Finally, it rocked backward and she knew that it had come to rest.

Their long journey was truly over.

Hannah looked down at Samuel's sleeping face. "We are here, my son," she whispered.

Samuel's tiny bow of a mouth crooked up into a baby smile that was gone almost as soon as it appeared.

"I am happy too!" Hannah looked toward the land. "Here is where the rest of our forever will happen!"

Nephi had anchored the ship in a small bay along the coastline. Long fingers of land jutted out into the sea on either end, partially enclosing the inlet. The waters were amazingly smoother here. The outcrops of land seemed to act as embracing arms that calmed and soothed the dancing waves.

Father Lehi walked to the center of the group. "Our Lord has brought us safely over the great Irriantum," he said. He looked around, gathering everyone's attention. "Let us give Him thanks."

There were few dry eyes when Father Lehi closed his prayer a short time later.

Lemuel came over to Hannah and gripped her hand. The two smiled at each other and Hannah felt as though her heart would burst with happiness and gratitude.

There was some discussion as to who would be the first to set foot on this new land. Finally, the small rowboat was lowered with Laman, Lemuel, and Nephi inside. Once the craft reached the water, it took little time for the three brothers to row their way over to the shore.

The entire ship's company watched as they beached the boat and made their way across the sand to the treeline.

Both Laman and Lemuel had taken their bows, and Hannah could see that they had strung them and now kept them ready in case of—something. Nephi had unsheathed his gleaming sword.

Hannah blinked. Until she had seen them do this, she had not had even an inkling of fear. Now she realized that, promised land or not, this was a strange place about which none of them knew anything.

The men were right to proceed with caution.

They skirted the treeline for a handful of paces, then Nephi slipped into the trees.

Laman and Lemuel remained on the beach, continuing to walk in the same direction. Several times, Nephi emerged and the three stopped to speak together, then continued on.

Finally, they reached the far end of the bay and turned to begin the walk back.

At that moment, a group of strange-looking animals stepped out of the forest.

Hannah and many of the people on the ship gasped aloud.

The animals were tall and walked with a strange, halting gait, vaguely reminiscent of the camels Hannah had known all her life. In fact, they resembled camels with their long necks and small heads. But they had no humps and Hannah could see that thick hair covered their bodies.

The animals paused when they saw the three men.

Nephi, Laman, and Lemuel did the same.

For several moments, the two groups regarded each other.

Then the animals moved toward the men.

Hannah could see the men brace themselves for an attack.

But the animals merely walked up to them, sniffed them in a curious way, then moved past them and off toward a meadow of grass that could just be glimpsed through the trees.

The men watched them go, then turned toward the ship and raised their hands in the air.

Hannah and everyone on board cheered.

From that moment on, the ship, waterway, and beach were a hive of activity.

People came and went and the one little boat was in constant motion hauling goods and supplies to the land.

A temporary camp was set up just inside the trees from the ship in a wide, flat, deeply grassed meadow next to a stream of clear water. A cheerful fire was soon burning in the center of the camp, and women bustled about settling possessions, grinding grain, tending children, and doing one of the myriad chores that had been theirs since the days of Father Adam.

Hannah looked up from her task of nursing Samuel and smiled.

Already it seemed as though they had been there for weeks, not the few hours of reality.

Some of the men and boys continued to haul crates and baskets from the ship, depositing them as directed by the women. Others were formed into scouting parties, all with at least one cautiously armed member, and sent along the beach and into the trees in every direction, exploring and mapping.

Possible building sites were to be charted and rated. The family did not intend for this camp to be their final settlement.

One of the groups of explorers came into the camp.

Lemuel was with them. He saw Hannah, came over, threw himself down beside her, and sighed happily. "I have to admit it. Brother Nephi was right," he said.

Hannah smiled. "Never thought I would hear you say that, husband."

Lemuel laughed. "Never thought I would say it!" He looked around. "This brings back memories."

"Of our camp back in the Valley of Lemuel?"

He nodded. "And of the countless camps between there and Bountiful."

"And the island where Samuel was born?"

He was silent for a moment. Then, "My favorite memory," he said softly. He looked at the baby now sleeping in his mother's arms, then reached out a hand and touched the soft cheek. "And the best thing I've ever done."

Hannah looked at Iscah as her sister wife directed two of her daughters in carrying a basket filled with blankets and bedding. "And your other children?"

Lemuel also looked at his other wife. "Of course. My daughters as well."

Hannah smiled. "Good."

Lemuel got to his feet. "Well, I'd best keep on. Father and Zoram need to know what our little party has discovered." He smiled at her and disappeared between two tents.

Later, as the family gathered for the evening meal, Hannah saw Lemuel speak to Iscah and grip her hand briefly as she handed him a meat-filled round of bread.

Hannah smiled. She was enjoying her husband's attentions, but she did not want them at the expense of her sister wife.

The next weeks flew past, with sites chosen for settlement and crops carefully planted. Then actual building began on permanent structures—houses and other buildings.

These first structures were crafted of wood and quickly erected with roofs of thatch. With the completion of each, people moved from their tents and happily took up residence in the more permanent buildings. Soon a street of tidy homes, each with its own small plot of ground for raising crops and animals, had appeared.

Hannah and Iscah shared a large acreage, with their small homes nestled together to one side. Their families gathered flocks of birds and a small herd of goats, and then helped erect pens and shelters for their animals.

Within a handful of weeks, Hannah was presiding over her own home.

Iscah's girls milked and brushed the goats from their little herd and kept both households supplied with milk and goat's hair. Lemuel's families worked together to twist the hair into yarn, to make cheese, and to dry and preserve fruits and herbs gathered in the rich woodlands that surrounded them. The stream that meandered through the village supplied fish caught daily by the boys and young men. Meat and leather came from animals hunted by the older boys and men in the thick forest.

Flocks of wild sheep were discovered in the underbrush, as was a herd of strangely colored cattle. Animals of both types were trapped and hauled back to the settlement. Soon their dwindling stock of wool had increased dramatically, and their goat's milk was greatly augmented with milk from their new cows.

Some of the strange animals that had been the first to greet them upon landing had been cornered and tamed and were proving remarkable for their abilities and their gentle nature.

The whole camp rejoiced when several of the older grandsons appeared one day leading two horses.

The boys had trapped the animals soon after the family's arrival and had been secretly training them for many weeks. The animals were still skittish and not entirely broken, but they were young and strong and would be of great help to the settlement.

Within a six-month period, Hannah's daily life was nearly as comfortable as it had been back home in Jerusalem.

But what made her joy complete was Lemuel's presence. Her husband was there often and spent many hours helping her and Iscah or having conversation with them.

It was the most happy and joyful time of her life with her fat, happy son, her comfortable home, her family, and her husband.

Surely, she had been greatly blessed.

CHAPTER 31

Hannah was sitting in her favorite spot beneath a great shady tree between her house and Iscah's. There had been a scurry of activity around Uzziel's home just down the street earlier, and Hannah suspected the birth of yet another child. She had sat herself here in the garden while she nursed Samuel to be accessible if the need arose.

It had not.

Mother Sariah paused outside Hannah's gate to wish her a good day and to tell her of the arrival of yet another daughter to Laman's house, then she hurried away.

Hannah had finished nursing Samuel, and the baby was rocking back and forth on his hands and knees in the soft grass, trying to work out just how to start moving forward.

"You have blessed me with a beautiful, strong, healthy son."

Hannah looked up, surprised. Lemuel stood beside her.

He grinned. No one could move quite as silently. His skills as a hunter seemed to have increased since their arrival here in the promised land, and he quite enjoyed his ability to move about undetected.

She smiled at him and shook her head. "One day you will startle me into an early grave, husband."

He frowned. "That is not my intent."

She laughed. "I would hope not."

He leaned over and picked up the baby. "A beautiful, strong boy." Samuel looked at his father and reached out to tug on Lemuel's dark beard. Hannah was struck by how similar they were, even with her son's round baby features: the same dark eyes and hair, the same curve to their brow, even the same straight nose.

Hannah smiled. "He is beautiful. He looks like you."

Lemuel looked at her, surprised. "You think this?"

"I do."

He regarded his son for a moment, smiled, and held the boy close. Then he turned abruptly and started off down the street.

Hannah got to her feet. "Husband?"

"I will return him to you shortly."

Hannah blinked and watched Lemuel carry Samuel to Uzziel's home. Laman was sitting under a tree there, and Lemuel stopped and spoke to him. Laman stood up and held out his arms, and Lemuel placed the baby in them.

Samuel squalled as he looked up and saw a stranger's face, but stilled when Laman began to rock him and speak softly to him.

Hannah started toward them, strangely disquieted by the sight of her son in Laman's arms.

It took a few moments for her to reach them, and during that time Laman held and rocked her son, speaking to the baby in low tones.

He turned to look at her as she joined them. "Well, sister Hannah, you have a fine son here."

Hannah summoned up a smile. "Thank you, brother Laman." She reached out her arms for her son.

He hesitated and, for a moment, she wondered if he would refuse to give her the baby. But he smiled, finally, and handed Samuel over.

"I have no sons," he said.

"I am aware," Hannah said, nodding.

"Uzziel has just given birth to yet another daughter."

Hannah nodded again. "Congratulations, brother Laman."

Laman cleared his throat. "I would see your son as mine. I would school him. Educate him."

Hannah felt her heart freeze within her.

"I have told Laman that he—Samuel—is *my* son," Lemuel said.

"And he will always be your son," Laman said quickly. "But I would take an interest in him, in his welfare and education."

"I will think on this," Hannah said, turning quickly and starting up the street. *When the sun rises in the west,* she added to herself.

From that moment on, Hannah lived in fear for her son. She often scolded herself for her distrust of Laman, pointing out to her suspicious mind his exemplary months of hard, willing work and seeming spiritual growth.

But her woman's heart remained suspicious still. Cautious.

Often her father's words, "You can be a strong voice in your son's life. Do all you can do," echoed through her mind. Was she obeying? Was allowing Laman access to her son at any and all waking hours "doing all she could do"?

Whenever her eldest brother-by-marriage picked up her son, a thrill of fear shot through her. Often it was all she could do to keep from snatching the small boy into her shaking hands and running as fast and as far as she could.

It did little good to speak to Lemuel. Her husband was flattered by Laman's attention and pleasing words. For the first time in his life, he had done something his elder brother could not, and he was basking in the experience.

Feeling once more bereft of husband and support, Hannah pressed forward with greater strength and did what she knew to be right. She taught her son the joys of work, read to him from the scriptures, and prayed with and for him.

Daily, she took Samuel and joined other members of the family as they gathered around Nephi, Father Lehi, or more increasingly, Lehi's next younger son, Jacob, to hear the Lord's words for them. She participated in the discussions: the meeting of minds and ideas with the coming of the future Savior at the core.

She encouraged Samuel in his first, halting expressions of testimony, rejoicing in every spiritual progression.

On Samuel's fourth birthday, Laman presented the boy with a beautiful bow, carved with his own hands, then offered to teach him to shoot.

Lemuel had heartily approved the idea, citing Laman's prowess with the weapon, and for hour upon hour, the three of them, the two grown brothers and the small boy, practiced in the garden. It was not long before Samuel was not only hitting the target, but doing so accurately.

Now when Laman appeared, Samuel lit up.

Hannah's heart sank within her at the sight.

More and more, the boy balked when she took him to Father Lehi for daily scripture study and prayer. More and more he wanted to "do what Father Laman is doing."

Hannah lifted her head. Someone was shouting in the square. No, several people.

She closed the gate to the goat pen and hurried toward the sound.

A group of family members were gathered together on the far side of the street. As Hannah drew closer, she could see that the people had formed a circle around something—or someone. She pressed into the crowd, finally emerging somewhere near the center. Then she gasped.

Samuel, a cut above one eye and blood streaming from his nose, was straddling Berachah's youngest son, Abishai, and pounding him with small fists. His victim had both arms over his face, trying to ward off the worst of the blows.

"Samuel!" Hannah cried out. She threw herself across the space and, grabbing her five-year-old son's arm, lifted him off the other boy. "Samuel! Stop this at once!"

Samuel blinked at her, wiping absently at his nose with one hand and smearing blood across his face.

Shaking her head, Hannah started to drag her son from the circle.

Someone stepped in front of her. Laman—arms folded and a grin on his face—said, "We will make a warrior out of him yet! He has the taste for blood!"

Hannah stared at her brother-by-marriage, feeling slightly sick to her stomach. For the first time, she suspected she might be losing her son.

Laman was beginning to cause trouble throughout the camp. Arguments and contention seemed to follow the man wherever he went. A group of the grandsons, Hannah's brothers' boys with Samuel among them, were beginning to follow the man about, listening closely to his every word.

It was not unusual for "wrestling matches" to occur at any time and in most any place.

One of Jacob's gatherings was broken up by two grandsons taking their opinions about the Second Coming from discussion to something far more physical.

Something as simple as returning from a day of labor could be turned into an excuse for contention, when those who had been farming met up with those who had spent their day hunting.

Family gatherings were beginning to take place with a conspicuous lack of certain family members. It was as though the family was being slowly, but effectively, pulled apart.

But even as the family unity suffered, construction on their village continued.

Nephi, in constant communication with the Lord, was designing stone buildings of fine, but curious, workmanship. His structures were beginning to appear on the other side of a large copse of trees—separate from the original town site. Shops and other places of business were the first to be erected. Soon, homes were appearing there also. Homes that housed Father Lehi, Nephi, and that part of the family who still professed belief in what they taught.

It was not long before the family was neatly separated into two, Laman and those who followed him on one side of the copse of trees and Nephi and his followers on the other.

CHAPTER 32

Hannah could hear someone shouting.

Her busy hands stilled in their task as she sat back on her heels and listened.

More shouting. And laughter. She breathed a short sigh of relief. Just someone returning from a successful hunt, probably.

Too many times in the past few months shouting had been much more than a simple exclamation of triumph.

Hannah shivered as she remembered Laman's face only a day or so previously. It had been dark with anger and twisted with hatred as the great man had paced about their settlement, screaming out his rage and fury after his latest dispute with Nephi. And from the heads nodding among the men and boys gathered to listen, his opinion was shared by many.

Even her own young Samuel had been loud in his agreement of his most-beloved uncle.

Hannah sighed and shook her head, wishing for the millionth time that Laman had had sons of his own or been happy with the numerous strong, healthy daughters presented to him by his beloved Uzziel. Then, perhaps, he would have left Lemuel's single son be.

Hannah felt the familiar prick of tears. Shaking her head, she rose quickly to her feet. Simmering silently in her house was going to do no one any good. She would go to the other settlement for a quick visit.

Spending time with her sisters always cheered her up.

The men were gathered on the far side of the compound still rejoicing over something. Bows and spears were figuring prominently in their motioning hands and expansive gestures. Her husband stood to one side, smiling and nodding happily, clapping long-fingered hands together softly.

Hannah stopped for a moment, studying the other figures carefully. Finally she saw an unruly mop of dark hair appear briefly in the crowd and she relaxed. Her son was obviously well and happy.

Hannah could only assume that the hunt had not only gone well, but very well. Already, she could see some of the other women sharpening knives and preparing platters and bowls.

As she watched, Thaddeus, now the settlement's tanner, came from his shop and almost ran across the compound, eager to see what hides would soon be on offer.

Hannah shook her head and moved quickly to the edge of the jungle, stepping gratefully into the cool shadows of the thick trees and brush that crowded the wide trail.

"Hannah!"

She sighed and turned.

Her sister's tall figure was mere foot-breadths away. How did she move so quickly and silently?

"The men have returned—"

"I heard," Hannah said drily.

Uzziel blew her breath through her nose in her usual response to foolish talk. "The men have returned," she said a little more slowly. "Your place is at the slaughter."

Hannah nodded and turned back toward the path. "I know, Uzziel. I am on my way to speak to Moriah and Anava. I'll only be gone a short time." She hated the sound of submission she could hear in her own voice. But then, Uzziel was Uzziel. "It will take hours for them to get to the practical part of the slaughter. You know how long they like to talk about it."

Uzziel was still for a moment. Then she nodded and stood back, letting Hannah resume her quick steps into the forest. "Make certain you are back before the shadows lengthen!" she called. "And do not believe anything they tell you!"

Hannah turned away.

The lush carpet of vines and leaves felt springy on the soft leather of her sandals, and Hannah's feet seemed lighter as she fairly flew down the path to the adjoining camp.

As always, she was struck by the difference between the two compounds. Though they were only a few hundred paces apart, they were vastly dissimilar in feeling. In Laman's camp, the people were more given to idleness—even the women seemed less and less willing to do all the work that needed doing. All about in Nephi's camp, people were weaving, sewing, tending garden plots and children, reading, teaching, hauling wood, building, and visiting together—busily and happily engaged.

Hannah sighed. Though she could not quite bring herself to admit it, she felt calmer and much more at home on this side of the trees.

"Hannah!"

She looked up and smiled. "Anava!" Her youngest sister, light brown hair neatly tucked beneath a bright cloth, was standing in the center of a large group of laughing children, not a few of which were her own. Slowly her slender figure worked its way to the edge of the group, and into Hannah's waiting arms.

The two sisters hugged each other tightly. Anava pushed Hannah's head covering back on her sister's dark hair and looked into her face. "How are you, my sister? It's been far too long since I last saw you!"

Hannah laughed. How much more easily laughter came to her when she was here! "I am well and healthy, sister."

Anava peered into Hannah's face and touched a spot near her sister's eyes. "But something deep down is sad, my sister. Something is troubling you."

Hannah shrugged. "It's the same thing that is always troubling me, sister. The further Laman leans from the teachings, the further his camp draws from peace and industry." She looked away. "And the further Laman leans, the further Lemuel follows."

Anava nodded, her gentle brown eyes filling with tears. "And your place is with your husband, so the further Lemuel goes—"

Hannah nodded.

Anava brushed at her cheeks, then she straightened and reached for Hannah's hand. "Well, let's not think of it right now. Laman and your Lemuel were both taught by the same father as my Nephi. They will remember their boyhood teachings and the miracles and signs they have witnessed. It will come back to them."

"Of course it will," Hannah agreed. But she could hear the doubt in her own voice.

Anava appeared not to notice.

Hannah summoned up a smile and looked around. "Everyone appears busy," she said.

Anava nodded and returned the smile. "Who knew that continual hard work and study would bring continual happiness?"

"Nephi did," Hannah said quietly.

Anava's smile widened. She looked around, and then pointed. "And he works the hardest of all!"

Hannah followed the pointing finger.

Using mason's tools, Nephi was smoothing the sides of a great squared block of stone. He, Sam, and several of the older grandsons were obviously in the process of creating the blocks to form the walls of the partially finished building beside them, a temple to their Lord.

Nephi, white teeth flashing in the sunshine, said something to his coworkers. All of them laughed. Then they began to fasten ropes around the block, ready to hoist it atop the finished rows.

The men appeared relaxed and happy, though as evidenced by their sweat-stained clothing, they had been working very hard.

Again, Hannah pictured the men in her compound and their disinterest in anything that required true labor and their joy and excitement as they celebrated the death of an animal. She shook her head and said, "Anyway, I did not come to talk about that. I came to talk of cheerful things."

Anava grabbed her sister's hand. "Then come with me. Mother Sariah will be so happy to see you!"

Hannah smiled, "But I saw her just a few days ago."

"She worries about Laman and your Lemuel and everyone in your settlement. Jacob and Joseph, as well as Nephi and Sam, visit her often, but Laman and Lemuel never do. I know she wants to hear how her other sons are doing. You are her last link. Heaven knows Uzziel never visits! And none of Uzziel's children do."

Hannah sighed. Her own Samuel was just as opposed.

Soon the two of them and Mother Sariah were a cozy little group in the cool shade of their mother-by-marriage's garden.

For some time, they simply exchanged news. Then the conversation turned, as always, to the actions of the people in Hannah's settlement.

"But why do they act that way?" Anava asked. "They have all been taught the same truths. They have all worshiped the same Lord."

Mother Sariah sighed. "Ah, but they have not all had their hearts touched. A door must be opened before one can step inside. A closed heart repels knowledge as well as beauty."

Deep in thought, Hannah walked slowly back to her settlement. She had seen and recognized the power of the Lord on numerous occasions. Why was it impossible for Laman and Lemuel and those who followed them to see what she could see?

Was it weakness to follow the Lord?

She shook her head and answered her own question. No. It was not weakness. It was true strength.

CHAPTER 33

"Hannah! Come. You are needed!"

She looked up. Without noticing, she had crossed through to the other settlement, and Uzziel was waving at her, directing her to join them.

A roaring fire had been built in the center of the square, and the carcass of one of the butchered animals was already spitted and roasting. Her sister was standing nearby where a second animal was being drained of its blood.

Hannah looked at the great bowl of crimson liquid and felt her gorge rise.

The bowl was set aside and Thaddeus, the tanner, went to work with his knives, skinning and preparing the beast.

Soon the second animal had been gutted and hoisted up beside the first.

The bowl of blood remained where it had been placed, Laman and Thaddeus seated near it. Laman, with a wide grin on his face, pulled the bowl over and dipped his fingers into the gore. "Let us begin a new tradition, son of my sister."

Thaddeus looked at his uncle. "A new tradition, Father Laman?"

"Yes, one that will mark us as true warriors." Laman lifted his dripping fingers and wiped the blood across Thaddeus's forehead.

The young man did not flinch, but continued to look at his uncle trustingly.

Laman dipped his fingers again and stroked them down Thaddeus's cheeks and chin, then moved on to his arms and hands. Soon the young man was coated liberally and was almost unrecognizable as something human.

Laman smiled and painted his own face. Then he stood up. "Come, my warriors of the day! Bring me your bravely beating hearts!"

One by one, the men who had participated in the hunt lined up and submitted to Laman's gory ministrations. Soon, nearly every man and most of the older boys in the settlement had been painted in the blood of their hapless victims.

Even a couple of the women had been given a token stroke or two over squeals of pretended protest.

Someone began to sing a song of hunting and huntsmen—a recent composition specific to their settlement—that was picked up by the other members of the group. Soon, everyone was singing at the top of their lungs.

One of the men jumped up and began to pound out the rhythm of the song with his feet. Within seconds, a crush of bodies were dancing and gyrating about the fire, their faces, arms, and hands dark with blood and glistening with perspiration.

It was like a scene out of some ancient, evil vision where demons walked the earth and insanity and malevolence reigned together.

With them, his face and body coated like the rest, was Hannah's husband, her eternal companion. And just there, next to the group of spinning, whirling men, stood her eight-year-old son.

Hannah hurried over to Samuel and grabbed his hand. "Come, son."

"Mother! No!" Samuel tried to yank himself away.

She tightened her grip and started to pull.

Then a hand, dark with blood, clamped down on her arm just above her wrist.

Hannah gasped and looked up into the hideous face of a nightmare that spoke with Laman's voice. "Leave the boy alone."

Hannah straightened. "He is my son, a young boy still. *I say he comes home with me*!" The last words were hissed directly into the face of the gory apparition before her.

Surprised, Laman let go and stepped back.

Hannah cast a glance at the man who stood directly behind Laman. Lemuel. Then, her heart a stone within her breast, she turned away and towed Samuel toward home.

As she turned, she caught sight of Uzziel a short distance away. Her elder sister, a dark streak down one cheek, was staring at her, her expression unreadable.

Four days later, Hannah, holding the hand of an unhappy Samuel, stepped from the forest into Lehi's camp. She took a deep, cleansing breath, then pulled her reluctant son up the street, stopping several people to inquire after Nephi or Father Lehi.

Finally, at Amanna's house, she found the person she sought, helping his brother Sam prune one of Amanna's fruit trees. "Brother Nephi," she said.

The man turned, set down the shears he had been using, and moved toward her, mopping his brow with a cloth. He gave her a warm smile. "Sister Hannah! What a great joy it is to see you!" He looked at Samuel. "Sam! We do not often get the pleasure of your presence!"

Samuel looked at the ground and said nothing.

"What is it that brings you to our door on this bright, beautiful, blessed day?"

Hannah gave Nephi a rather strained smile. "Samuel is eight, brother Nephi. It is time to think of his baptism."

Nephi looked at her. "Baptism! And Lemuel? He is not—?"

Hannah sighed. "Lemuel leaves this sort of thing to me."

Nephi looked at her for a long moment. "I see," he replied. He took a deep breath, summoned up a smile, and turned back to Samuel. "Well, this is exciting! Eight!"

Samuel shrugged.

"We should plan a celebration!" Nephi said. "Samuel. What would you like do?"

Samuel shuffled his feet and looked at the ground, murmuring something.

Nephi reached for the boy's hand. "Sorry, son, I was not able to hear you."

Samuel looked at him. "*Not* get baptized?"

Nephi raised his eyebrows. "Is that really how you feel, son?" he asked quietly.

Samuel shrugged again, then looked at Hannah and said, "I-I suppose not."

Nephi studied him for a moment. Then, "Baptism is the first real contract you will make with your Lord, son. It is not to be made without thought, and certainly not to be made if it is something you do not want."

"I-I do not know."

"Well, no need to make up your mind in this moment," Nephi said, smiling. "But it is important. Remember, son: *For the gate by which ye should enter is repentance and baptism by water.*"

"What does it mean?" Samuel asked.

"Son, if you wish to enter into the kingdom of the Lord, you need to be baptized."

Samuel was silent for a moment. Then he looked at Nephi and took a deep breath. "My father says—" He paused and looked down once more.

Nephi waited a moment. "What does he say, son?"

Again, Samuel lifted his head and looked Nephi in the eye. "Why do you hate my father and Father Laman?"

Nephi blinked. Then he put a hand on Samuel's shoulder. "Son, I do not hate my eldest brothers."

"They told me you do! They told me you would force me to make oaths that would bind me to foolishness forever! Oaths that you have not authority to make! Because you are the younger brother . . . " Samuel's voice trailed away and he stood there, trembling.

Hannah gasped and clapped a hand over her mouth.

"Samuel, son," Nephi said quietly, "the priesthood of the Lord is given as soon as you are of age, if you are striving to be worthy. *Where* you are born in a family is no consideration."

Samuel looked at him but said nothing.

Nephi sighed. "Perhaps we should speak of this again later."

Samuel stuck out his chin. "I will feel the same, N-Nephi."

"*Uncle* Nephi, son!" Hannah said. "You must show respect to your elders."

"Why?" Samuel looked at Nephi again. "*He* never does." He slipped between them and was gone.

Hannah felt as though her heart had been crushed within her. She sank to the packed earth of the street and buried her face in her hands as she sobbed.

Nephi put a gentle hand on her shoulder.

"Is he lost to me, brother Nephi? This son I waited for and prayed for my entire life? Is he lost?"

Nephi was silent for a few moments.

Hannah lifted tear-drenched eyes and repeated, "Is he?"

"I do not know, my sister," Nephi said at last, squatting down beside her. "Certainly your husband and our elder brother have had a negative influence on his young mind." He smiled suddenly. "But he *is* young. We still have time to speak to him and maybe change his thinking." He placed a hand on her head. "I will think and pray."

"Thank you, my brother."

"Hannah!" said another voice.

Hannah scrubbed at her face, then lifted her head and looked at Moriah.

Moriah looked from her sister to Nephi. "Is there something amiss?"

Hannah took a deep breath and glanced at Nephi. "Yes, sister, but it is being cared for."

"Well, then, do not sit in the dust. I have fresh bread and freshly churned butter. They are so delicious together! Come inside for some refreshment."

Hannah grasped Nephi's outstretched hand and allowed him to help her to her feet. Then she smiled at him gratefully and moved toward her sister. "That sounds lovely, Moriah."

"Sons! Uzziel has at long last presented me with sons!"

Hannah looked up from her spinning. A crowd was gathering outside Uzziel's house. Laman could be seen in their midst holding two swaddled bundles, one in each arm.

Hannah hurried over.

"She finally got it right, brother?" Lemuel said.

Laman threw his head back and laughed, a great roar of sound.

Both babies jumped and started to cry.

Lemuel looked down at them. "Hear how strong their lungs are?" he demanded of the assembled crowd. "They will grow to be mighty hunters like their father!"

Hannah turned away. She was not needed at this gathering. And she really did not want to be there. She returned to her spinning.

A short time later, Lemuel joined her.

Hannah looked at him in surprise. Except to come for Samuel, her husband had not approached her in weeks.

"Wonderful news," he said.

Hannah nodded. "It is."

Lemuel was silent for a few minutes.

Hannah kept spinning.

Finally, "Why can I not—?" he paused, biting his lips.

"What is it, husband?"

"Nothing." Lemuel paced back and forth a few times.

Another period of silence.

Then, "I am not strong like you! I cannot—" Again, he stopped.

Hannah set her spindle in her lap and looked at him. "What is it you are trying to say, husband?"

He snorted softly. "I am not strong like you. I cannot stand against him."

"Who?" Hannah asked, though she was already fairly certain of his answer.

"Laman."

"Are you speaking of your eldest, wisest brother?" Laman said.

Lemuel's head snapped around. Laman was standing a couple of paces away. "Y-yes, brother, I was."

"And what did you say about me?"

Lemuel was silent for a moment. The he sighed. "Only that you are a difficult man to resist," he responded.

"And who would want to resist me?"

"Who, indeed?" Hannah said, looking at her husband.

"Come, brother," Laman said. "And bring your son. I have aught I would say to the two of you."

Hannah watched her husband hurry off after his brother.

"So in essence, even though he now has sons, Laman still wants Samuel to be his heir. Is that not reason to rejoice?"

Hannah sighed. "Is it, husband?"

Lemuel looked at her, his eyes narrowing. "What are you saying?"

"I do not think Laman is a proper influence for our son. I do not think inheriting a legacy is a reason to rejoice unless it is a legacy worth inheriting."

"Ah, wife. How sensible you sound when I do not have Laman here to speak sense into my other ear."

"What he speaks it not sense. When he speaks we hear the whisperings of the father of all lies."

"You are wrong."

"You did not always think so. Do you remember the island?"

Lemuel was silent.

"Do you remember our talks? The Spirit you felt?"

"I remember the joy of a son born."

"Yes! The joy and blessing of a son!" Hannah reached out and gripped her husband's hand. "And remember the promises whispered there in that fragrant bower only twelve summers ago? About being a better husband and listening to your wife?"

He looked at her. "It is just—too—hard." He got to his feet and left.

CHAPTER 34

"But where is Father Lehi?" Hannah asked. "I have not seen him for weeks."

"He does not leave his bed much these days," Anava said. "He is very weak and can only sit up for a very short time."

Hannah caught her breath. "I did not know."

Anava nodded and looked toward the window. "He lays there and talks to the Lord. Mother Sariah tries to help him and give him food and drink, but he will take very little. He talks to Nephi about his work and how there is more to be done." She shook her head. "How he can expect to do more work now I will never—"

"Anava?" Moriah was at the door. "Oh, and Hannah! Good! Father Lehi has asked for the family to assemble."

Anava scrambled to her feet. "The whole family?"

Moriah smiled at her. "Everyone."

Throughout the following days, Hannah was dismayed to notice that Father Lehi's words spoken when the entire family had gathered—words that had pierced her very soul—seemed to have no effect on the others in her settlement. In her conversations with Lemuel, Iscah, and others, no mention was made of Father Lehi's warnings, possible consequences, or blessings promised upon obedience. And certainly no one felt any need to make changes in their lifestyle. The hunters still went daily into the forest to find game. The women worked the hides, hunted firewood, and gossiped.

Even her beloved Samuel was unaffected by the things he had heard and the Spirit that had touched Hannah so profoundly.

Her despair was complete.

Hannah, spinning wool in the afternoon sunshine, heard the faint sound of someone screaming.

She gasped and jumped to her feet, dropping her spindle into the grass at her feet.

Another scream followed the first.

And then Hannah recognized them for what they were. Death screams.

"No!" she gasped. Without another thought, she was running down the street toward the other settlement. As she ran past, others looked up from whatever they were doing.

"Death screams!" she panted.

They looked toward the other settlement. Some got to their feet and started after her.

Uzziel, her face set impassively, simply watched her go.

The street in the other settlement was thronged with people, all rushing toward Nephi's house.

There, they gathered in the garden.

Nephi came out of the house, and it was quite obvious to Hannah that he had been weeping. He scrubbed at his face with a cloth. "F-father has been taken home," he whispered.

At his words, Hannah sank to the earth, her strength suddenly taken from her. Tears followed and, for several minutes, she sobbed bitterly.

Anava and three of her daughters came out of the house and, going to Nephi, put their arms around him. The five of them wept together.

All about her, Hannah could hear the sounds of weeping, but she dared not look up for fear of losing control completely. In her mind, she was seeing Father Lehi as she had first known him as a small girl, a giant of a man, kind and strong. There followed scenes of generosity, of wisdom, and of counsel. She remembered the night he had come to them for help when he had been beaten and when he announced that she and her sisters would marry his sons. She remembered his patience during the long hard journey to Bountiful and his suffering aboard the ship.

And always, *always*, his great and abiding faith.

Tears did not seem adequate for such a man. And yet, they were all she had to give. Tears and obedience to the things he had taught. Hannah straightened and brushed at her face. To the extent of her ability, she could obey.

"You shall be blessed of the Lord, my daughter. In your age, you shall be blessed again." Almost, she could hear Father Lehi again say those last words to her.

Through her tears, Hannah smiled.

Father Lehi's body was interred the next morning.

The men from Laman's camp had come across a series of natural caves in some cliffs a short distance from the settlements. A suitable grotto had been chosen and it was to this that the family bore Father Lehi's body shortly after sunrise on the day after his death.

None had eaten since the great man's passing, and most had continued their tears and lamentations throughout the night. Many were now dressed in rough cloth and had obviously been pouring some of the area's dark, rich soil on their heads.

The service was not long, but due to the loud lamentation, some of which was hers, Hannah was able to hear little.

During a momentary lull, she heard Nephi utter the words, "Oh that my head were waters, and mine eyes a fountain of tears, that I might weep day and night."

She sighed. Her feelings exactly.

Following the memorial, the family returned to Nephi's settlement for food and refreshment.

Hannah found a spot in the corner of the garden outside Amanna's home.

Mother Sariah sat down beside her, and Hannah reached for the elderly woman's hand. "Oh, Mother. I am so sorry for your loss!" she said.

Mother Sariah looked at her and smiled rather sadly. Then she lifted her head. "It is not a loss, daughter. Rather, it is a separation. And only for a short time."

"Mother Sariah, you cannot mean you are considering following Father Lehi!"

She smiled again. "I know I will be following him, my daughter. Gladly. But not today. Probably not tomorrow. In the Lord's time." She shrugged. "You cannot think I will long survive him. I am already a great age."

Hannah shook her head. "To me, you will always be that beautiful woman who accompanied Father Lehi when he first called upon my family."

Mother Sariah squeezed Hannah's hand. "And who always loved doing it." She smiled again. "Some of my most fond memories are of visits to your family!"

Hannah was quiet for a moment. "Were you pleased, Mother Sariah?"

The elderly woman looked at her, surprised. "Pleased, daughter?"

"When Father Lehi decided to marry your sons to Ishmael's daughters."

Mother Sariah smiled. "What makes you think it was his idea, daughter?"

Hannah blinked. "You—it was you?"

Her mother-by-marriage smiled. "Of course. I could think of no other young women more worthy of my sons!"

At that moment, Uzziel walked past, her head high, her young sons herded before her. Mother Sariah's smiled dimmed somewhat as she watched them go. "Of course, everything has not turned out as we hoped." She took a deep breath and turned back to Hannah. "Still, when I look at you, I realize that it was right."

The elderly woman leaned back, bracing herself on her hands and arms. She looked up into the trees above them. "Has the baby moved yet?"

Hannah frowned and looked at her. "The baby? What baby?"

Mother Sariah turned her head and fastened her eyes on Hannah's face. "Your baby, daughter."

"My baby?" Hannah felt suddenly faint. "*My baby*?"

Her mother-by-marriage smiled. "Your baby."

"But I—I am not—" Hannah's eyes went wide and she stared at Mother Sariah. "I—I do not—"

"But there have been signs."

Hannah felt her face growing crimson. "Yes. No—I do not know." She took a deep breath. "I have never been—regular, Mother Sariah. Never really had—cycles. And with my other confinement, I was so ill."

Mother Sariah nodded.

"So you know that I really would not be sure."

Another nod. "Yes, daughter." Mother Sariah smiled. "But you must be nearly far enough along to feel the baby move?"

Hannah shook her head. "How can this be?" she whispered almost to herself. "It has been weeks since Lemuel last came to me." A thought struck her and she caught her breath. "Father Lehi knew, did he not?"

Mother Sariah smiled.

"What is being discussed so quietly here?" Lemuel sat down beside Hannah. "Mother? What are you saying to my wife?"

Mother Sariah looked at her son and took a quick breath. Then, just as she opened her mouth to speak, she glanced at Hannah, who shook her head slightly.

Mother Sariah let out her breath and smiled at her son. "Nothing of importance, my son."

"Ah. Because you two looked quite intense."

Mother Sariah smiled slightly. "That is how we normally look, son." She glanced at Hannah. "Serious and intense."

"Ah. Well, I need to speak to my wife, Mother, so if you will permit, I will take her from you."

Mother Sariah laughed. "When do you need *my* permission to speak to *your* wife?"

Lemuel stood up, waited a moment for Hannah to get to her feet, and started off along the street.

Hannah hurried to catch up to his long strides. "What is it, husband?"

Lemuel paused a short distance from the gathered crowd and turned to her. "I think it is time for Samuel to participate in his first real hunt."

Hannah frowned. "But he has gone along on hunts for—"

"His first *real* hunt."

She stared at him, confused.

"He will be the hunter."

"He will be the one leading the way, following the tracks? Making the killing shot?"

"Yes."

"But husband, he is only in his thirteenth year! Surely one more year—"

Lemuel sighed. "Laman told me I'd have trouble with you."

Hannah controlled her anger with difficulty. "Laman?"

Lemuel lifted his head and turned to look at the crowd of people a short distance away. "He said you would not agree."

"And I do not! Husband! Have you ceased to make any of your own decisions? Will you let brother Laman control both you and your son?"

"It is wonderful that he still takes an interest in Samuel. He has his own sons now. He could forget our son entirely!"

"I wish he would!" Hannah hissed at him. "I wish your precious brother would concentrate on his own family and leave yours alone. Heaven knows he has so much larger a family than yours!"

"But not—" Lemuel bit his lip.

"Not what?"

Lemuel sighed. "Wife, Laman befriended Samuel when he did not have sons of his own. Now that he does, well, he is afraid of offending a young man he has grown very fond of."

Hannah stared at him. "Laman is afraid of offending someone?"

Lemuel's eyes closed and he rubbed them with long fingers. "You have never tried to understand my brother."

Hannah's eyebrows went up. "What is there to understand? He takes what he wants, does what he wants, and ignores whom he wants, then squeals when, on occasion, he is forced to pull back."

Lemuel was silent.

"There was a time, husband, when you agreed with me."

He looked at her, and then over toward the crowd again.

Hannah followed his gaze.

Laman was standing at the edge of the gathering, his eyes on the two of them.

Hannah suddenly felt tired. She sighed. "I know that you will not stop until your precious Laman gets complete control over Samuel. But wait a little, husband. Wait until he is at least in his fourteenth year to make him a hunter."

She turned and walked off toward the copse of trees that separated her settlement from this one.

"Hannah!"

She turned.

Moriah was running toward her, her sandals making little puffs of dust in the hard-packed street.

"What is it, Morrie?"

Her sister smiled. "It has been such a long time since you called me that."

Hannah shrugged and turned away. "I guess we do not see as much of each other as we used to."

Moriah put her hand on Hannah's arm. "Is there aught you would share with me, sister?"

Hannah sighed and looked at her. "So Mother Sariah has told you already?"

Moriah stared at her. "Mother has told me that *you* may have something to say." She frowned and tightened her grip on Hannah's arm. "Is there something I should know?"

Another shrug. "You'll hear soon enough. Mother Sariah thinks I may be with child."

Moriah's eyes went wide. "*Hannah! How wonderful!* You must be thrilled beyond expression!"

Hannah lifted her head. "I do not know how I feel about it. I am not even sure it is true."

"But Mother Sariah—"

"Walk with me, sister. I must get out of this heat."

Moriah fell into step with Hannah, chattering happily. "But this is wonderful news! Just think! After all of this time!"

Hannah paused for a moment, then walked on. "Yes. I had not thought it would happen to me a first time and certainly not a second."

"Remember how happy Lemuel was when Samuel was born?"

Hannah nodded, feeling suddenly close to tears. "I remember."

"He was nearly beside himself with joy. He could not seem to spend enough time with the two of you. He wanted to confide every thought to you! Why, the rest of the family was sure that, finally, he had forgotten his fascination with—" She gulped and stopped.

Hannah stopped again and glanced up the street toward the gathered family. "Yes. I hoped as well—" She shook her head and continued walking.

They had reached the trees and felt instantly cooler.

Moriah put out her hand and grasped Hannah's arm again, stopping her. "Sister, are you happy?"

A tear trickled down Hannah's cheek. Then another. Finally, she spoke. "No, I am not."

Moriah gathered her younger sister into her arms. "I can see it in your face, favored one. You are in pain."

Hannah gasped and leaned against her sister's shoulder as the flood gates opened.

For several moments they stood there, the quiet trees around them, while Hannah grieved for her years of uncertainty and heartache.

"Come over here, sister," Moriah said, steering Hannah further into the trees and away from the path.

A short distance away, they found a flowering thicket with a gnarled old tree growing out of the center. The roots of the tree offered a perfect spot to sit and confide.

After a time, Hannah dried her tears on the hem of her tunic and straightened. "Father told me that I needed to do all I could do," she said.

"Yes, favored one. He said the same to all of us."

"No. Just after Samuel was born, I saw Father and he told me I needed to make sure I had done all I could."

"*After—?*"

Hannah looked at Moriah. "In a dream, I saw Father and Mother. But it was so real. *They* were so real. Father reminded me of the reasons he and Father Lehi chose me to marry Lemuel. And he told me I could make the difference in my husband's and Samuel's lives, but I must be strong and immovable."

"And you always have been."

Hannah smiled rather sadly. "I have tried. But have I done all I can? With Lemuel and Samuel both now following Laman, can I say I have done my best?"

Moriah frowned. "Lemuel *and* Samuel?"

"They are as deeply under the grip of Laman's appeal as Lemuel ever was on his own."

Moriah sat back, a stricken look on her face. "No!"

Hannah nodded. "Yes." She looked away. "Daily, I see them slip further from me. Further from the truth. Further from the Lord."

"But they will come back."

Hannah shook her head. "Father told me that if Lemuel was ever lost to his brother again, he would not be brought back."

Moriah was silent.

Hannah turned back to her. "I have lost my husband a second time, Morrie. I am losing my son. What can I do?"

Moriah shook her head. "I do not know."

Hannah slid her hand over her abdomen. "And if Mother Sariah and Father Lehi are right and I am carrying another child, what of this one? Will I see it follow Laman down the path of evil as well?" She looked at Moriah. "And at the judgment day, will the Lord see fit to lay the blame at my feet, where it belongs?"

"A just Lord will not put so heavy a burden on you. He will know how faithful you have been, how you have done everything you could to—"

"Ah. But have I done everything I could?"

CHAPTER 35

In the days following Lehi's death, relations became more and more strained between the two settlements.

With Lehi alive, Laman had been more or less judicious with his opinions and desires. Now that his father was gone, Laman's restraint seemed to have gone too. His voice was often heard loudly protesting what he saw as his younger brother's usurpation and greed for power and Nephi's mindless following of ancient and irrelevant practices.

He and Lemuel had long since stopped attending any spiritual meetings, and now they took delight in disparaging those from their settlement who did go.

Because of this, Hannah soon became the lone representative from her side of the forest. At first, as she made the long, lonely walk down the center of the street toward the other settlement, she had been met with embarrassed glances or averted eyes. Then, as the days wore on and the guilt lessened, people ceased to notice.

Once or twice she tried to convince Samuel to come with her, but without success. Her son was much more interested in training for the hunt than in something as unreal as his spiritual welfare.

So it was with an aching heart that she made the almost daily trek to the other settlement, alone, to receive the spiritual guidance she so much desired.

One morning, as she made her way along the street, Lemuel called to her. Turning, she saw him lounging with Laman in the shade outside Uzziel's home. Samuel was with them. Slowly, she turned and let her steps carry her over to them.

"Wife. Where are you bound?"

Laman and Lemuel laughed. Samuel said nothing, but looked from his mother to the two men.

Lemuel looked at Laman and tapped his brother lightly with a fist. "Going to partake of a spiritual feast?"

Laman laughed again. "Yes, good sister Hannah, instead of filling your head with an imaginary feast, is it not your duty to stay here and make sure your husband and your son are filling their bellies with an *actual* one?"

Hannah took a deep breath and spoke evenly. "There is food prepared for them, if they so choose." She looked toward her house. "I have left bread and meat and cheese if they have appetite. And there are fruits and herbs—"

Laman held up a hand. "I have already provided for them, good sister." He put an arm around Samuel's boyish shoulders. "When I see my good sister neglecting her menfolk in order to dabble in things long since abandoned by *wiser* people, I cannot turn them away in their hunger."

Just then, Uzziel came out of the house, carrying a platter on which she had stacked bread, meats, and cheeses. She paused when she saw Hannah. "Hannah, sister. Would you stay and sup with us?" She looked up the street. "Or are you too determined to waste your time with long-dead practices and teachings?"

Hannah straightened and faced her. "They are not long-dead, my sister. They are living, beautiful teachings that you know will bring you closer to the Lord!"

Laman and Lemuel laughed. Laman leaned toward her. "Is that what you want? To become closer to the Lord?" He looked at

Lemuel. "All she needs to do is come with us on a hunt. She'll see a faster way of bringing creatures closer to the Lord!"

Hannah looked at her son. "Samuel, would you like to come with me?"

Samuel looked from his father to his mother. "I do not—"

"Do not pressure our son!" Lemuel shouted, coming to his feet.

Hannah looked at her husband calmly. "Why is it when you teach him the things you desire, that is acceptable? But when I try to teach him what I know to be true, that is pressuring him?"

Lemuel was silent, his mouth twisted into an ugly line.

"I think someone's wife needs to know her place," Laman said, grinning. He looked at Lemuel. "And who better to teach her than her husband?" He turned back to her. "But if you insist on going, dear sister, and my good brother, Lemuel, has not the strength to stop you—"

Lemuel shifted but said nothing.

Laman went on, "—I have a message for you to give to our younger brother who thinks to rule over us." He smiled. "We have had much trial because of him." He looked at her. "Now, we will slay him."

The words were said so calmly that, at first, Hannah did not think she had heard correctly. Then she saw the threat in his dark eyes.

Laman was deadly serious.

She gasped.

He smiled. "We will slay him that we may not be afflicted more because of his words."

Horror washed over her at the chill, heartless words. She could think of nothing to say in response.

Laman went on, "We will not have him to be our ruler; for it belongs unto us, who are the elder brethren, to rule over this people."

Hannah shook her head and backed away, feeling hopeless and near to tears. Turning, she ran the remainder of the way up the street to the barrier trees.

Behind her, she could hear the two men laughing.

Nephi was speaking when Hannah joined the group a few minutes later. He looked at her and smiled. She could not help but compare it to the smile his eldest brother had given her such a short time before. Her eyes blurred with tears.

She quietly took a seat beside Amanna and Sam on the outskirts of the group. Amanna's youngest daughter, Naama, was seated next to her mother, fiddling with a shining pendant on a fine gold chain about her neck. For a moment, Hannah was distracted by the gleam radiating from the intricately carved charm when the sunlight struck it.

There was a chorus of soft "amens" from the assembled family members as Nephi finished speaking.

Hannah said it absently, her thoughts in a whirl.

"My family," Nephi began to speak again. "There is something more I would speak of."

"Nephi! You are here! Safe!"

All eyes turned as Moriah's eldest son, Ezekiel—breathless and dusty and streaked with green where fronds of vegetation had swiped against him—skidded to a halt in front of his uncle. "I thought—"

"Sit down, son, and catch your breath," Zoram said, rising and going over to him.

Ezekiel shook his head. "I have to tell you what I heard!"

Nephi joined them. "What is it, son?"

"I was on the day's watch. Well, Joseph and I were. And we needed to move the flock into the next canyon where the pool is. We were gathering the animals and one of the lambs had gotten herself caught in some bushes. I went to free her and while I was there, I heard two men talking."

Nephi nodded. "Yes?"

"They were talking about you, uncle, about how they were going to get rid of you and anyone so misguided as to follow you."

There was a gasp among those assembled.

Ezekiel put a shaking hand on Nephi's arm. "They said it was the only way to make things right."

Hannah got to her feet and approached Nephi. "Brother, I would speak with you."

Nephi looked at her. "What is it, sister Hannah?"

"As I was leaving our settlement," she nodded toward the copse that separated them, "I was given a message by Laman."

Nephi nodded. "Yes, sister?"

In as few words as possible, she told him what Laman had said.

Nephi was silent as several people started speaking at once. Finally, he held up his hands and the talking ceased.

"Are you not going to tell them, brother?" Sam asked quietly.

Nephi sighed. Then he nodded. "My family, the Lord has warned me in a dream that my brethren desire my death." He sounded sad and tired.

Mother Sariah got to her feet. "You know what we must do, son."

A tear made its way down Nephi's face, losing itself in his beard. Another followed the first. He reached out and gripped his mother's hand and nodded.

Then he turned to the rest of the group. "We will leave here. We will separate ourselves from our brethren and find the place which the Lord would have us inhabit."

Hannah sank to the ground. They would leave.

But what would happen to her?

The next few days saw feverish activity in Nephi's settlement: foodstuffs prepared and stored and flocks of sheep and herds of goats, cattle, horses, cureloms—the strange animals who had greeted them on arrival—and cumoms—their cousins—gathered into the closer fields.

Hannah helped where she could, walking quietly back and forth from one settlement to the other, knowing that the coming separation was a necessity, but knowing as well that, when the prophet of the Lord and his people moved on, any hope for her Samuel—and herself—went with them.

Each day her steps grew slower and her heart heavier.

She did find it curious that none of the people in Laman and Lemuel's camp seemed to be aware of the commotion in the other site. Maybe consuming strong drink, feasting half the night, and sleeping most of the day would account for it.

Maybe they simply did not care.

This morning, three days after Nephi's announcement, she was in Amanna's house, folding cloths and blankets into a basket.

Amanna came into the room with her youngest daughter, Naama, trailing behind. "Of course he will come, dearest one," Amanna was saying. "He will not allow you to slip out of his grasp quite so easily!"

"But mama! Father Nephi said he would remain—"

Amanna held up her hand. "Father Nephi merely meant that he would stay behind with the flock and, after the main caravan had pulled out, fall in behind them."

"Oh." Suddenly the girl was all smiles.

The two of them turned to Hannah, whose eyes had filled with tears.

"Hannah?" Amanna asked anxiously at the same time as Naama said, "Aunt Hannah!"

Hannah summoned up a laugh and scrubbed impatiently at her cheeks with the blanket she had just folded. "It is nothing, dear ones. Merely tears of happiness."

Amanna studied her suspiciously and Hannah, feeling the heat in her cheeks, turned back to her task.

"We were discussing my upcoming marriage," Naama said happily. She danced about the room. "Uncle Zoram bargained with Father for my hand just last night."

"And who is the lucky young man?" Hannah said.

The girl smiled widely. "Uncle Zoram and Aunt Moriah's son, Zalman." She leaned closer to Hannah and pointed to the gold pendant that hung from the chain about her neck. "He made me this!"

Amanna snorted. "Gifts from an unmarried man to an unmarried girl!"

Hannah remembered seeing the necklace a few days earlier, but she exclaimed dutifully over the beautiful pendant, noting the delicate, intricate work.

"And this is what he presented to me last night!" The girl held out her hand.

Another gold chain encircled the slender wrist. From it dangled several more of the pendants, similar to the first and just as carefully crafted, but smaller.

"Oh!" Hannah exclaimed. "It is beautiful!"

"He loves me," the girl said simply. She hugged her arms about herself and danced out the doorway and into the garden.

Amanna laughed. "I have not been able to get a bit of work out of her all day!"

"I remember a couple of other girls as foolish," Hannah said, smiling.

"That was a long time ago," Amanna said.

Hannah nodded. "A very long time."

Amanna move closer and pulled the blanket from Hannah's grasp. "Sister, I would talk to you."

Hannah looked at her. "Yes?"

Amanna sighed. "Come over here. Sit."

The two of them sat down on the thick mat and Hannah turned to Amanna expectantly.

Her sister had folded her slender fingers together and was looking down at them. Finally, she raised her head. "Sister, I want you to come with us."

Hannah blinked. Whatever she had been expecting, it was not this. For just a moment, her heart sang with hope. Then, "Amanna, I—" She took a deep breath. "You know that my husband would never consent to coming with you."

"Yes." Amanna looked down at her hands again. "I was not thinking of him when I invited you."

"And my son. My Samuel. Lemuel would never consent to his leaving, either."

Amanna looked at her, her dark eyes filled with tears. "I know."

Hannah was silent for a moment. "You would have me come without my husband and without my son?"

Her sister was silent. Then, slowly, she nodded.

Hannah shook her head dismissively and got to her feet. "I would never consider it, sister. I could not leave my family!"

"You would be coming *with* your family!" Amanna said, rising also.

Hannah turned to face her. "Amanna, gentle one, I waited too long and fought too hard for my son to lose him now." She turned away.

"But Hannah, if you stay, you will surely fall prey to the same devils that beset Laman and Lemuel and our sister Uzziel!"

Hannah stopped and turned. "Have you so little faith in me, sister?"

"No, I have great faith in you. But think on this. You will be alone to the end of time in an evil, godless, and friendless place."

Hannah was silent for a moment. Then she lifted her head and looked at Amanna. "I cannot leave my son," she said.

"Even if his sins will, one day, be heaped upon your head?"

Hannah's eyes filled with tears. "His sins? He has not even reached his fourteenth year. Have we decided his fate already? Have we stopped h-hoping?"

Amanna shook her head and put her hand on Hannah's arm. "No, of course not, sister."

"Then how can we even consider abandoning him?" Tears were flowing freely now and she brushed at them impatiently.

"Of course you are right," Amanna slid her arm around Hannah's shaking shoulders. "We will speak of this no more."

Hannah nodded and moved away from Amanna, toward the door.

"Hannah."

She turned.

Amanna was looking at her intently. "I am sorry."

Hannah nodded again and stepped through the doorway into the garden.

A fire was burning brightly when Hannah reached her own settlement, but, though there was a whole side of beef roasting, no one was dancing or singing.

Instead, she could see the men gathered together on one side. A meeting.

She glanced about the town site. A few women were visiting together by lamplight in their gardens, but it appeared as though none had been invited to listen in on what the men were discussing.

It suddenly seemed of vital importance that she hear.

Hannah slid into the shadows and moved carefully closer to the fire. When she was within earshot, she sank down onto her heels, wrapped her arms around her legs, and stayed very still.

"So are we all agreed?" she heard Laman's voice ask.

There was a murmur of assent from those assembled.

"They are stupid and will not be expecting anything, and none of them have the expertise with weapons that we have, so I am certain we will be able to carry this war into their very homes."

Everyone cheered.

"But remember this. Nephi is mine. I want him brought out alive." Laman looked around the group. "If he is harmed in any way, I will personally kill the man responsible."

Hannah caught her breath.

Laman lifted his head and turned in her direction, peering intently into the shadows around her.

Hannah froze. Her heart was hammering painfully in her chest and just for a moment, she felt she had a great deal in common with one of Laman's hunted deer.

After an eternity, Laman again turned back to the men. "Nephi is to be unharmed when he is brought before me. Understand?" He smiled, his teeth gleaming red in the firelight. "Any harm he receives will be by my hand."

The men around him were loud in their agreement.

"Good." Laman stretched to his great height. "So—tonight." He looked up at the moonless sky. "At my signal."

There was another loud cheer, and then the men were calling out for food and drink. Instantly, the square was filled with women carrying platters of bread and cheese, wineskins and animal-horn mugs. Someone tested the meat and pronounced it ready, and the feasting began.

Her body cold with horror, Hannah edged away from the blaze, careful not to move too quickly or draw attention to herself. Every nerve was jumping and urging her to fly, but she resisted, knowing that if she made one mistake—if she betrayed herself—she would certainly be prevented from warning Nephi as she intended.

When she reached the shadow of the first of the houses, she slowly stood up. But as she turned to go, she glanced one last time toward the fire.

Laman was looking right at her.

CHAPTER 36

Hannah started walking toward the copse of trees that separated the two settlements.

She heard the lightly running footsteps and saw the shadows break away from the light and disappear into the darkness, but she pretended not to notice, continuing her casual stroll in the direction of Nephi's settlement.

But just as she reached the trees and started to think she might have been mistaken, something struck her in the middle of her back.

Her breath knocked cleanly from her lungs, Hannah landed heavily on her face.

Several pairs of hands rolled her over and hoisted her into the air as though she weighed no more than a bit of thistledown. Still struggling to breathe, she was thrown roughly over a muscular shoulder.

The little amount of air she had managed to draw in was again driven from her lungs, and everything faded into blackness.

Hannah gasped and opened her eyes to her room. She turned her head. She was in her own house on her own sleeping mat.

How foolish she had been, suspecting the men in the settlement of—

Her thoughts broke into fragments as she tried to sit up and realized she could not move. Someone had bound her so tightly with cords that she was incapable of shifting anything other than her head.

At that moment, she knew that the nightmare she had witnessed had been far too real.

"Welcome back, wife."

Hannah turned her head. Lemuel was sitting on their house mat, legs crossed, looking guilty of nothing more than wanting his dinner.

"Husband! What has happened? How could you let—?"

His eyebrows went up and he held up his hand. "Let?" He shook his head. "After you spied on us for your false prophet? After you have done everything in your power to ensure the upstart is successful in his attempts to rule this family? Something only an elder brother is entitled to."

"But husband, you know that—"

Again he stopped her. "Finally, wife, you have had your say. No more will I be forced to listen to your prattle." He smiled. "At last you have found your place."

"But husband—"

Lemuel got up and walked over to her. Then, slowly and deliberately, he drew his hand back and slapped her across the face. Hannah's head flipped to one side and she felt a sharp pain in the back of her neck.

Shocked, she stared up at Lemuel with wide eyes.

Lemuel smiled again and brought his hand back, this time slapping the other cheek with equal force.

Any thought she may have fostered of convincing her husband to listen to reason fled. Hannah felt the tears well up in her eyes and drip slowly back and into her hair and ears.

Lemuel nodded and resumed his place on the mat.

Iscah appeared with a platter, and Hannah looked silently at her sister wife. Begged with her eyes.

But Iscah turned her back and proceeded to serve their husband his dinner, waiting quietly with her hands folded together while he ate.

Sometime later, when Lemuel had eaten his fill, Iscah collected the platter and turned to go. She paused for a moment beside Hannah. Looking down at her, she said, "See what comes of dishonesty, sister? See what happens when you conspire against what should—and must—be?" She tucked the earthenware platter under her arm and, nodding to Lemuel, disappeared into the night.

Soon after Iscah left, Samuel appeared at the door.

"Samuel!" Hannah gasped out.

Lemuel turned to look at her, and Hannah closed her mouth and shrank as far from him as her bonds would allow.

He turned to Samuel. "What is it, son?"

"It is time. Laman told me I must watch over the *traitor*," his mouth twisted over the word, "while you help him and the others take care of what needs to be done."

Lemuel got to his feet and put a hand on his son's shoulder. "Watch her carefully, son. She cannot be trusted."

Samuel nodded. "I know, Father. I will not disappoint you and King Laman."

King Laman? Hannah closed her eyes. Surely this could not be happening. Surely their Lord—But then she remembered something her father said on that fateful day of Samuel's birth. "*Should Lemuel ever fall again under the power of Laman, there will be little anyone can do to bring him back to the path laid out for him and other righteous men. He, like his brother, will finish out his days in wanton and evil acts, leading his posterity—and your Samuel—astray to the end of time.*" Hannah shivered as she remembered his next words. "*The regrets from a life lived thus will be indescribable.*"

Already, the life lived was indescribable, and they had not even gotten to the regrets.

She turned to look at her son, seated now where his father had sat moments before. Not quite thirteen years old, he had grown tall, but still possessed the light frame of a very young man. He was looking far too serious for one so young.

"They are wrong, you know," she whispered.

"Silence, traitor!"

"Samuel. Please listen to me!"

"Silence!" His young voice cracked on the word. He got to his feet, took the lamp, and disappeared through the door, leaving her in darkness. A faint glow came in through the open door, and she realized he had taken up his post just outside.

During the next few hours, Samuel regularly came to the door, holding the lamp to check on her. But before she could do much more than call his name, he was gone again.

The settlement was silent. Even the usual sounds in the forest seemed more muted in the stillness.

Hannah tried wiggling her hands and arms in a vain attempt to loosen her bonds, but she was dealing with the same knots that had held a mighty prophet of God for four days. All she succeeded in doing was rubbing her wrists raw.

The time passed slowly and Hannah found herself both listening for, and dreading, sounds that would indicate that the men returned.

Finally, toward dawn, she thought she heard something. She stiffened and held her breath, peering intently into the blackness above her head.

Loud, angry voices. Shouting.

She could not make out what they were saying, and she again cursed the bonds that held her.

Someone called to Samuel and his voice answered from right outside her door. Then she heard him get up and move off.

A short time later, a large shadow blocked out what little light came in through the door. Someone brought a lamp, and Hannah shrank back as Laman's features were revealed. "How did you do it, traitor?" he asked.

Hannah stared up at him. "Do what?"

He came inside and others crowded around the door, Lemuel and Samuel with them. "You know what! How did you do it?!"

"I-I do not know what y-you are talking—"

"They are gone. All of them. Gone!"

Hannah gaped at him blankly. "Gone?"

Laman began to pace in the small space. "Even their food, their flocks and herds, all gone." He spun around and pierced her with his eyes. "How could they have known if you had not told them?"

"How could I possibly have told them? Stop a moment and think, brother La—"

"It is *KING LAMAN* now," he screamed, spittle flying. "*KING!* And you'd better remember that your life is now in my hands!" He stopped for a moment. "You are right. There is no way you could possibly have told them—unless you are consorting with the demons of evil!" He spun around. "That is it! Of course. Our brother Nephi did. You do. It all makes sense!"

He flung himself out of the house and into the garden.

Hannah shivered. The nightmare continued.

It was midmorning before someone remembered her and came to release her.

It was one of Iscah's daughters, the youngest, Tabitha. The girl, just a year or so older than Samuel, looked frightened to death and stayed only long enough to loosen Hannah's bonds, then fled like a startled deer.

Hannah, feeling decidedly sore and weak, took care of her immediate needs and then slowly found her way out to the street.

Laman and Lemuel and many of the others were in the square, discussing what had happened the night before.

Talk ceased and everyone stared at her as she started up the street toward the copse of trees.

A couple of the men got up as though they would go after her, but Laman stopped them. "Leave her be. What can she do? She can be of no further use to the upstart."

Hannah continued walking. The relief of stepping into the cool trees was of short duration, however. As soon as she crossed into the other settlement, she could feel the silence and emptiness settle over her like a weight.

She stopped. All about her were the memories of life and industry, of laughter and family. All gone. All swallowed up by the silence.

Odd. Now that Nephi and his followers had gone, now that the life had been sucked from this place, this settlement felt like the other one—Laman's kingdom just past the trees.

Hannah walked from house to house. All were neat, tidy, and empty.

She paused outside the partially finished temple and ran her hands over the smooth walls; the stones so carefully fitted together that it was nearly impossible to find the line between them. The walls looked almost as though they were hewn out of one solid block.

The tools had been taken, but the other materials, partially finished blocks of stone and timbers, all were neatly set aside as though the workers would return at any time.

But the workers would never return.

Her tiny hope that the men in her settlement had been playing a monstrous joke or had been somehow mistaken was snuffed with finality. There truly was no one left.

Except her.

Hannah sank to her knees in the dust and allowed the tears to fall.

"You should be happy to see the end of them, Mother. As I am!"

Hannah looked at her tall son standing in their home. The lines of his face still held the boyish curves of his babyhood.

Not quite a child, not yet a man.

She sighed. "Do you not believe, son? Not even the smallest portion?"

He snorted. "Believe in what, Mother?" He straightened boyish shoulders. "The foolish traditions of our fathers? The commandments that enslave and oppress?"

"They do not enslave us, Samuel," Hannah said quietly. "They free us."

"Free us from our coin and our Sabbath," another voice said.

Hannah turned.

Lemuel was leaning against the doorway to her house. "We are ready to leave for today's hunt, and we need our mighty hunter to lead us. I wondered where he had gotten to." He looked at his wife. "Now I see that he has been drawn again into your net, wife."

"I only wanted to see my son!" Hannah's voice had risen.

"You only wanted to further his brainwashing!" Lemuel retorted. He straightened away from the door and stepped inside. "But now you see a young man who will not be led about by the nose."

"I never—!" Hannah began.

"And dragged about talking 'baptism.'"

"That was years ago!" Hannah frowned. "And brother Nephi would not allow his baptism."

Lemuel smirked. "Well, the upstart did get it right—once."

Hannah looked at him. "He would not allow his baptism because he did not want him to be condemned for failure to keep the covenants he would make."

Lemuel shrugged. "Old and outdated covenants with no real power in them."

Hannah stared at her husband. "Lemuel, you *know*—"

"I know that I was fooled for a long time. But now I am on the right course."

Hannah shook her head. "Husband, you are on the wrong course. Remember how you felt at the island—"

Lemuel made a slashing gesture with one hand. "Do not speak of those blind and treacherous days!"

Hannah turned her back on her husband and faced Samuel. "Son, I need to know how you feel."

Samuel started to look over her shoulder, toward his father.

"No, son. Just for this moment, do not look at your father. Look at me. How do *you* feel?"

Samuel met her eyes and, for a moment, she thought she saw something stir. Then the beloved face hardened and the round chin came up. "Mother, I want nothing to do with your foolish traditions." He looked steadily into her eyes. "I want to be a man. A real man, like Father and Uncle Laman. I do not want to waste my time in praying and prostrating myself before some false god. I want to do those things that bring me pleasure." His eyes strayed toward the doorway. "Out there." He looked back at her. "Not forced to kneel for hours on the hard stone of some stuffy building."

Hannah's eyes were blurred with tears, but she could still see him as he leaned forward into her face and put his hands on her shoulders. "Mother, I do not feel what you feel. The only time I am truly happy is when I am on the hunt."

Hannah's tears were flowing freely now. She gasped for breath. "But you are so young now. Perhaps—"

"Mother. I will never change how I feel. I am happy. I see no reason to change. Ever." He let go of her and turned away.

Hannah sank to the floor, sobbing bitterly.

She did not hear her family as they left her home.

EPILOGUE

The fire had grown hotter. The faces of the hunters were a mottled patchwork of blood and sweat.

Hannah sat to one side, isolated from everyone in the camp, dead eyes on her lost son, capering and cavorting with the rest.

Laman held up his hands and the young men stopped their dancing and flung themselves down before him, prostrating their young bodies in the dust in a show of abject adulation and reverence.

Hannah put one hand over her mouth and closed her eyes against more threatening tears.

When she opened them again, Laman was smiling and touching each young man on his naked head, calling them to rise and come unto him.

Each did willingly, kneeling before their uncle and happily kissing his hand. Then, as they regained their feet, they began to chant. "Hail to our rightful King Laman! Glory be to him!"

Soon the entire crowd had joined in. "Hail to our rightful King Laman! Glory, glory forever!"

A couple of people were watching her, but she had no intention of chanting something she knew in her heart was so very wrong.

She looked at her husband, painted like the rest and enjoying his position as second-in-command. She turned her gaze again to her son. Samuel. Named for a great Israelite prophet, a champion of the Lord, now consumed with following his uncle into the depths of evil and despair.

Laman. Her head turned again and she focused on the great, hulking, black-haired man standing so arrogantly to receive his due. A surge of hot anger poured through her, forcing her suddenly to her feet. For a moment, she rocked there. Then, "No!" she screamed at the people and the fire and Laman. "No! You cannot have him!"

Several heads turned in her direction, but she ignored them as she leaped toward the fire and her son.

The heat was instantly unbearable and it became difficult to breathe. Briefly, she wondered how the others could stand it.

Time seemed to slow down and it was as though she was suddenly pressing against a great force. Doggedly, she kept moving forward, her eyes on the bloodied figure of her son, standing with the others in front of Laman.

Finally, she was close enough to grab his arm and she did so with desperate fingers. "Samuel, you must come with me!" she cried out.

Samuel turned his head slowly and looked at her. Then his lips curled in distaste and he lifted his arm, trying to break her hold.

But Hannah clung to him with every ounce of her fading strength. She could feel the gummy gore and sweat that drenched his body and smell the heavy scent of the swine blood.

She drew in a slow, painful breath. "*Samuel!*" she screamed. "*You must come with me. Now!*" Every word cost her more of her precious strength.

Samuel's head was shaking back and forth and he tried again to unfasten her from his arm, shaking her like she was some distasteful parasite that had attached itself to him.

Laman and Lemuel were moving toward them, both of them shouting something, but their words were swallowed up by the roar of the fire and the sudden strange buzzing in Hannah's ears.

She felt the hands of her husband and brother-by-marriage grip her by the shoulders just as Samuel shook his arm again. This time, Hannah felt her grip loosen, her fingers sliding along her son's arm toward his hand.

"*No, Samuel! No, Son! Please! Please! Pl—*"

Something hit her across the back and she fell to the ground, losing both her grip on her son and what was left of her breath.

Dazed, Hannah shook her head and tried to regain her feet, but something hit her again and pain blossomed in her head as her strength abandoned her entirely.

Confused, she tried to focus on the figures that had gathered around her, but the pain from the second blow, coupled with the lack of air near the fire made it impossible. Someone grabbed her by the ankle and began dragging her along the ground.

Her tunic and under tunic slid up past her waist, and stones and twigs scraped painfully across her naked back and legs as she was dragged along the ground toward the trees.

Feebly, she tried to struggle—kick at whoever held her ankle so firmly, but all she managed to do was bring someone else forward to seize her other ankle.

Helplessly, she was dragged into the forest.

For an instant, she felt relief as the soft grass rubbed against her scratched back and legs and her breathing eased in the cooler air.

Her ankles were released suddenly and her legs dropped like stones. Weakly, she tried to push herself to her feet, cover her naked limbs.

Then the first stone hit her.

It caught her tender bottom lip, splitting it open. Gasping aloud, she raised her hand to cover the wound and felt the fresh blood drip through her already gore-stained fingers. Lifting her head, she looked at the shadowy figures that had formed a circle around her and tried to comprehend what was happening.

When the second stone hit her on the shoulder, knocking her back onto the grass, she knew. Her heart stood still. Her judgment had been decided, her fate sealed. She was to die at the hands of her family.

The crowd gathered close and more stones were thrown, hitting her painfully in the leg, chest and head. She turned, frantically looking for the tall, familiar figure of her son in the group, but her eyes refused to focus.

Someone appeared with a torch, but the light did little to help her see.

More stones were thrown.

Then, finally, she saw Samuel step to the front of the group, Laman and Lemuel behind him.

She stared at her son—unable to speak through her bloodied and swollen lips—trying to put every emotion she could muster into her eyes.

Laman handed Samuel something and the boy hefted it with one hand, then lifted it high so it gleamed in the torchlight.

Another stone.

Hannah's eyes fastened on it as he carried it closer.

Then she looked at him and shook her head.

Samuel looked down at her, and their eyes met for a moment—his black and cold, hers wet with tears and heartbreak.

Then he dropped the stone and Hannah knew no more.

Someone was squabbling, arguing over something, shrill voices jarring her awake from a soft, dreamless rest.

Hannah opened one eye to a blur of green. She frowned. This was not her house. She tried to open her other eye, but it refused to obey her; she tried to reach out to touch it but cried aloud at the pain of lifting her arm.

Then memory washed over her. Cold and bitter, it flowed through her like a knife, cutting her to her tender soul.

Her family—her husband and her *son*—had stoned her. Left her for dead.

Was she dead?

She tried again to lift her arm and cried out at the pain. No. She was still on earth. Surely there was no pain and suffering in the spirit world.

Tears began to flow. There was nothing for her in this world. Why had the Lord seen fit to leave her here? Had not she done enough?

Had not she suffered enough?

The harsh voices, still arguing heatedly, invaded once more.

Hannah listened for a moment, but could not make out the words. Slowly, carefully, she turned her head.

The world was rosy with new morning light. The sun had not yet risen, but the air was full of the promise of another day. Hannah's eye widened as she realized it was not a group of people as she had expected. Rather, a couple of vultures were squabbling over whether or not she was dead—enough.

At her movement, they hopped backward a few paces, their eyes on her, their cries silenced.

Hannah rested for a moment, then moved her head again. This time it was easier. She tried her arm and it, too, seemed to be hurting less. Cautiously, she looked all around the clearing. Nothing else stirred. Her family had obviously left her for dead and gone back to their settlement.

And knowing their penchant for late-night celebrations and aversion to the early morning hours, she assumed they would not be stirring for quite some time.

She tried to push herself upright, but she simply did not have the strength.

Carefully she ran her hand along her body, seeking out injuries. There were several sore spots along her chest, arms, and legs. Her back had been rubbed raw where she had been dragged. And her face and head ached badly from the blows they had received; she had been devastated physically, emotionally, and spiritually.

Hannah took a deep breath, listening to the air flow through her body. She felt her heart beating steadily inside her. Strangely, when tears would have been customary, she felt peace settle over her.

The Lord had preserved her life.

But why?

Where could she possibly go?

What would she do?

Her family had chosen the path of sin and would receive the wages of such. If she returned to them—and if they let her live—she would partake of it with them. She, the daughter of Ishmael and follower of the Prophet Lehi. She, who had wanted only goodness in her life, goodness and righteousness and the light of her Lord and Savior.

She, who had instead received the great weight of iniquity, heavy as the stones her family had used to try to end her life.

The weight of her husband's and her son's sins already seemed to press down on her.

How would it feel to have the weight of sins from generation upon generation upon generation?

Suddenly, Hannah went still. She stopped breathing. Her hand crept to her belly. Had she really felt—? There it was again. A flutter. Just the tiniest movement.

Was it possible? With all she had endured?

She waited. Surely she was mistaken. Surely—no. It happened a third time.

Could it be true? Was this the child that Lehi had foreseen? That Mother Sariah had confirmed?

She held her breath for another period of waiting, then sighed as it came again. Another confirmation.

The child was real.

Real.

In an instant, the course of Hannah's whole life changed. Her work was *not* done. The Lord was calling her again, giving her another child to raise, this time in righteousness.

Forgetting her pain, Hannah found the strength to push herself upright, to work her way to her knees. With many stops to rest, she slowly got to her feet, afraid that any movement of hers might stop that light fluttering, might prove she was only dreaming.

At last, she stood on her feet. Once more, she waited, one hand on her belly.

There it was again.

Hannah covered her bruised and split lips and stifled a sob. Suddenly her mother's words, spoken in a dream became clear. *"Bring your son to salvation. Your* son. *Remember what I say this day. It is important—when you have a great choice to make."*

She did have a choice to make. For her unborn *son*, she must choose to abandon the family who had abandoned the Lord. And her.

She must choose to follow Nephi, her prophet. With the Lord's guidance, she would find him.

She paused once and looked back at the quiet settlement. Smoke from the ashes of the once-great fire curled lazily into the rosy dawn. Nothing else stirred.

Hannah turned away and, taking a deep, strengthening breath, stepped onto the path leading into the light, her footsteps slow and unsteady, but her mind sure.

ACKNOWLEDGMENTS

I feel that if someone has a gift, one should acknowledge that gift to the person who bestowed it. So to my Heavenly Father, who gives me the words, thank you with all my heart and soul.

I would also like to acknowledge my Stringam, Berg, and Tolley families. It is with your encouragement and faith that I keep on writing.

And thank you to my team: Emily Chambers and Hali Bird, who believed in my book; Priscilla Chaves, who gave it a face; Jennifer Johnson, who made it readable; and Vikki Downs, who sent it around the world. You are the very best!

DISCUSSION QUESTIONS

1. How does life today differ from that of Lehi's in 600 BC?
2. Name some of the family customs discussed in young Hannah's life.
3. What were Hannah's and her sisters' duties?
4. What was normal marriage age for a Jewish girl in biblical times? For a Jewish man?
5. What was Hannah's diet like?
6. How were people's clothes made in Hannah's time?
7. Were women important in the average household?
8. If you were required to leave your home forever, what would you take with you?
9. What were the hardships of a nomadic life? Would you have survived those hardships?
10. How do you react when someone corrects you?
11. Consider your immediate family. Could you survive a year with them on a small ship? A lifetime in a remote location?

ABOUT THE AUTHOR

Photo by David Handschuh, www.davidhandschuh.com.

Diane Stringam Tolley was born and raised on the great Alberta prairies. Daughter of a ranching family of writers, she inherited her love of writing at a very early age. Diane was trained in journalism, and she has penned countless articles, short stories, novels, plays, and songs and is the published author of two Christmas novels: *Carving Angels* and *Kris Kringle's Magic*. She and her husband, Grant, live in Beaumont, Alberta, and are the parents of six and grandparents of seventeen.

SCAN TO VISIT

WWW.DIANESTRINGAMTOLLEY.COM